"There's a slash from here . . ." He pointed to a space in the low center of his chest, and watched her eyes follow it. " . . . to . . ." He drew his finger slowly down, down down to a spot her eyes couldn't follow. " . . . here."

Her gaze stopped and lingered on the place where his finger stopped.

Then she slowly raised her head. Their gazes met. Collided, more accurately.

He wondered if his pupils were as large as Mrs. Fountain's pupils currently were.

"And everything gets so very . . . stiff . . . you see," he added. Somberly.

She visibly drew in a breath.

"I know how to address the stiffness," she said gravely.

His eyes widened. An interesting sensation had begun to trace his spine.

"Do you? I am all ears, Mrs. Fountain." His voice was a hush.

She hesitated again. She bit her lip thoughtfully and leaned forward just a very little.

"Well, you first need to warm it . . ."

And th▓▓▓▓▓▓▓▓▓▓ and covered his with her other hand.

" . . . to▓▓▓

He couldn▓

By Julie Anne Long

Julie Anne Long

It Started with a Scandal

AVONBOOKS

An Imprint of HarperCollinsPublishers

AVON BOOKS
An Imprint of HarperCollinsPublishers
195 Broadway
New York, New York 10007

Copyright © 2015 by Julie Anne Long
ISBN 978-0-06-233482-4
www.avonromance.com

First Avon Books mass market printing: April 2015

Avon Trademark Reg. U.S. Pat. Off. and in Other Countries, Marca Registrada, Hecho en U.S.A.
HarperCollins® is a registered trademark of HarperCollins Publishers.

Printed in the U.S.A. 5550 5431

10 9 8 7 6 5 4 3 2 1 4/15

TO THE FT'S

Acknowledgments

M Y GRATITUDE TO MY delightful, insightful editor, May Chen, who unfailingly gets me, which is such a luxury; to the gifted, hardworking staff at Avon; to my Agent, Steve Axelrod, and to all my amazing readers who make my job such a pleasure.

It Started with a
Scandal

Chapter 1

&

"IN LIGHT OF YOUR . . . circumstances . . . Mrs. Fountain, I'm certain you're aware that it is a bit unusual for you to be granted an interview at all. But this is an exceptional . . . situation . . . and the Redmond family did put in a good word."

So many words requiring delicate choosing and pillowing with little silences. *Circumstances. Situation.*

Withstanding all of them the way she had for years, Elise gritted her teeth. "I understand," she said somberly.

" . . . that is not to say that you could not satisfactorily perform the duties, and I should hope you would not be influenced by Mrs. Gordon, whose temperament proved unequal to the job . . ."

Mrs. Gordon must have been the sobbing woman Elise had passed as she'd come up the walk. Mrs. Gordon had been carrying a valise and muttering "heartless bastard" viciously under her breath.

" . . . because the successful candidate will possess a clear head and a mature outlook . . . ," Mrs. Winthrop continued. She paused briefly in her torrent of words to narrow her eyes at Elise.

Elise had donned her most severe gown and ruthlessly pinned her hair motionless with approximately three hundred pins. She nodded, serenely confident that she looked mature and that nothing as frivolous as a curl would escape.

And she kept her fingers laced tightly in her lap, as if this alone could keep her nerves from shattering. It had at least disguised the trembling.

Would that she'd managed to keep her *stays* laced just that tightly six years ago.

Alas, spilt milk, and all of that.

" . . . and as you know, I'm employed by the Earl of Ardmay, and they have volunteered me to undertake the selection process as a special favor to their family . . ."

Mrs. Winthrop had not ceased speaking since Elise arrived fifteen minutes ago.

" . . . and as for the current staff, there will be no steward or butler, as this is a relatively small household and the tenant is temporary. So you would head the small entire staff, which is comprised of—"

Something unmistakably large and glass, hurled from a considerable distance with considerable force, exploded into thousands of jingling fragments.

Both women froze.

It was *exactly* what Elise expected her nerves would sound like when they finally shattered.

In the stunned silence that followed, the rain hurled itself at the window like a warning. *Get out! Get out while you can!*

Ah, if only she'd a choice.

Mrs. Winthrop cleared her throat at last. "He likely won't ever aim *at* you. All the same, there's naught wrong with his arm and it's best to be well clear of him if you think he might be in a throwing mood."

Elise hoped this was black humor. How on earth to respond? She glanced down at her bloodless knuckles as if they were crystal balls. No help there.

She decided to nod sagely.

"I understand they're blessedly rare. The throwing moods," Mrs. Winthrop expounded.

"And we must always count our blessings."

It emerged more quickly and dryly than Elise intended.

In other words: More *herself* than she had intended.

This she knew, because Mrs. Winthrop's eyebrows launched like birds flushed from shrubbery.

She eyed Elise sharply for a moment.

Elise held her breath.

Then Mrs. Winthrop smiled a vanishingly swift smile. It was like a cinder thrown off a distant campfire, when Elise had been lost in the metaphorical dark woods for weeks.

"All right then, Mrs. Fountain, I should be pleased to introduce you to his lordship, Lord Lavay, who is a prince of the House of Bourbon. If he's . . . amenable."

THE LOQUACIOUS MRS. Winthrop went curiously silent as she led Elise through a labyrinth of Alder House's too-dark hallways. The candles hadn't been trimmed; a few were fitfully, smokily, burning in their sconces. Elise frowned. The house was handsome enough, but in the rooms they swiftly passed, the fires burned low or not at all. She surreptitiously dragged a fingertip along the top of the wainscoting; she could feel dust cake it.

She saw no evidence of the rumored household staff.

They scaled a flight of marble stairs with a smooth, modest banister, and Mrs. Winthrop finally paused on the threshold of what appeared to be a study.

It was as dark and soft as a cave, but a huge leaping fire picked out glints from around the room, and Elise's eyes tracked them reflexively: the polished legs on a plumply upholstered settee and a pair of gorgeous chairs, the inlay on a small round table, the gilt on a framed map and the stand of a handsome globe, an empty crystal decanter, a tiny bottle of Sydenham's Laudanum on a sideboard, only half full.

She stopped when she reached the mirrorlike toes of a pair of Hessians by the hearth.

And followed them all the way up.

Inside them stood a man.

A very tall man.

He in fact all but loomed; the firelight threw his shadow nearly to where she stood at the door.

Elise took an unconscious step back from it, as though it were a spill of lava.

His face was aimed rather pointedly at the window, as if he was expecting someone.

She followed his gaze curiously.

She just saw the same ceaseless slanting rain, like bars on a cell.

A spray of sparkling shards surrounded his feet. The remains of a vase, from the looks of things.

"Lord Lavay . . ."

Elise shot Mrs. Winthrop a worried look. The seemingly indefatigable Mrs. Winthrop's voice had gone faint. As if she suddenly didn't have enough air to form words.

The man turned. Slowly, as if he was the earth itself on its axis. Or as if an invisible sculptor was rotating him to present a finished work.

Voilà! Elise thought to herself. An attempt at bravado.

It was too late. She'd already sucked in her breath and tightened all of her muscles, like a creature who had stumbled across a predator in a clearing and wished to make herself unnoticeable.

He was so clearly of that singular species, The Aristocracy, that she might as well have bought a ticket to see him, the way she had once when her father had brought her, as a little girl, to see the Royal Menagerie in London.

He wasn't young. There was no softness to his face—not in the set of his mouth, or the burn of his gaze, or the severe right angles of his jaw. His beauty was austere and inarguable, and there was a palpable force to him, as if he had sprung from the earth due to violent underground activity, a bit like a mountain range. She thought about the things she'd been told about him.

Privateer. Soldier. Prince.

Power, violence, privilege.

He looked like all of the things he was purported to be.

Do we carry around our pasts so visibly? she wondered. Because if so, *she* was certainly in trouble.

There was no denying that he frightened her.

And after a moment, this made her angry. She'd been so certain she was impossible to frighten after the events of the last five years. She could not afford to be frightened. She thought she *deserved* never to be frightened again.

She squared her shoulders.

Life is full of tests, children, she'd once primly told her students.

That was before she'd been tested.

THE WOMAN MRS. Winthrop had brought into his study was petite and colorless. Her face and the folded knot of her hands were twins, both white and tense. Her dress was demure, long-sleeved, high-collared, fashioned of serviceable gray wool. Her hair was dark. She could be any age.

Her eyes dropped instantly upon meeting his. It was deference or fear, or perhaps fascination. He was accustomed to all of them. None of it interested him.

She was, unsurprisingly, unremarkable in every way.

Apart, that was, from her posture, which was almost aggressively rigid. It reminded him of a drawn saber.

This made him smile faintly.

He sensed it wasn't a pleasant smile when both women gave a little start.

"I'd like to introduce Mrs. Elise Fountain, my lord."

Miss Fountain dropped an elegant enough curtsy.

"You may leave us," he said to Mrs. Winthrop without looking at her.

Mrs. Winthrop bolted like a rabbit released from a trap.

Mrs. Fountain's gaze rose again, rather like a man struggling up the side of a cliff, then it wavered and held.

It TOOK ALL of Elise's fortitude to resist craning her head after the fleeing Mrs. Winthrop.

"Please sit down, Mrs. Fountain."

She went still. His native French still haunted his consonants and turned the vowels into veritable caresses. She could almost *see* the elegant, endless spill of a fountain when he said her name.

"Mrs. Fountain. Has Mrs. Winthrop brought to me an applicant who does not speak English?"

The tone was silk over steel, exquisitely polite.

And yet she could easily imagine him ordering, in
the very same tone, the beheading of whoever had
brought him such a stupid and mute candidate.

"Forgive me, Lord Lavay. I do know how to sit."

She tried a little half smile. She knew she possessed a portion of charm, though it was a trifle
rusty from disuse, given that she'd locked it away
after it had gotten her into trouble.

"If you would be so kind as to demonstrate
your ability to do so."

He gestured to a chair upholstered in chocolate-
colored velvet. She might as well have been a chair
herself for all the charm he exerted. She felt positively neutered. Which was perhaps all for the best.

She sat gingerly and, she hoped, gracefully, on
the very edge of it, the better to bolt if necessary,
and folded her hands.

Oh God . . . the chair was so *soft*. It cradled her
bum almost lasciviously. Its tall, spreading fan of
a back beckoned like a lover's arms. And her life
had seemed so narrow and *spiky* for so long, in
every direction she'd turned, that the comfort surprised her by nearly doing her in.

She slid a tentative inch backward as Lord
Lavay lowered himself into the chair opposite her,
slowly.

He's in Sussex recovering from an attack, she'd
been told.

She began to think it was an attack of apoplexy.

She could see their two faces reflected in the
polished wood of the table. His clean-hewn as

wood itself. Hers small and white, looking a little too insignificant.

"Splendid. We have established you do indeed know how to sit. A very good thing, as I do not tolerate liars." He smiled again faintly here, which she supposed was meant to soften that little thrown-down gauntlet of a statement.

She offered a tight little smile of her own. *Demonstrating my ability to smile.*

"What do you believe are your qualifications, Mrs. Fountain?"

What an interesting way to put it. As if he alone would judge whether she possessed any qualifications at all.

"I have been trained—" She was shocked to hear her voice emerge as a reedy croak, probably due to the thin atmosphere his lofty presence created. She cleared her throat. "I have been trained in the managing of a fine residence, from adhering to budgets to deciding upon household purchases to preparing pastries and remedies and simples, to hiring and discharging—"

"Where?"

She blinked. "I'm sor . . . ?"

"The *residence*," he articulated slowly. "Where was this, as you say, fine residence?"

She'd been with the man for fewer than five minutes and she wanted to kick him.

"Northumberland."

"For whom did you manage this residence?"

She hesitated. Her heartbeat ratcheted up.

"The home belongs to my parents. I was raised and educated there."

She did not say she was no longer welcome in it.

If he wanted the whole story, he was going to need to drag it from her one question at a time.

His gaze was so intense it was as though he held the tips of two lit cheroots to her skin.

Perhaps he already knew, despite what Mrs. Winthrop had said. Sometimes it felt as though the entire world knew.

But surely she wasn't as important as all that?

And surely there were enough Redmonds and Everseas about to keep the scandal mill fed?

Her heart was thudding so hard it felt like someone was throwing angry kicks at her breastbone.

She surrendered and slid those last few inches into the chair's embrace. Lavay's shoulders were vast beneath that sleek, flawlessly tailored coat. She wondered if any woman had ever taken comfort there. Or perhaps the sole point of his existence was to make women feel awed and insignificant.

"And why do you now seek employment as a housekeeper for a fine residence?"

She hesitated. At least she now knew a good use for that word she loathed.

"My circumstances have since changed."

His brows flicked upward in apparent surprise.

Since she was now convinced this would be the last time she ever saw him, she was emboldened to stare back, which wasn't easy to do, because he

somehow managed to be both exhilarating and terrifying. His eyes were an unusual color, russet and
gold, a bit like brandy shot through with sunlight.
She wondered if they brightened when he laughed.

If he laughed.

Faint mauve shadows curved beneath his eyes; his
skin seemed stretched with fatigue. What appeared
to be a new scar, faintly pink and narrow as a knife
tip, scored his cheekbone for about two inches. How
that must have hurt, she thought. Though it didn't
really mar his looks. It was more like an underscore:
this man is beautiful *and* dangerous.

She suspected she now understood what
"attack" meant. Something like sympathy surged
through her. There was, of course, always the possibility he'd been attacked by the last housekeeper
for being insufferable.

In the silence, a log tumbled from its perch and
the fire gave a vehement pop.

"Circumstances," he said ironically at last,
"have an unfortunate tendency to do that."

His mouth dented at the corner. If this was a
smile, it hadn't reached his eyes. Irony seemed his
native language.

She was stunned.

She feared she stared at him dumbly in the silence that followed.

Which was so taut that when he gave his fingers
a single drum on the table, she almost jumped.

"The current staff is lazy and recalcitrant, and
because I have had sent to me a few possessions

I value, such as silver and porcelain, thievery is a concern. But then good servants are always difficult to come by, even for such a one as me. I have high expectations and low hopes of seeing them met. What qualifies you to command loyalty and efficiency from a staff, and what makes you think you will be able to meet my expectations?"

The unspoken words being, *where others have departed sobbing.*

And "such a one," was it? Surely the world could not withstand another such man.

She drew in a long breath.

"I've taught classrooms full of unruly children possessed of a variety of natures, and I know how to make them listen and learn and like it. I understand the concerns and politics of household staff and am prepared to address and manage them. I have experienced a number of, shall we say, economic conditions, and can adjust to any of them. I am scrupulously organized. All in all, I have a very good brain. And I am afraid of nothing."

Except you.

She'd just told a brazen lie to the man who claimed he would not tolerate them.

She suspected he looked at men just this way before he decided whether or not to run them through: it was sort of a mildly interested, fixed expression. She was not a woman to him; she was a problem to address, a code to decipher, a decision to coolly make. At one time her vanity might have been wounded.

Now nothing else mattered apart from what Lord Lavay did next.

"You may have the position on a trial basis for a fortnight, Mrs. Fountain." He said it almost idly. "You will start immediately."

She froze.

And then an almost violent relief sent heat rushing into her face and blurred her vision. For a merciful second, an infinitely safer, softer version of him swam before her eyes.

He drew one of those crumpled-then-smoothed sheets of foolscap toward him and perused it. As if he'd already forgotten her.

She freed her hands from their demure knot and absently swiped her damp palms along her skirt before folding them again.

She was proud that her voice was clear and steady.

"Thank you. You shall not regret your decision, Lord Lavay."

"I seldom have cause to regret my decisions." He said it coolly, almost absently, eyes on the correspondence, not on her. Indulging a serf just this once. "You may leave now, Mrs. Fountain."

As she departed, she surreptitiously dragged her hand across the top of the chair as if it were an exotic pet. A thank-you for the comfort.

PHILIPE GLANCED UP in time to see Mrs. Fountain take a quick little extra step at the doorway of his study as she departed.

It looked suspiciously like the beginning of a . . . frolic.

He frowned.

God, how the little details of running a household bored him. Odd, when the details involved in running a ship were so very similar and he relished those. It was just that one was a job for a man, and one was a job for a woman.

He doubted Mrs. Fountain was that woman.

Why should she succeed when three others had already failed? He'd sacked two of them, and the third had fled.

He of course already knew certain things about her, the things the worthy Mrs. Winthrop had chosen to divulge, anyhow—that she was capable of the job, at the very least, and the fact that the quality of her character had allegedly been endorsed by the Redmonds. His closest friend, the Earl of Ardmay, happened to be married to a member of that esteemed family.

If there was any advantage to all of the people and events that had led to his convalescent exile in Pennyroyal Green, Sussex, England—cutthroats and kings, seductions and beheadings, exquisite pleasure and excruciating pain, sword fights, gunfights, pirate fights, the utter destruction of his way of life until all that was left of him was the stony-cold, ruthless determination to restore it—it was that he could read people as fluently and swiftly as he read five languages. Questions were merely a way to distract his subject while he quietly summed them up.

Mrs. Fountain's posture, her diction, her ability to look him in the eye and string together formal, persuasive English sentences, to use a word like "politics" . . . all of it betrayed more breeding than the usual housekeeper possessed. She was proud. Proud people often did excellent work; proud people often thought they were above their work. Proud people would find it difficult to use the servant's stairs. His intuition told him she had a temper.

And she blushed and pet the furniture, as if she'd never seen velvet before.

Mrs. Fountain was also, he suspected, a trifle desperate.

He knew a bit about desperation.

But while she'd spoken, a spiral of glossy black hair had escaped from its bondage of hairpins and settled against her temple like a treble clef. She hadn't seemed to be aware of it. It had been so at odds with her precise speech and rigid spine that his mind had blanked and he'd almost forgotten what he'd been about to say. He'd almost forgotten to even think.

He sighed. He'd unnerved her. It didn't matter. She would doubtless be gone within a fortnight, and hopefully the desperate Mrs. Fountain wouldn't take the rest of his silver with her.

Charm had begun to seem superfluous in light of other urgencies. Certainly it had been no defense against the band of cutthroats who'd attacked him in London and left him with a lot less blood, a little less money, a few more scars, and in debt to the last person on earth to whom he wished to owe his life.

And he always, without fail, honored his debts.

He stood again, slowly, stiffly, and turned toward the window.

The rain had ceased, and the sun was beginning to drop, and the sky was blushing.

Pink had rushed into Mrs. Fountain's cheeks when he'd told her she could have the job. It had been rather like the sun rising to illuminate a delicate landscape. He'd ducked his head, feigning distraction, to spare her dignity.

But not before he'd noticed a tiny impression, a dimple, in her chin. He'd imagined pressing the tip of his finger into it, just so.

Perhaps further indication that he was right to ease up on his laudanum.

Chapter 2

❧

"ALL RIGHT. SHOW ME the Starry Plough, now, Jack."

They were sprawled on her bed in the dark, their heads aimed toward the window, the night brilliant and thick with stars. Her arm was draped around him, his hard little head rammed into her armpit, and he was drumming his heels on the bed and making flatulence noises with his mouth.

He was never really still. He was just six years old, and she supposed he was still discovering all of the things he could do with his limbs—dance, leap, create, destroy, annoy. And he was never really quiet, except when he was asleep. And then he slept with a loose-limbed, flushed-cheeked abandon that humbled and astounded her. Ever since he was born, life had been exquisitely beautiful and terrifying all at once, and probably would be forever. He was the gift that had cost her nearly everything else.

"It's riiiight . . . *there*, Mama." He pointed up through the dormer window.

"Oh, *very* good. But shhh. What did I tell you about those noises? Perhaps we can sing a song instead if you must make noise. Quietly."

"The song about Colin Eversea?"

"Where on earth did you—*definitely* not that song."

"From Liam," he benignly answered her unfinished question.

Of course. Young Liam Plum worked at the pub and helped out at the vicarage. He was allowed to ring the church bell, which filled Jack with awe and envy, and he cheerfully helped out with odd jobs about the village. He was quick and clever, and he wasn't much older than Jack. He'd been rescued from life in the London slums by Captain Chase Eversea and his wife, Rosalind, and his education at the hands of the streets was, diplomatically put, diverse. Jack took lessons with Liam held by the vicar at the vicarage, and he was allowed to help with chores there, too.

"He's famous, Colin is," Jack told her with a superior, confiding air. "I saw him once, riding a horse. Big cove."

"Cove" sounded like another word he'd learned from Liam. She would have a discreet word with the vicar, who had such exquisite manners and a refined vocabulary.

Colin Eversea was indeed famous for being the most dashing man to ever escape the gallows, in an explosion and in front of an audience of thousands, no less. A flash ballad had been written about him, and it had proven so popular that it was still sung in pubs and on street corners by cheery drunks and by university students and anyone who felt like singing while they worked, it seemed. New verses were added all the time, most of them quite prurient.

"You're quite correct. I remember when we saw Colin Eversea on the horse. The Eversea family is everywhere here in Sussex, rather like the Redmonds. They're very important people in this town, and every time you see them you will treat them with great politeness and respect. If you see him again, bow and call him Mr. Eversea, not Colin, and you certainly won't refer to him as a 'cove.' Or sing that song to him."

"*Mr.* Eversea," Jack tried dutifully.

"Well done. Just like a gentleman."

She could feel him beaming. He squirmed a little, pleased to be praised.

"And now that we're speaking of large and important people, I've something exciting to tell you, Jack. We are going to move from here into a large, beautiful house that's rather close by, and I am going to look after it for a . . . for a large man."

Jack took this in silently.

"We're going to leave Miss Endicott's and this room forever?"

If he'd sounded more plaintive than curious, her voice might have cracked when she spoke next.

"Yes. It's time to go." She said this with a lilt. To make it sound like a game.

He stopped drumming his heels. "Why, Mama?"

"Because the gentleman knows we'll do the best job caring for the house and for him, and I shall make a handsome salary. And we'll have rooms just as lovely as this one, and you'll even have one of your own. It will be better and so much *fun*."

Jack took this in thoughtfully.

"It was better when Charybdis lived here, anyway."

They'd shared this small room at the very top of the house. The teacher who had last occupied it married a marquess, of all things, and had taken her soft and temperamental cat, Charybdis, with her.

"Will we be able to see the stars?"

"Most definitely. We can watch the stars through our windows there, and maybe in the spring go outside at night to watch them, too."

If she lasted in the position that long.

By God, she *would* last that long.

"He's large? Is he a giant? Has he a goose what lays golden eggs?"

It was typical of Jack to sound hopeful, rather than concerned, about the prospect of a giant. She suspected he got that sort of courage from her, given that his own father was hardly an example of it. Then again, she'd never thought of herself as particularly courageous until Jack had come along.

And now *he* was her courage.

"A goose *that* lays golden eggs is how we'd say it if he did have one, but he does not. He's quite imposing." She never chose smaller words for Jack when she could find a grander, better, more specific one, because he was clever and he adopted new words the way some people adopted puppies or kittens. "He's grand and wealthy. Not quite as grand and wealthy as the one on the beanstalk. He's a prince, however."

Now, in the dark of her room, the title struck her as almost absurd. Not even in her wildest imaginings had she ever gone to work for a prince of any kind.

Then again, she would never have imagined what had happened with Edward Blaylock.

Or Jack.

Jack took this with equanimity. He was a child, and as far as he was concerned, anything could happen. He hadn't yet had the word "impossible" inflicted upon him. A unicorn could appear in the garden and he wouldn't make a fuss. He'd ask to bring it a carrot.

"If he's prince, will he be king?"

He ought *to be, with an ego like his,* Elise thought. Perhaps that was the trouble. All that power flowing in his blood, built up over generations, and currently no place to wield it except upon household staff.

Her predicament (the word she had come to prefer in her mind, rather than "circumstances") had turned her into quite a philosopher, when by nature she'd always been a pragmatist. For instance, one allegedly wasn't rewarded for all of the good one did until one departed the Earthly Plane. But if you committed *one* (albeit epic) transgression, a lifetime of damnation seemed required. Surely she was a cautionary tale for all those unruly young ladies at Miss Endicott's academy, and they ought to have kept her on as a teacher for that reason alone?

She'd tried that logic on Mrs. Endicott, who was accustomed to Elise's leaps of reasoning and usually enjoyed them.

Alas, there had been nothing either of them could do this time. Elise had been Elise one too many times; she'd said the wrong thing to the wrong person, and the wrong person had been subtly, nastily vengeful. It didn't matter a whit that Elise had been in the right.

And Elise, pragmatist to the bone, had understood this. It had likely only been a matter of time, anyway.

Mrs. Endicott had called in a favor from a particular Redmond family member who'd felt he owed her a favor—she'd been under great pains not to say *which* Redmond—and was able to secure Elise an interview for this position.

And this housekeeping position for the surly prince was all that remained between Elise and destitution and a life she refused to imagine.

Because she couldn't go home again.

If she was careful, Lord Lavay need never see Jack at all. The servants quarters and the rest of the house were parallel worlds. Some underservants of larger houses lived a lifetime without ever seeing the lord of the manor.

"He's not that sort of prince, Jack. The sort who will become king. But he *is* very important and he has chosen us, which is an honor. He knows we will do the very best job of caring for his house. And for him."

"Is he nice?"

She quirked her mouth wryly.

But here in the dark, with the person she loved most in the world and the promise of a roof over her head for at least another fortnight, it was easier to be charitable. But now she wondered whether the prince had ducked his head to allow her to turn a scorching red and subtly fall apart without a witness. Though such graciousness seemed at odds with his otherwise pitiless scrutiny.

"He's well spoken and well bred. If you're very polite, too, you may grow up to have a big house."

It was never a mistake to seize an opportunity to instill incentive in the child, she thought dryly.

"That's good, then," Jack said cheerfully, giving what amounted to his blessing. "Can we read 'The History of Mother Twaddle and the Marvelous Achievements of Her Son Jack' by Benjamin Tabart again?"

It was the story of Jack and the Beanstalk. She'd named him John, but they both preferred Jack because of this story. She'd also named him for his father and her father, neither of whom she'd seen in six years.

She leaned across him to light the lamp and opened the book.

"Make it a song, Mama!"

"Oh, very well. Let me think a moment . . ."

Jack's breath seemed held.

And then she had it. As she tucked him snugly in, she sang:

When Jack went to market with his cow
And came back with beans instead
His mother cried, "Oh Jack how
Could you be so touched in the head?"
But Jack planted the beans and one day found
A stalk soaring into the heavens.
He climbed up and . . .
He . . . climbed up and . . .

She'd sung herself into a corner, blast, with the word "heavens," but that was all right, because Jack was asleep before he'd had a chance to say his prayers.

She'd say prayers enough for both of them.

She went to take one last look out the window. She wouldn't miss the view when she looked onto the downs because, if she craned her head, she could see the trees that marked the clearing. She remembered the delicious surprise of the sun and breeze on parts of her body that had never been exposed to sunlight, let alone a man's eyes. Edward's eyes, so like Jack's eyes, as he'd moved over her, and how perfect and simple her joy had been, and how very, very ill advised.

She supposed she'd done the metaphorical

equivalent of trading her magic beans, as it were, and she'd gotten Jack in return.

And now all they had to do was win over the giant.

AS ORDERED, SHE arrived at Lord Lavay's residence the very next morning. She eyed those servant's stairs, her hand firmly gripping Jack's.

How ironic that they should go irrevocably up and up to the very top of the house, when her social status seemed to be doing just the opposite.

Suddenly the reality of her "circumstances" gave her vertigo and there was a rush of blood to her head. She acutely understood the impulse to throw a vase.

She would do it. She could do it.

The little hand tucked into hers was the reason she did anything.

"Hurrah! We get to sleep at the top of the house, Jack, where the view of the stars is the best," she said. "I'll race you."

Jack won, much to his gloating delight, and they patrolled their new home.

The room was spacious enough, at least compared to her former room at Miss Marietta Endicott's Academy, and it might have been reasonably comfortable if it hadn't been as cold as a tomb. The hearth was dead, dark, and dirty. The heavy curtains were flung open on the main culprit, a large window with an aging frame through which winter air squeaked; if she lasted longer than the fortnight, it would presumably allow in a lot of sun come spring; the aged, if thick, carpet bore witness to this. It had likely once been an un-objectionable deep green, but it was now a faded memory of that. She peered out on rain-soaked grasslands and soft rolling hills interrupted by clusters of oaks and birches. She could see all the way to the vicarage. The view had its charms.

When she gave the curtains a vigorous tug to close them, a little puff of dust rose, and she coughed irritably.

She knew the small staff was kept on by the owner of the house at reduced wages while the house was empty of a tenant. When it was let, the tenant—in this case, Lord Lavay—paid them full wages. He'd been here for more than a month.

But what the devil did the staff *do*, precisely?

She was going to enjoy finding out.

It was going to be lovely to have a long list of things to accomplish, to have people to order ab— er, organize. She didn't have the constitution for limbo. And since the future was certain for at least the next fortnight, she could afford to be cheerful. She was going to be the best bloody housekeeper who ever lived.

She turned around, and that's when she no-ticed the great cluster of keys on the desk, which seemed a rather insecure place to leave them, given that they would unlock the stores, the porce-lain, silver, and linen cupboards, and every other important locked thing in the house. Symbol of her new status. She hefted them, and they jingled pleasingly and portentously.

She sat down hard on the bed, and it bounced promisingly. Her spirits bounced a little, correspondingly. There was a small writing desk, an unprepossessing wooden chair, a lamp, a modest little vase. A bit of polish and airing, some flowers stuffed in that little vase, a few of Jack's drawings framed and hung—*voilà*! Then, perhaps, this room would feel like home.

She sprang to her feet and peered into the little room adjoining hers.

Jack was standing on his bed, his knees bent in preparation for a good bounce.

He froze when he saw her.

"It would be such a shame to break the bed when you've only just arrived, and then to have to sling you up outside in a hammock. Perhaps you oughtn't bounce?"

He grinned at that. "All right, Mama. Could I really sleep in a hammock?"

"Only sailors sleep in hammocks. You have a comfortable bed. Pretend you're sleeping in a cloud in the sky, because I'm certain you will feel just that way."

He mulled this over. "Could I sleep in the barn? In the straw. I saw the barn."

"You could if you were a goat, but sadly for you, you were born a boy."

He laughed. "You're funny."

"I am. I really am," she agreed. "We'll build

a fire, Jack, because it's a bit cold up here in the clouds. One day soon you can help the maid do it. Every boy should learn how to build a fire."

"Hurrah!" he exclaimed. He dropped to his bottom and mischievously bounced a bit on the bed, then sat obediently still when she raised her eyebrows in warning.

"Well, my darling son, do you like your room?"

It was very like hers, only much smaller and less drafty, mercifully.

He looked around coolly. "It's grand," he said loftily. It was his new favorite word. Everything was "grand." He thought it made him sound very adult. "When will I see the giant?"

"The giant will stay in his part of the house, and we shall stay in ours. You'll be far too busy having lessons and helping the vicar, who may even allow you to ring the bell, to see Lord Lavay. And we mustn't ever bother him. Promise me, Jack?"

"Oh. All right, Mama. Because he'll eat us? I can run fast. Faster than Liam."

He didn't seem worried about the possibility of being eaten.

The vicar's wife's sister had told her that little boys often passed through a period when they considered themselves utterly invincible.

"He has plenty to eat, so he doesn't need to eat people." *Not literally, anyway*, Elise thought. "All the same, it's best to give him a wide berth so he can go about his important business."

Whatever that was. She thought of that crumpled-then-smoothed letter on the table, the heaped correspondence, the smashed vase.

Jack sprang from the bed to the window. "I can see the church from here! And a cow! And someone on a horse, and a carriage, and a . . ."

" . . . and you can see Meggie and Liam Plum coming to fetch you off to the vicarage for lessons. See those little dots in the distance?"

"Hurrah!"

And with that, Jack scrambled back down the stairs, Elise following him at a more dignified pace.

They both had lessons to learn today.

Chapter 3

❦

In the kitchen, Elise found a cluster of people sitting around a great long slab of a table, each of them holding a hand of cards. Cheroots dangled from the lips of two of the women. Smoke rose spectrally.

The stink of unwashed dishes wafted in from the scullery. A light scum of dust and grease seemed to have settled over the entire kitchen, which clearly hadn't been sprinkled with sand or swept in some time. It was appalling, and grand, because she loved nothing better than an opportunity to improve things.

She gave her impressive cluster of housekeeper keys a portentous jingle.

Not one of them budged. One of them slapped down a card, and the others muttered. They were transfixed by the game. Someone shoved over what appeared to be pennies.

Elise aggressively cleared her throat.

They all pivoted in startled unison.

"Five-card loo, is it?" she asked brightly.

They stared at her, slack-mouthed and blank-eyed, apparently at a loss as to how to answer this question despite the fact that it was, of course, five-card loo.

"Wots it to yer?" a woman finally drawled around her cheroot, which bobbed on her lips. Her face was broad and impassive, her forehead vast enough to project silhouettes onto, and one could have yoked her to a plow. Elise was impressed. She hoped this was the washerwoman, because this woman would beat and slap the very devil out of the linens, and Elise suspected they were all going to need it.

"Good afternoon. I'm the new housekeeper, Mrs. Fountain. That is what it is to me."

In unison, five pairs of brows went up. The large woman narrowed her eyes.

What Elise wouldn't have given to know what they were thinking.

The large woman extracted the cheroot from her mouth and gestured with it languidly. "Well, 'ow do ye do, Mrs. Fountain. Ye'll need to throw in a shilling if ye'd like to join the game." She gave a slow smile. Her eyes were hard and assessing.

"I beg your pardon?" Elise said tautly.

" 'is lordship won't be 'ere but a few months. We servants ought to stick together. Come, 'ave a seat, Mrs. Fountain. Kitty, the teapot." She pushed out a chair with one of her legs while the one called Kitty shoved over the teapot and what looked like a flask of whisky.

"This will be the easiest job ye've ever had."

We servants was still echoing in Elise's head.

I'm one of them. She looked at the soiled caps and aprons, the sleeves shoved up to work-roughened elbows, the pasty complexions resulting from a life spent toiling inside.

Heat climbed her neck, and she prayed it wouldn't travel as far as her face.

I can't I can't I can't.

She felt as though she was pinned down by those words. *We servants.*

Begin as you mean to go on, Elise, her father always said.

And nothing else mattered, she reminded herself, except Jack.

"Yes, we ought to stick together," she said firmly. "And now you will stand, if you please. All of you. Now."

The queen herself had never sounded so uncompromising and certain of being obeyed.

"Beggin' yer pardon, Mrs. Fountain. We will do what?" The woman's voice was idly sinister.

"You will stand and curtsy when you greet me, and I shall return the courtesy. Anyone who wishes to keep his or her job will anyhow," Elise said pleasantly, but it was etched in steel. "And as you make your bow, kindly state your name and position in the household so that I may come to know you."

Their gazes ricocheted among each other like billiard balls. Some kind of silent communication was taking place.

They all settled on the large woman, who appeared to be the default leader. A position she had perhaps won through arm wrestling.

"Perhaps later, Mrs. Fountain." She mimicked Elise's pleasant tone but managed to make it sound a bit sinister. "We was just takin' a bit of rest, now, as ye can see."

"A rest from what, pray tell?" Elise asked, even more sweetly.

They were going to outdo each other in fake sweetness.

"Why, the strain of losing pennies to Ramsey. It fair shreds my nerves, so it does."

Judging from the direction all their eyes took, Ramsey was the man with the stack of pennies.

There was laughter that trailed into coughing when Elise trained her cold eyes on them and quite pointedly did not laugh.

"Come now, Mrs. Fountain. We came wi' the house, like. We're fixtures, like the furniture. We've always taken care of it."

Fixtures, her hindquarters. They were less a staff than an infestation.

"Ah, if you're like the furniture, that must mean you haven't been cleaned adequately in some weeks?" Elise said this brightly. "Or that perhaps you're all dim, like the hallways? A bit greasy, like the hearth here in the kitchen?"

And now five sets of decidedly unfriendly eyes were regarding her with unblinking hostility.

Elise returned the stare evenly. She was outnumbered but she was angry now, and she was as motionless as a stalking cat. She knew how to intimidate in precisely the same way a cat did. No one knew what a cat was capable of.

"Heh heh," one of the maids said uneasily. Some hybrid of laugh and grunt.

Clearly they couldn't decide where she got her confidence, and it was the reason, for instance, cats were able to intimidate larger, blustering animals. They possessed surprisingly sheathed pointy ends.

On the one hand, a good battle was *precisely* what she needed, and she would be damned if anyone would prevent her from keeping a roof over her head and Jack's.

On the other hand, her heart was knocking against her breastbone again. Surely she'd wear it out early at this rate. It hadn't experienced this much activity since she and Edward . . . though this wasn't the time to think about that.

She thought quickly. Lord Lavay had been right about one thing: skilled and loyal servants were rarer than hen's teeth. But she also knew from experience that hierarchy died hard among servants, and perhaps this lot had simply been jarred loose from the natural order of things through neglect and the absence of someone at the helm, the way old fence posts will start to lean every which way after a time.

She gave the keys an insinuating jingle.

"Come now. We servants deserve respect from each *other*, don't you think? And respect starts with a bow and a curtsy. Shall we at least begin that way?"

She looked to the maid who had given the tentative laugh. Her face was pale and pinched beneath a floppy cap, and her eyes were enormous. She looked eager for approbation. She stood and curtsied. "I'm Kitty, mum, Kitty O'Keefe. A parlor maid. Pleased to meet you."

Elise nodded serenely and curtsied.

The man who appeared to be winning all the pennies lumbered to his feet. Tall and lanky, his eyes were pale gray, his nose like the prow of a ship, which lent him some dignity he probably didn't deserve.

"Ramsey, William Ramsey. Footman." He bowed. Hmm. Not a bad bow, really. An elegant footman might be hiding in there somewhere.

"Mary Tamworth," said another woman. Fair hair straggled from beneath her cap, and she was tall and angular, with long arms and bony wrists. Perfect for reaching into candle sconces and trimming wicks, Elise thought.

"James Pitt, footman." James Pitt stood as tall as Ramsey and, on the whole, wasn't bad to look at, with even features and lively dark eyes. He appeared to possess all of his teeth. And he bowed elegantly, too.

"Excellent," Elise said brightly, as if they'd been eight-year-old girls who could be refined through a good dose of discipline, encouragement, and by distracting them with an endless stream of things to do.

The compliment seemed to mystify them more than anything. Mary Tamworth looked vaguely pitying. As if Elise was a slow child who hadn't yet caught on to the rules of the game, and they were all humoring her.

Elise turned to the large woman.

It threatened to become a staring contest until "Dolly Farmer," she muttered, ironically, around her cheroot. It was more a pronouncement than a statement. As if she'd been reciting the name of a famous battle, which Elise had begun to suspect this would become.

And then she rose from her chair.

And rose and rose.

And rose.

Upright, Dolly was nearly as tall as she was broad, her arms as broad as bread loaves, her bosom a mountain range.

She looked down at Elise with hard, amused eyes.

"I be the washerwoman and cook, Mrs. Fountain."

She executed a dainty, mocking curtsy.

"And rug beater I should think, Mrs. Farmer. We'll be doing a good deal of that in the days ahead. Beginning today."

"D'yer think so, Mrs. Fountain?" Dolly sounded almost amused.

"Yes."

She stared the woman down in silence, until the woman's feet actually began to shuffle.

"Now, perhaps you haven't had the proper training to care for a gentleman of Lord Lavay's stature, but we can set that to rights straightaway. Has the house been empty long, then?"

"Canna be empty if we're all in it now," Dolly said laconically.

Several of them snickered.

"Empty of a tenant like Lord Lavay," Elise repeated evenly. "You are all, of course, here on his sufferance, and now mine."

That quieted them.

Suddenly the servant's bell jangled violently.

Elise jumped. And then spun about.

She would have thought to have heard more snickering.

Instead everyone froze.

"His lordship is calling for you, Mrs. Fountain," Kitty O'Keefe whispered. "That be *your* bell." And then she actually crossed herself.

"Oh, *honestly*. I'm not going to the front, for heaven's sake. He might be a prince, but I daresay he puts his trousers on the same way as every man you've ever met, one leg at a time. I've met him and discerned that no spiky tail protrudes from them. And one cannot wear Hessians if one is sporting cloven hooves."

Too late she realized this made it sound as though she'd reviewed the back of his trousers, which she had not.

She had, however, reviewed the front of them long enough to note that his thighs filled them out eloquently.

Inconveniently, this is what filled her mind's eye now.

Dolly Farmer was eyeing Elise as though she

read every one of those thoughts. Her eyes were glinting.

"He does go on in that Frog language when 'e's angry, which is always. He doesna blink when he talks. He shouts. Asked Mrs. Gordon if she was stupid as easy as if he was askin' 'bout the weather." This came from Mary. "Insultin', that. Hurts a body's feelings."

And he also throws things, Elise almost added with a sort of grim cheer, picturing that stare of his. He'd probably aimed it at subalterns to get them to tell the truth.

"I would shout, too, if the candles in my hallways weren't trimmed and replaced, and the fires were out, and the house was dirty. I speak a number of languages. I imagine I can carry out Lord Lavay's wishes regardless of how he chooses to express himself. And his wishes, my good people, are our command."

The bell jangled again, vehemently.

The sound her nerves would no doubt make if people could hear them.

She cleared her throat. "Very well. When I return—"

"If," someone muttered.

"I expect the scullery to be so clean, or on the way to being so clean, that we'll all be happy to eat off the floor there. I'll share my receipts for soap—"

"*We* use sand and the like to clean." Dolly crossed her arms across her chest like bandoliers.

Elise fixed her with a look so quelling that Dolly at last blinked.

"So you *do* know how to clean." Elise clasped her hands together in feigned delight.

Dolly narrowed her eyes and tipped her head back, peering down at Elise, assessing her.

"I'll share my receipts for soap," Elise repeated precisely, as if she hadn't been interrupted. "We'll be using soap from now, as we don't have to fetch water from a well. But for now, sand will do to clean the kitchen and scullery if we haven't enough soap. You all look the sort who take pride in a job well done, so I know I won't have to ask you again."

This was patently a lie and quite the risk, but Kitty, for one, clearly fancied this version of herself—she stood a little taller, smiled a little, hiked her chin—and this was what Elise was counting on. All she needed was one malleable link in the chain in order to bend the rest into her idea of order. She knew this from experience with classrooms full of girls.

"Aye, Mrs. Fountain," Kitty said. Curtsying again, superfluously.

"And while Dolly and Kitty are cleaning the scullery, I want the candles trimmed, replaced, and lit in the sconces of the main hallway. This place is as dark as a tomb, and whilst we needn't be extravagant, it ought to be welcoming to visitors, not to mention all of us. This I leave to you, Mary. James, Ramsey, I'd like you to build fires

in the main rooms and in my rooms, and if the
hearths need cleaning, do it. There is no reason
for *any* of us to remain in a cold, dark house. I
shall review your performance upon my return. I
know you won't disappoint me."

Dolly Farmer slowly took her cheroot from her
mouth and ground it slowly into a saucer of what
looked like Sevres china. Elise imagined that
Dolly was picturing Elise's face.

"Anything you say, madam," she purred.

"IN THE FUTURE, I do not want to ring more than
once, Mrs. Fountain," Lord Lavay said by way of
greeting. He hadn't even turned to face her, so he
must have heard her slippers on the hallway.

And then he did turn.

Slowly.

She wondered if he did that for effect. Perhaps
he understood that the common, mundane female
of the serving class, such as herself, would need
time to prepare herself for his impact, and it was
an act of generosity.

But learning to withstand his presence was
going to take every bit of her hard-won fortitude.
His impact went right to the base of her spine. The
effect was something baser, an unnerving and
unwelcome reminder that she was a woman, perhaps above all, and still young.

The filtered sunlight coming through the window
contrived to outline him in gilt and showed her fine
lines raying from the corners of his eyes. He either

squinted down the barrels of rifles or spyglasses or smiled on occasion, and she was counting on the former. He probably wasn't quite forty years old, but he was older than thirty, she would wager on it.

"Mrs. Fountain," he said abruptly. "Did you not hear me? Were you perhaps dropped on your head as a child?"

Ah. What a mercy he was so reprehensible.

"My apologies, Lord Lavay," she said calmly enough. "My hearing is perfect. I was making the acquaintance of the staff and giving them instructions, and I came as soon as I was able."

"They are a motley lot," he said grimly. "Skulking about. Clearly incompetent. Sometimes the fires are lit in the morning, sometimes they are not. Sometimes I am brought coffee to drink, sometimes I am not. This room . . . the furniture wears a coat of dust, the hearth, it is dirty . . ." He gestured with a sort of exasperated ferocity that made him look particularly French. "The house is built well enough, but it is not gracious." He made this sound like a capital crime. "It is not beautiful."

The last word was *almost* wistful. Perhaps more weary than wistful.

Intriguing.

She sensed that now was not the time to tell him the staff had been playing five-card loo and smoking, drinking, and eating his cheese in the kitchen. The appearance of the house would not be improved by the appearance of servants' heads arrayed on pikes outside the gate.

But she couldn't alienate her staff, either, because the house would never get clean.

"They lack direction," she said smoothly.

His head jerked up abruptly, and he studied her. She could have sworn something like amusement flickered across his face.

"Do they," he said evenly.

She merely gazed steadily back at him.

Had he rung her simply to rail at her? She supposed it was her job to listen, regardless.

When he didn't seem inclined to speak again, she decided to be bold.

"Lord Lavay. I should like some clarification regarding my position, if you would be so kind."

"Clarification? Your role is to ensure the house runs flawlessly. I should like it to be comfortable, and by comfortable I mean clean and as luxurious as conceivably possible in this godforsaken corner of England. I expect the staff to wait upon me when I entertain visitors and hold social occasions, which I expect be conducted with grace and style. I do not want to be troubled with the details of how this is accomplished unless absolutely necessary. You will be held accountable for the activities or inactivity of the servants. You will achieve all of this within the budget I provide to you. And you will keep the books." And here he produced and thrust at her, to her surprise, a sheet of foolscap. "I believe the budget is both reasonable and scrupulously accurate—I assure you I can assess how much wheat a ship's crew needs for its voyage down to the grain, no more, no less. In other words, you will perform the usual duties of a housekeeper, Mrs. Fountain, with which I hoped you were familiar when I hired you for a fortnight's trial."

He said all of this with barely restrained patience and a hint of condescension that made her want to kick him. Likely she'd only break her foot and he wouldn't even wobble in those Hessians.

Fortunately, while her temper occasionally caused her trouble, it also made her more eloquent.

And for heaven's sake, Pennyroyal Green was hardly *godforsaken*. Church attendance had never been better since the handsome Reverend Sylvaine had taken over the vicarage.

Even though every muscle in her body had tensed beneath this barrage of arrogance, she managed to keep her voice steady.

"Thank you. The point of clarification I sought regards the staff. Do my responsibilities include hiring and firing employees at my discretion?"

This won her an upward brow flick.

"You will work within the budget I have prepared for you," he repeated, sounding mystified as to why he should have to repeat it. "And this means if you believe you can meet my qualifications with additional, fewer, or different staff members and do so within the parameters I've outlined, then . . . do feel free to wreak havoc upon the ranks."

It was almost *wit*. But he was somewhat white

about the mouth, she saw. His ill temper would be the death of him. Perhaps he strode the world in a perpetual state of apoplexy, aghast at its imperfections, hoping to set an example with his own flawlessness, doomed to disappointment.

Pride goeth before a fall, always. She possessed many fine qualities, but she could also be perverse and obstinate, which even those who had claimed to love her were forced to admit. She would not be defeated by this man.

She cleared her throat again.

"Lord Lavay . . . your last home . . ."

"Was on a ship," he said impatiently. In other words, the way he said and did everything. "I thought that was clear."

" . . . and . . . and your home before that . . ."

There was a pause. Long enough to be interesting.

"France," he said flatly, at last. He made it sound as if France were a lover who had betrayed him, so he'd been forced to kill her, but he loved her still. "I had homes in Paris, Provence, Versailles. My sister is in Paris presently. My estate . . . my home is in Provence."

Had. It was a painful verb. She'd once had a home she'd been welcome in, a job she'd enjoyed, a lover she'd thought she could trust. She sympathized with his use of the past tense.

She knew all too well what had happened to French aristocrats during the revolution. Likely those properties had been confiscated, stolen, or destroyed. There had been execution after execution. A torrent of death and destruction, with aristocrats fleeing the country if they could.

Circumstances, he'd said, had an unfortunate way of changing.

She sensed this man would not welcome her sympathy. Possibly all of the events had rolled right off him anyway, like pillows aimed with trebuchets at a castle wall.

"I will have them all again," he said idly.

She felt it then: a small thrill, as if his certainty, his confidence, his strength, had seeped into her blood. This was the sort of man, she was certain, whose men would follow him anywhere.

There would be consequences for crossing him. Or disappointing him.

She'd always thought of herself as strong willed. But the force of his character was a bit like walking into a stiff wind. It took all of her will not to sound timid.

"I thought perhaps if there was a particular way in which I could make this house more comfortable for you for the duration of your stay—"

He held up his hand abruptly. "Surprise me, Mrs. Fountain." He said this sardonically. "If you succeed where others have failed, I *will* be surprised."

She dug her nails into her palm. She counted to ten, silently and swiftly. She forced herself to take precisely three deep, even breaths before she spoke.

"Thank you for your vote of confidence, Lord Lavay."

She was proud of how benignly, even deferentially, this emerged. Because she'd never meant anything more sarcastically.

He narrowed his eyes a little. As if he could all too well hear the version in her head. The bloody man was excellent at not blinking. Probably from looking through spyglasses and down the barrels of rifles and the like.

And then he sighed, a great inflation of his lungs that made his vast shoulders move in a fascinating way beneath his coat.

"Perhaps this will be a useful way to think of your duties here, Mrs. Fountain—you are the first mate and I am the captain of this particularly drafty Sussex ship. You will see to the stores and to the morale and health of the crew."

She was so startled and enchanted by this analogy that she smiled.

Something shifted in his expression then. His cool perusal took on a thoughtful, faintly surprised, almost troubled quality. A faint frown formed between his eyes, then he turned slightly away, toward the window.

She was reminded again of a prisoner in a cell. Which was absurd, since he was master of the house, and surely he could leave at any time.

She could have sworn he'd *just* realized she was a woman, and not necessarily a homely one.

Her vanity might have preened if the idea hadn't been so alarming. Perhaps he rationed charm, if he possessed any, and only bestowed it on those he found worthy, and was silently chastising himself for wasting some of his on her.

But these flashes of whimsy, the dry humor . . . it was a bit like peering at the real man through a thicket of thorns.

Another odd silence followed.

"Did you . . . ring for a particular purpose, my lord?"

"Yes."

And he said nothing more.

She flailed inwardly, wondering if she should speak again.

His voice was a trifle gruff when he spoke, and he turned his head slightly away from her.

"If you would be so kind as to pick up the quill on the floor next to the desk."

Her eyes widened, then fell to the floor.

A quill pen did indeed lay on the carpet, half under the desk.

She looked up at him, confused.

He was still looking away.

And then she flushed.

Was this a demonstration of his supremacy? An arbitrary command to perform a menial task in the middle of the day, just because he could? Did he want to peruse the way the muslin of her dress draped her hindquarters when she bent?

Alas, no enlightenment was forthcoming. He simply waited.

"Of course, my lord." Because this was the answer she ought to give every one of his requests.

Her cheeks hot, she took the two steps toward the desk, and as she bent to kneel—slowly and gracefully—she saw what appeared to be the same wrinkled sheet of foolscap she'd seen yesterday, spread out next to another sheet, upon which a few words could only have been scrawled while drunk, so ragged and blotchy were they. She saw also a blob of wax and a seal and ink and sand, an empty brandy decanter, and the little bottle of laudanum, which was still half full.

She knelt long enough to notice that the carpet here was dusty, too. Good God.

She stood slowly and placed the quill gently on the desk, as if returning a baby bird to its nest. On the way back up she noticed one of the words on the foolscap: *Marie-Helene.*

She turned to face him again, schooled her face to inscrutability, and folded her hands in front of her.

"Will that be all, Lord Lavay?"

"Yes," he said.

They regarded each other from across the expanse of (dusty) carpet.

"Would you like me to refill the brandy decanter?"

"You will not last long in your position if you need to ask me how to do everything, Mrs. Fountain."

Mother of *God.*

The tops of her ears were hot from the effort to contain her temper, and no doubt they were radiant little red beacons, thanks to the fact that she had pinned her hair into lying flat against her skull.

He was watching her curiously. Probably waiting to see if the top of her head would lift right off and steam pour out.

"The carpets in this room need beating, too," she said quite neutrally.

And at that he turned abruptly, plucked up the quill, and twirled it in his fingers.

She was almost positive he'd turned in order to hide a smile.

"Are you implying that something else in this room would benefit from a beating, Mrs. Fountain?" he said idly, dragging the letter toward him.

But when he looked toward her again, quill in hand, his face was quite impassive. The sun shining through the window was giving him a bit of a golden crown. It looked completely appropriate.

"You are dismissed," he said, as irritably as if she ought to have known that, too.

Chapter 4

❧

SHE HALF DREADED RETURNING to the kitchen, but she moved down a hallway now softly aglow; mirrored sconces with branching arms sported neatly trimmed, lit candles. She would have felt more triumphant if the candlelight hadn't helpfully illuminated the dusty floors and dingy walls, and if her face hadn't felt hot and tender with temper, as if she'd literally been flayed. She slowed to a more dignified pace when she realized she was in fact storming away.

She half hoped the staff hadn't finished in the kitchen, because a dose of good hard labor was a wonderful way to burn away her mood. She prayed for a clear day tomorrow so she could beat the devil out of a carpet.

Only two things kept her from loathing him.

The expression on his face when he'd said "France."

And the expression on his face when he'd said "home."

She knew full well what it was like to yearn for home and to know it would be denied.

Those things, like the shadows beneath his eyes, were the way into him.

She hoped.

Oh, she hoped.

It was either that, or he was simply additional punishment for her afternoon of bliss in the arms of a feckless solicitor in training.

She was even more mortified to realize she'd worn her dark green wool dress this morning not entirely because it was warm. She knew what it did for her complexion and her eyes. As if he'd ever notice such a thing.

"You will not defeat me, Lavay," she muttered darkly.

Muttering so soon, and it was only her first day on the job.

Jack was her invincibility. She thought of Jack and she gave herself a little shake, as if she'd been shot with quills by Lavay and was now shedding herself of them.

"Thank you, Mary," she said warmly as she passed the maid, who was trimming another pair of candles. Mary nodded to her and offered up a tentative smile.

Elise was heartened. She *could* charm. She *could* inspire. She *would* win over everyone in this bloody house, the dour Lord Lavay included. Perhaps all they needed was appreciation and guidance and affection.

The farther away from Lavay she got, the more her mood elevated. The scent of lye preceded her before she reached the kitchen, along with a gust of crisp air—the windows had been partially opened in order to allow things to dry.

The maids were hunched over, scrubbing diligently, Kitty at the stove, Dolly at the floors, swirling a mop with the same vigor a soldier would use for stuffing gunpowder into a cannon. Both had their sleeves pushed up, and both were putting their all into it, sweating. Both gave every appearance of having done this before, given that the kitchen already looked cleaner. The table had been wiped clean of the remnants of the game of five-card loo, cheroot ashes, violated Sevre china plate, and cheese rinds included. Sand had been sprinkled over the hearth.

"Excellent work, ladies," she said warmly, in her best, encouraging schoolteacher voice.

Kitty peered over her shoulder but didn't stop moving. "Thank you, Mrs. Fountain." She offered a smile.

Dolly fixed her with those glittery eyes. "Yes, thank you, Mrs. Fountain," she said sweetly. "We aim to satisfy."

Perhaps she *had* been just that inspirational.

And perhaps Dolly was mocking her.

Elise sighed.

As long as they were cleaning.

And at least she had permission to give Dolly the sack if necessary.

Taking advantage of the filtered sunlight pouring in through the windows, she sat down at the spotless table and unfolded the budget handed to her by Lavay.

Apart from the slightly shaky penmanship— did the man have an issue with drink?—on figures and lists of items, the budget was virtually a work of art. A thing of beauty. Precise and specific and absolutely rigid.

So like the man himself.

Her heart sank again.

He had thought of everything—from candles to cheese to coffee, from linseed oil to lye, to eggs and wheat and boot blacking, and, of course, salaries, which were sufficient, just barely.

She'd not thought to ask what he might like for dinner, and the notion of approaching him again so soon was daunting. Like going out in the sun again while still sporting a vicious sunburn.

"Dolly, what does Lord Lavay eat for his evening meal?"

"Anything put in front of him, Mrs. Fountain."

She tried again. "Has he expressed a preference for any particular kind of food? Perhaps . . . cakes? Peas in sauce? Partridge? A ragout of beef? A nice steak? Filet of unicorn?"

"He expresses himself by swearing, Mrs. Fountain."

"Surely he has more refined appetites than that."

Dolly paused. "Canna speak to the lordship's . . . appetites . . . Mrs. Fountain. But he eats what I puts in front of him."

Elise looked up at her sharply again, eyes narrowed.

Dolly's eyes were just sliding away from her.
She had a sly little smile on her face.

Did Dolly always sound insinuating, or was it
deliberate? Perhaps it was a regional accent, that
tone? Perhaps everyone from, oh, Dorset, sounded
insinuating?

It had begun to sound like they hurled food
into his room and fled, like animal keepers in a
menagerie.

"What does he like to drink or eat in the morning?" she continued, her patience fraying.

"Coffee," Kitty said eagerly, happy to be able to
supply the answer to at least one question.

"Does he often receive visitors?"

"The Earl of Ardmay," Kitty provided eagerly,
on a reverent hush. "And the countess. Miss Violet
Redmond!"

Elise nearly choked.

Of course he'd receive an *Earl*. He was a bloody
prince of the House of Bourbon. And hadn't she
heard that he'd served as a privateer along with
the Earl of Ardmay on a ship?

"And ladies, too," Dolly added laconically.

Ladies, was it?

"Ladies?" she repeated, hoping for clarification.

"Aye," Dolly said.

Elise didn't think this part of Sussex teemed with
prostitutes, so perhaps Dolly meant it when she said
"ladies." Likely she meant Mrs. Sneath and com-

pany, who would descend upon any new residents in Pennyroyal Green, particularly surly lords, radiating goodwill and charity, and bearing preserves.

"And what do you feed the visitors?"

"If there are cakes, we feed them cakes."

"If? There should be no 'if.' There should always be cakes." It was the role of the housekeeper to make sure of it.

"Are there cakes now?" she heard her volume and pitch escalating.

"Cakes and the like be the job of the housekeeper, Mrs. Fountain," Dolly explained on a patient drawl, as if Elise was hopelessly daft. " 'ave a look inside the storeroom."

Elise got up and did that quickly. It would have given Old Mother Hubbard's cupboard a bit of competition for meanness. A few sad potatoes attempting to reproduce, their eyes sprouting, a scattering of rapidly wrinkling apples, sacks of flour and grain, some jars of preserved meats, pickled and dried vegetables, sugar, a wildly disproportionate number of jars of preserves for the number of people who lived in this house, half of what appeared to be a purchased loaf of bread wrapped up, a wheel of cheddar, hacked into already.

She began to feel a certain sympathy for the man, who, for heaven's sake, was entitled to a few expectations. He didn't *have* to eat as though he was on a ship.

She sat down and looked at the budget again. She did her own swift calculations.

There wasn't a ha'penny in there for anything one might construe as a "luxury." Then again, in some homes, soap was a luxury, not to mention footmen.

Her failure was built right into the budget.

As if they'd heard her thoughts, the footmen ambled into the kitchen, laughing and jostling each other.

They both looked startled to see her. Clearly they'd temporarily forgotten a new housekeeper had been installed.

"The five-card loo game has been cancelled permanently," she said pleasantly.

They eyed her cautiously, as if they'd been out for a stroll and stumbled across an unfamiliar mammal and were uncertain as to whether it would bite.

They, she was forced to admit with despair, did not look like footmen, though they were each certainly tall enough. Footmen ought to match, and they were only an inch or so apart in height. Their coats were clean, though they were different cuts and colors. She couldn't detect any loose buttons. She saw no iron mold on their neck cloths.

Surprisingly, their boots shone.

"Your boots are very shiny," she dubiously allowed. "Your neck cloths are white." As if they'd heard the whole of her thoughts up until then.

"I've me own receipt for blacking. Me secret's vitriol and egg white," Ramsey declared proudly.

"I use cream of tartar and salt for marks on the

neck cloths. My own family receipt," James countered, as though in competition. "Not that His Highness notices or cares. The Redmonds and Everseas, now the livery they wear . . ."

He trailed off wistfully.

"Elegant as the devil," James said to Ramsey, and Ramsey nodded in wistful accord.

They heaved identical sighs.

"You will call him Lord Lavay," Elise corrected reflexively, somewhat sternly. "Not 'His Highness.'"

Ramsey blinked.

Hmm. So they weren't *entirely* untrained. They even took a little pride in their skills. They possessed a bit of vanity. Perhaps they even yearned to be truly useful. She felt a pang of sympathy. The two of them were a bit like the bruised apples left over on a costermonger's cart, the ones you bought if that's all you could afford. The ones you could make into . . .

"Apple tarts!" she said suddenly.

She knew how to make a *brilliant* apple tart. Calculated to enslave any man. And there were just enough ingredients to make a dozen of them before she did her shopping.

Ramsey looked injured. "No need to be insultin', Mrs. Fountain."

"Not you. I was just . . . never mind. Would you be so kind as to tell me whether either of you possesses a spine? It's difficult to tell, you see, when you slump so. I can see you both have fine sets of shoulders, so show a little pride and throw them back, please."

Imagine that. Lord Lavay's irritability was contagious.

And effective. Possibly both startled and flattered by this command issued with such out-of-context irritation by their new commander, they did what they were told.

She squinted, imagining them in livery. If Lavay wanted gracious living, he couldn't have this misbegotten pair attending his suppers or admitting his guests, or, as he so charmingly put it, skulking about. And imagining how happy they would be in new livery gave her a little glow.

"And where have you been just now?" she demanded.

"The lordship has visitors. We've been to let them in."

She shot to her feet. "Who?" she squeaked. "I didn't hear a bell!"

"The Earl and Countess of Ardmay." They each gave a one-shouldered shrug.

And just then her servant's bell began to leap and jingle.

And for a moment her gut clutched as she remembered again that she was a servant now, who could be summoned by a bell.

Everyone froze, and their heads swiveled toward her.

There was a silence.

"They usually drink Darjeeling tea, Mrs. Fountain," Kitty whispered pityingly.

As if she knew Elise was done for, and already missed her.

PHILIPE HAD RECEIVED his guests, the Earl and Countess of Admay, in one of the drawing rooms, which, magically, featured a roaring, leaping fire.

He stared at it, nonplussed, unwilling to be seduced by hope. It might be an arbitrary fire. They did spring up from time to time in the house. Perhaps it was boring to do nothing at all, even for servants.

He turned to his guests, who were already relaxing on his settee as if they'd done it a dozen times before, which they had.

"If you turn one more expression of pity on me, I shall have you ejected, Lady Ardmay."

Lady Ardmay was the former Violet Redmond. He only called Violet "Lady Ardmay" when he was irritable, which was nearly always these days.

"By whom? One of those unpromising footmen who opened the door? Honestly, Philipe, they look as though they committed a crime in St. Giles and are merely using your house to hide from the law. I do wish you'd come to stay with us so we could look after you."

With the besotted earl and Violet and their new baby daughter, Ruby?

He'd almost rather be attacked by six cutthroats again.

Philippe had first met the Earl of Ardmay when the earl had simply been Captain Asher Flint and the two of them had served together on Flint's ship, the *Fortuna*.

"I shall ring for tea if you like," he said. "Would you care to wager whether anyone appears?"

"Oh, of course. I'd forgotten you'd hired a new housekeeper. The one our dear Mrs. Winthrop helped you engage."

Philippe rang the bell vehemently.

"Doubtless Mrs. Fountain is in her quarters packing her trunks in preparation to flee," Lavay said idly.

"And it isn't *pity*, Philippe. It's concern," Violet said, trying to steer back to the topic.

"Pah," he shrugged with one shoulder. "One and the same, Countess. I thrive, as you can see."

"Of course," Violet lied, exchanging a glance with her husband, which Philippe did not miss.

"How much?" Philippe asked the earl regarding the wager.

"A quid."

Just as a breathless Mrs. Fountain appeared in the doorway.

"Yes, Lord Lavay?"

Her cheeks were flushed, and two black spirals of hair bobbed at her temples. Doubtless they'd seen an opportunity to escape when she'd taken the stairs at a run. Mrs. Fountain, it seemed, could no more keep her hair completely tamed than she could her temper or pride.

But there was something valiant about the attempt to do all of that.

She suddenly looked so young.

He turned toward the window reflexively, in

welcome, as if sunshine had suddenly poured through a break in the clouds.

But no. Still gray. He frowned faintly, puzzled.

Odd that the sensation should arrive along with Mrs. Fountain.

He reached into the pocket of his coat and, with a one-shouldered shrug, handed a pound note to the earl, who accepted it with alacrity.

Mrs. Fountain's eyes followed the transaction, her face inscrutable.

"Will you be so kind as to bring tea for the earl and countess, Mrs. Fountain."

"Of course. It should be my honor."

She curtsied as if she were meeting the king, a low, graceful affair that seemed to go on forever. They all watched her go down, and then up. Rather soothing, all in all, like a leaf losing its grip on a tree, he thought, amused.

"Would you care for a light repast?" He turned to Violet and the earl.

Mrs. Fountain froze.

Knowing there was likely nothing worth serving in the house, let alone to an earl and a countess, Lavay was quite wickedly curious to see what she'd decide to bring up on a tray.

"Nothing for me, thank you. We cannot stay long," Violet told him.

"Very well, I'll return promptly."

Mrs. Fountain offered another curtsy, a mercifully quick one, and slipped out as quickly as she'd arrived.

"It looked for a moment there as if she was praying," Violet mused.

"For my demise, no doubt," Lavay said. "Care to wager on whether she returns?"

The earl grinned. "I could use another quid. I'll wager she does."

They waited a few moments for the click of Mrs. Fountain's slippers on the hallway marble to fade off into the distance.

"There are worse fates than marriage, Philippe," Violet said lightly.

Philippe shot her a filthy look. "Next time, I'm going to instruct those motley footmen not to let you in the door."

"And thank you, my dear," the earl said dryly. "Nothing like being damned with faint praise."

Violet just laughed. She sent her husband a smile that would have curled any man's toes and made him long for a dark room and a soft bed, then she gave his thigh a companionable pat. Neither of these men intimidated the infamous former Violet Redmond in the least. She'd once shot a pirate to save her husband's life. Hence they were less circumspect than they might have been when they talked business about her.

Their business was usually violence and money.

Philippe had fisted his hand; he forced it open into a straight palm now. It had been stitched quickly, like the other wounds, and the scar pulled like the very devil had its claws in, setting off a cascade of cramping muscles that had led

Philippe to invent new curse words for the sole purpose of getting through the pain.

"Seven of them and you would have been dead, Lavay. And you're the only one who could have survived six of them," Ardmay said. "Apart from me."

Philippe nodded. False humility bored both of them. They'd experienced too much, together and apart.

The two of them together had earned significant fortunes as privateers, and even more when sent on assignment at the caprices of the king, investigating conspiracies against the Crown and hunting pirates who'd threatened the safety and profits of England's merchants, and therefore the comfort and safety of her citizenry.

They had been so successful as privateers that the Crown now took advantage of their unique abilities in other secret circumstances requiring strategy, charm, brute strength, a willingness to stride into hideously dangerous places, and uncommon skills with weapons. It had been lucrative for each of them, together and apart.

It had also been nearly fatal for Philippe.

But there had been great satisfaction in the work. For Philippe, every capture, every sword that clashed with his, every thug they thwarted, every death or loss prevented was a way to offset the ones that had nearly destroyed his family and way of life.

And it *had* been profitable.

But they had failed to bring the pirate Le Chat to justice.

Truthfully, they hadn't so much failed to capture him as allowed him to walk away.

The true reason for that was quite complicated. Each person sitting in the room possessed a piece of the true Le Chat's secret, and none of them had shared it with the others.

Philippe had a particularly ironic, somewhat galling reason to be grateful the real man lived still and ran free. In his pocket now, on a torn strip of foolscap, was a direction that no one else in the world knew, written by a man known in merchant circles as Mr. Hardesty but who was, in truth, someone else altogether.

If you think you know how to repay me for your life, Lavay, you can find me here . . .

Oh, but the reward money for bringing in Le Chat. It would have solved . . . nearly everything.

If he thought about it too long and hard, the impulse to hurl the nearest smallest object would overtake him.

To think he'd once been renowned for his charm.

His stack of correspondence was growing higher by the day, it seemed. And several letters virtually throbbed with urgency.

"Is this how you want to restore your fortune, Philippe?" Violet persisted. "You'll be dead before you do."

Philippe snorted. "Thank you for your faith in me, Violet."

But he'd become more and more certain that she was right.

She smiled at the use of her given name.

"Think of the pleasures you'd miss on earth if you were dead. Please allow us to hold a ball, or at least an assembly, in your honor," she pressed.

"Perhaps," he said shortly. "I should like that. Not just yet, however." He could not now imagine being able to dance, since his injuries made him stiff, and he wasn't about to confess it. How ironic it was that waltzing seemed as important a skill as fencing. Navigating society often seemed akin to fencing in fine society all over the world.

There was an odd little silence, during which Violet exchanged another glance with her husband. She cleared her throat.

"Lady Prideux wrote to me. She was most recently here at Miss Endicott's academy to see about a bit of a business regarding her youngest sister. She will be in London again soon if there is incentive enough."

He vaguely recalled that Lady Prideux's sister had been installed in Miss Endicott's esteemed academy, a school locally known as the School for Recalcitrant Girls. But Violet's tone was a bit too casual, which meant her motive was ulterior.

He smiled wryly. "I've a letter from her, too."

But then, it was difficult not to smile when he thought of Alexandra; she was inextricable from memories of happier times. Their families had been much thrown together when they were younger, and there had always been unspoken assumption among them that she and Philippe

would one day marry. She'd grown into a viva-
cious and beautiful and preternaturally confident
woman, and she amused Philippe. Her family
was not quite as elevated as the Bourbons; their
fortune not quite as intimidating; their reach not
quite so vast; their power not quite so threatening.

Which was why more of them had kept their
heads and money during the revolution.

The Bourbons were back in power in France,
and even as a little girl Alexandra had always
loved the notion of influence and power. And
though Philippe was far away from the throne, he
still bore the name.

Hers was yet another missive he didn't know
how to answer, though he was growing more certain by the day.

He flexed his painful hand just as Mrs. Fountain appeared in the doorway, a tray bearing a
teapot and cups in her hands. They all fell silent.

Walking as though balancing on a tightrope,
her back straight as a mizzenmast, she crossed
the distance between the doorway and the table
around which they were all arrayed.

In the silence they could all hear the cups rattling ever so slightly on the tray.

Her hands were shaking.

A peculiar impulse surged through him to
reach out and take the tray gently from her. *I'm
not as fearsome as all that.*

And yet, he suspected that wasn't entirely true.
He had somehow, over the years, become precisely that fearsome.

"Thank you, Mrs. Fountain," he said gravely when the tray was at last safely arranged on the table.

She ducked a curtsy, turned herself around as carefully as if she'd still been balancing a tray, and elegantly carried herself out.

He found himself standing motionless, wondering if she would take that little extra step in the doorway again, unable to resist the beginnings of a frolic celebrating the fact that she'd managed to get the tray into the room without dropping it.

But she removed herself in a dignified manner.

He was so completely absorbed in watching her go that he almost gave a start when the earl cleared his throat.

Philippe swiveled to see Violet and the earl watching him. The earl's palm was extended.

Philippe fished about in his coat pocket and came up with another pound note. He was bemused to realize he was faintly pleased he'd lost the wager.

Chapter 5

❧

JUST AS TWILIGHT BEGAN to paint the remaining clouds in broad swaths of mauve, Elise burst out of the house through the kitchen and aimed herself at a run toward the vicarage—if she half walked, half ran, she could do it in ten minutes, she'd calculated. Her life had become all about minute calculations just like that. The cold air felt wonderful on her much-abused cheeks, which had flushed and blushed with every gradation of temper and emotion more times today than cheeks were likely designed to do.

She wondered what Lavay would say if he saw her running like a madwoman, probably losing more pins than she could afford to lose from her hair. But she hadn't a choice about running, either. She'd taken her opportunity to bolt when the footmen had admitted a dark, slim, cold-eyed, granite-jawed gentleman who had not wanted tea or anything else besides, who had been greeted by Lavay himself at the door. With a single, characteristically charming "I do not want to be troubled," Lavay had shut the door to his study behind him. Hard.

Too late for that, she'd thought cheekily. *I suspect you already are troubled, Lord Lavay.*

She'd run past a big black horse tethered loosely to the shrubbery, as though the rider had leaped off and flung the reins in. Her head almost whipped right off her neck when she thought she saw the king's coat of arms on the saddlebags: she glimpsed a rampant lion and an azure field as she raced by.

But there wasn't time to investigate that. Who knew what Lord Lavay got up to.

Her concerns were more mundane.

Thank God Thank God Thank God Thank God the Earl and Countess of Ardmay hadn't wanted anything to eat. She could not recall ever feeling so awkward and terrified and gauche, so at sea, not even on her first day teaching at Miss Marietta Endicott's Academy. All day long she'd felt like an actor who hadn't been handed a script before opening night and who'd been thrust onstage before a critical, drunken crowd armed with things to throw. Fortunately, she'd had worse days. The day she'd informed Miss Marietta Endicott she'd been with child, for instance. *That* had certainly been without precedent.

She'd get through it the way she'd gotten through everything, by relying on nerve, pride, brio, and breeding, all of which, ironically, could conspire to get her sacked. Especially the pride part.

The *nerve* of him betting against her.

Which, she suspected, was exactly what he'd been doing when he'd exchanged a pound note with the Earl of Ardmay, another large man, more rough-hewn and more exotic, somehow, than Lavay. Who was not so much rough-hewn as sleek and hard as a rock polished over and over by wave after wave of time and experience. Her father had attended to the ills and injuries of all the local Northumberland gentry, but never before had she seen the likes of the Earl of Ardmay or Lord Lavay.

Before she'd bolted, she'd left Dolly with instructions to put together a meat pie for him out of the ingredients in the pantry.

The vicarage was a relief after the Dour House of Lavay: noisy, bright, warm, and full to bursting with children—redheaded ones, mostly, belonging to Mrs. Sylvaine's sister, some of them destined for Miss Marietta Endicott's Academy, Elise was nearly certain. Somewhat incongruously, what appeared to be flower arrangements far too spectacular for a vicar to afford were scattered about, stuffed in vases and jars. Every color was represented.

This was new.

"A rather exuberant approach to decorating, Reverend Sylvaine."

His laugh tapered into a sigh. "I was just remarking on its resemblance to a jungle. I think those are of tropical origin." The towering and handsome Reverend Adam Sylvaine gingerly poked at a spiky affair the livid color of a sunset. "My cousin Olivia sent them over, with instructions to distribute them over graves in the churchyard. It seems some of her suitors haven't yet heard the news that she's engaged—and even if they have, they will persist in sending hothouse flowers. Landsdowne may be forced to call them out eventually."

Elise laughed. Lord Landsdowne was Olivia Eversea's fiancé. The one all of London never dreamed she'd have, ever since Lyon Redmond— Violet Redmond's brother, the oldest Redmond and heir—had disappeared, taking, it was said, her heart with him forever. No one had truly believed she'd consider another man.

No one had counted on how determined Landsdowne was.

"I brought apple tarts, Reverend!" She proffered her cloth-wrapped bundle. "I will exchange them for one child."

The reverend's wife, Evie, laughed, then raised her voice. "Jack, where have you gotten to?"

Whereas Elise had done *it* for the pleasure of the thing, the reverend's wife, the former infamous Evie Duggan, had done it for money. She'd been a professional courtesan; surely this ranked higher on the scale for Fallen Women, if such a thing existed? The difference, however, was that Evie had never truly been respectable and had disappointed nobody, whereas Elise had been and had disappointed everybody.

But now Evie was happily married to the vicar Adam Sylvaine, who had single-handedly restored church attendance in Pennyroyal Green and Greater Sussex through charm, selflessness, sheer pigheadedness, and devastating good looks. Together, they were kindness and acceptance personified. They were among the few who knew the truth about Elise's . . . circumstances.

Evie craned her head. "Jaaack—oh! He's right . . . here!"

A blur shot into the room and flung his arms around Elise's waist.

"Mama!"

She seized Jack and lifted him up in a squeeze. He was almost too heavy for that now.

"Good evening, my love. We must fly. Thank you, Reverend, for everything. May I ask you a question? I fear it's more in the way of another favor . . ."

"Anything we can do for you, Mrs. Fountain, as you know."

"My new position . . . well, it seems I won't be able to come fetch Jack home in the evenings from now on. I'm taking a bit of a risk now. I shall have half a day away on Sunday. Do you know of anyone who would be kind enough to escort him home? In exchange for . . . apple tarts?"

Her entire life was stitched together by an intricate network of barters and favors of time and skill and knowledge, of baked goods and canned goods, unused bolts of cloths and hand-me-downs, and herbs and cheeses and books and advice and tutoring.

"I'm a big boy, Mama! I can walk home on my own!"

"I'll do it."

Standing in the doorway was Evie's brother, Seamus, who whisked Elise with a surreptitious but adroit look that implied he wouldn't mind throwing his arms around her waist, too.

The refreshing thing about Seamus Duggan was that he never pretended to be anything other than what he was, which was a Charming Rogue who would do anything to avoid an honest day's work if a bit of fun could be had instead.

The dangerous thing about Seamus was that he was handsome in a way that caused female heads to whip around violently to get another look, and he was, in truth, a delight: quick to laugh, a bit too ready to fall in love, a bit too ready to forget that he was allegedly already in love when someone new caught his eye, always up for a lark or a prurient joke or a fight.

Hence his nickname locally: Shameless Duggan.

The vicar had taken him in hand and kept him too busy to get into too much trouble. It remained, however, a slippery and delicate challenge, akin to being careful not to hold a bar of soap too tightly.

Children loved him. Ever since he'd arrived in Pennyroyal Green, nearly all the older boys had doubled their profanity vocabularies and knew where babies came from, and he was kind to shy little girls.

He leaned against the door frame of the kitchen, green eyes sparkling, mouth curved in a teasing smile. Elise couldn't help but smile back at him now. All the ready smiles in this house were balm right now.

She'd seen Seamus with his sister's children. She was absolutely certain Jack would be safe with him, and that he wouldn't learn anything *too* untoward.

"Kind of you, Mr. Duggan, thank you."

"I'll escort ye back even now, if ye wish, Mrs. Fountain."

"That won't be necessary, Seamus," all the adults said simultaneously.

His smile broadened. "But it's truth. I'd be pleased to walk him home of nights, Mrs. Fountain. 'Tis no trouble at all."

"Thank you, Mr. Duggan. We must fly . . . and one more favor, Reverend Sylvaine. Would you . . . would you mind terribly if I took away a few of these bouquets?"

"You would be doing a favor for *me*, Mrs. Fountain."

PHILIPPE AWOKE THE next morning wearing a faint smile. He'd had such a pleasant, if homely, dream: he'd lifted his head at the sound of a coal hod clanking, seen the back of a woman wearing a soft white cap, heard the rustle of a fire being lit, and had felt all was right with the world.

An hour or so later he woke again because he was actually a little *too* warm. And he normally slept shirtless, so this was seldom the case.

He lifted his head off the pillow and peered.

The fire *was* blazing.

So it hadn't been a dream. In the air he drew an invisible point with his index finger. One point to Mrs. Fountain for getting the servants to do their jobs. For at least today.

He got himself upright and froze, his hand automatically reaching for the pistol he kept on the night table. He hovered. He thought he'd heard whispering outside his door.

Since The Attack, mornings were the hardest— every appendage he possessed was reluctant to bend, and everything else was stiff, and not necessarily in an exciting way—but his survival instincts managed to overcome pain, and he crept to the door and put his ear against it.

"Now remember, Mary, he's just a man. He puts his legs in his trousers one at a time. In all likelihood he won't bite."

"Perhaps he hasn't all of his teeth, anyway. He's not young, Mrs. Fountain."

Was that stifled *giggling*?

He couldn't hear what Mrs. Fountain said to that.

"But he'll be awake when I go in this time. He was asleep when I built up the fire." This was Mary the maid. *Coward!* he thought, half amused.

"Very well. I'll do it. But you will do it from now on."

An instant later there was a smart rap on the door.

He managed to fling himself back into the bed and pull the covers up to one armpit.

"What is it?" he demanded. His voice was a

hoarse rasp. Everything that ought not have been jostled was singing with pain from the sudden brisk motion.

The door swung open, and in bustled Mrs. Fountain. "*Good* morning, my lord. I'll just leave this tray here and pull the . . . pull the . . ."

He squinted up at Mrs. Fountain, who looked fresher than anyone ought to at this hour of the day, at least in the filtered morning light.

She seemed to have frozen.

She looked down at him longer than she ought, too.

She seemed too young for apoplexy, but one never knew.

"What the devil is that?" he rasped.

"That?" she parroted. Almost literally parroted, as her voice was a bit of a dry squawk.

"Come now, we've established you're not deaf, Mrs. Fountain. On the tray."

He began to sit up, and the sheet slid from his torso like avalanching snow.

"Coffeeandantwoappletarts."   The   words rushed out as if they'd merely been briefly dammed by something else.

"Apple—"

"I'll just leave it here, shall I?" she said brightly and pivoted, turning her back to him.

He could hear the tray rattling in her hands as she walked over to settle it on the nearby writing table.

And then she flung the curtains aside.

"Arrgh!" A torrent of sunlight struck him square in the face.

At least it wasn't raining.

She departed so quickly that she was nearly a blur, the door clicking shut adamantly behind her.

ELISE PAUSED WITH her back to the door, one hand clutching the knob, as if to prevent him from getting out.

Or perhaps to prevent herself from getting back in.

She stared unseeing for a moment at Mary, who hovered anxiously in the hallway.

Or not necessarily *unseeing*. Elise didn't expect to forget what she'd seen in there any time soon.

"Did he take it from you, Mrs. Fountain?" Mary whispered, as if they'd been holding out a beefsteak to a finicky captured wolf. "Shall I do it tomorrow?"

Elise thought quickly.

"He's definitely a bit surly in the morning," she said slowly, with a great show of martyred magnanimity. "Perhaps I ought to do it instead."

IT SEEMED TO take an inordinately long time to dress in the mornings, given that nothing on his body really wanted to bend the way it ought. Hastening the process caused him to pause, tense, and turn the air blue with swearing until he was ready to try again. Getting his coat on was the most difficult. Shaving with his left hand was another matter altogether. He had never anticipated needing to stay in Sussex longer than a fortnight, so he hadn't anticipated the need for a valet. He'd once heard Hercules, the temperamental cook on their ship, wistfully describe a wife as someone who would "help you get yer boots off."

He imagined describing it just that way to Alexandra, Lady Prideux, his potential bride, and hearing her peals of laughter. Alexandra was accustomed to having an army of servants to do her slightest bidding.

He flexed his right hand, which really was the cause of most of his irritation and frustration.

Philippe halted on the threshold of the study. Something was definitely different.

He entered cautiously. Just two steps.

And then he moved through it slowly, as if in a dream. Little reflected fragments of himself caught at the corners of his eyes.

Everything—every inch of the surface of his desk, the frames on the walls, the intricate turns on the chair and settee legs, the crevices of the buttocks of the hearth cherubs—had been dusted and polished. The room almost *pulsed*, it was so brilliantly clean.

An enormous rectangle of sunlight lay over the carpet. The curtains had clearly been taken down and the dust shaken from them, and were now tethered away from the windows by their golden cords. They were at least a shade brighter than they had been yesterday. The carpets had been beaten within an inch of their lives. The scrolling browns and creams and oxblood were rich again, and his feet sank into them as he prowled his environs, both hopeful and suspicious as a cat.

But another scent mingled with the lemon and linseed and burning wood.

A peculiarly disorienting smell, which, for a moment, made him think that this was certainly all a dream, from the giggling outside his door to the preternaturally bright room. Sometimes at sea he'd awaken with a smile on his face, that scent just drifting away from his awareness.

And then he saw it.

There, on the mantel, was a jar bursting with a profusion of lavender and hyacinth.

In other words, the flowers of Provence.

He gave a short, stunned laugh.

He drew another mark in the air for Mrs. Fountain.

He strolled over and touched them gingerly. They were just a little wilted, as if they'd been clutched in a hot fist for some time before being transported to the study and arranged neatly in the jar. Or perhaps the bountiful fire was doing its part to hasten their demise.

Still, they were beautiful.

Something in him eased. As if one item, the size and weight of a lavender and hyacinth bouquet, had lifted from his invisible burden.

He rotated slowly again, scanning the rest of the room for any other little surprises.

The brandy decanter was full and gleaming.

And tempting.

He turned his back on it as if it was a doxy crooking her finger, then rang for Mrs. Fountain.

Chapter 6

Mrs. Fountain still looked untenably fresh and guileless, given that she had clearly risen well before dawn to flog the worthless serving staff into cleaning.

"Good morning again, Mrs. Fountain. I would like you to retrieve my correspondence from Postlethwaite's Emporium in town today. The mail coach should have been in."

"Yes, sir. Of course, sir. Is there anything in particular you would like for dinners this week? I will do the shopping in town today."

"I should like boeuf Bourgignon, but I will be content with recognizable meat, served perhaps alongside peas, or some other recognizable vegetable. And wine. And perhaps bread. Surprise me, Mrs. Fountain."

"The meat pie last night . . ."

"Was edible. In the absence of an excellent chef, I infinitely prefer simpler food prepared well rather than awkward attempts at complexity."

"Thank you for your clarification," she said evenly. "I will inform the cook."

She didn't say *You rude bastard* aloud. But the air pulsed with it.

He was almost amused.

"And I feel I must give you my verdict on the apple tart," he said gravely.

"Very well." She straightened her spine and folded her hands before her like a penitent.

"And as you know, I feel strongly that one ought not to lie if it can be avoided."

"You made that clear, sir, yes."

And now her breath was clearly held.

He was not a sadist. He did, however, possess a sense of drama. So he allowed the silence to continue for a beat or two.

"It was Heaven on a plate, Mrs. Fountain. Thank you."

Her face went slowly luminous.

She was as radiant as . . . as radiant as . . .

Well, as radiant as the furniture in this room.

How had he forgotten the simple pleasure of making someone else happy?

"I'm very pleased you are pleased," she said somberly. But her eyes were fairly dancing.

"I should like my days to begin just that way from now on if I don't rise before dawn. With perhaps the exception of the assault of sunlight. Perhaps a more gradual introduction of light in the room would be more merciful."

"Very well, my lord."

"That is all," he said and turned from her, toward the correspondence he would once again attempt to answer. And likely fail.

When she didn't move, he turned, a quizzical brow cocked.

"Lord Lavay" came her voice, tentatively. "If I may ask another question."

He sighed. "I must request again that you issue questions with great economy, Mrs. Fountain, as my patience is not infinite."

Another silence, of the mustering-nerve sort.

"I should like to outfit the footmen in livery."

He stared at her blankly.

"Livery?"

"Yes." Her spine had gotten straighter, as if she were a tree preparing to withstand a storm.

"Livery," he repeated flatly, his tone suggesting that he was giving her one more chance to apologize for a grave insult before he challenged her to a duel.

"Yes."

He was stunned silent.

"Next you'll be asking me to supply them with whores and liquor."

"Well, no," she said.

"Why on earth do the footmen need to be more decorative than they are? They are merely functional, and barely that. I scarcely even need two of them. This is not the ark. We are not about to embark on a journey requiring a matched set of every kind of servant."

"Because people who take pride in their work will do a better job for you, and livery will help them take pride in their work."

His temper began to sizzle. "Thank you, Mrs.

Fountain, no one knows this better than I. I was the first mate of the *Fortuna*, and I have employed staff. Besides, God only knows the rewards I've received for the things I've bought for mist . . ."

. . . *resses* remained unsaid, but it was another syllable that pulsed silently in the morning air.

An infinitesimal nonplussed silence followed.

But the momentum of indignation and zeal for her mission carried Mrs. Fountain forward. "Yes, sir. Which is why I am puzzled you *required* an explanation for the livery."

His eyebrows shot up in warning.

He had a sense the words had slipped on through the frayed hammock of her control.

Because in the silence that followed, he could almost hear her silent *bloody hell*.

" . . . given that someone of your prestige and rank, and the house, deserves to be served and represented in elegance and style, as do your guests," she concluded adroitly. "And if you begin by providing the footmen with livery, they'll think you think they matter to you, and it is very difficult to put a price on loyalty. Though perhaps you know its price. I did not see 'loyalty' in your budget."

He ought to be furious. It was perilously close to insubordination.

But damned if he didn't rather admire it quite a bit.

And at least it wasn't dull.

Some trees toppled when continually battered by storms. Others just grew deeper, stronger roots.

He suspected he knew which kind of tree Mrs. Fountain would be.

"Nicely saved, Mrs. Fountain."

She smiled a tight, demure smile.

He sighed. "Very well. You may decorate the footmen. In fact, your arguments are so persuasive I now request that you decorate the footmen. But I will not release additional funds in order for you to do it, if that's the reason you've come to see me. Consider it a test of your ingenuity."

He watched her face, which was more expressive than she probably hoped or realized, as realization set in. Rather the way an anvil sets in when you drop it on your foot.

"Thank you, Lord Lavay. There's nothing I enjoy more than a test of my ingenuity."

"And God only knows, I shouldn't be able to sleep nights if you didn't *enjoy* yourself, Mrs. Fountain," he said softly.

In truth, he was rather perversely enjoying *himself*.

A feeling that lasted all of twenty seconds, eradicated by a single mistimed glance at the table at the unanswered letter from Marie-Helene, and one from his solicitor in Paris that he'd perhaps been dreading most, and one from his grandfather.

He felt his spirits darken as surely as if another of those thunderclouds had rolled through.

She saw the glance and cleared her throat.

"If you'd like to throw something, Lord Lavay, I will send in Mary to sweep up the wreckage.

But I feel I must tell you that it would require approximately fifteen minutes of her time, including searching out little shards that may cling to the carpet or draperies, and given her salary, the cost to you would be . . ." She tipped her head back to think. " . . . a shilling ha'pence."

He stared at her, astounded. "I see you've familiarized yourself with my budget."

"It is truly a thing of beauty," she said with every appearance of sincerity.

"And you performed those calculations rather quickly in your head."

"As I claimed in my original interview, I have a very good brain. I wouldn't dream of lying, Lord Lavay, as I know how you dislike liars," she said gravely.

"Oh, I do," he said just as gravely. "I do."

While the rest of her face was very solemn and deferential, serene as a nun's, her eyes gave her away. That shine might very well be caused by the light coming in the window, but as he hadn't been born yesterday, he recognized wicked humor when he saw it.

He wondered how long he'd tolerate this exchange if those soft eyes weren't aimed at him.

This was a woman capable of immense charm, he suspected. But it was pinned in as tightly as her hair. She fair crackled with the effort of restraint.

She was, in fact, an altogether pleasing study in contrasts: the dark, dark eyes, the pale, pale complexion, her lips red and rather plush, her brows slim black slashes, like punctuation marks.

She *had* been a schoolteacher, after all.

He saw that her dress had been turned and restitched, skillfully, but the faintest faded line remained at the hem. He noticed those kinds of things. And because he thought he was coming to know his housekeeper, he was certain she would prefer he didn't notice those kinds of things. She was proud.

"I do like the flowers," he said, almost gently.

She swiveled toward them, then swiveled back to him, flushed and pleased.

"I'm so very glad, my lord. I must point out you haven't room in your most excellent budget for flowers. Since doubtless fresh flowers cannot be obtained when one is at sea on a ship, you did not consider them. Although, I feel I must point out we are not precisely at sea here."

He was perilously close to being amused by how *ingeniously* Mrs. Fountain was conducting what amounted to an epic power struggle in the most passive manner conceivable. She was, in fact, attempting to take the piss out of him without him realizing it.

Except that he was fairly certain she was aware that he did realize it.

"So many things you feel the need to point out, Mrs. Fountain," he murmured.

She looked uncertain at that.

"How *were* they obtained?" He was genuinely curious.

"Ingenuity, my Lord."

"Is that so, Fountain? You must be positively savoring your new position, then. So many opportunities for ingenuity."

He fancied he could hear the wheels of her very good brain rotating in search of just the right response.

"My position is everything I'd hoped for," she said bravely at last.

And this seemed sincere, too.

He sighed. The familiar ache had begun to sink its claws into him, and he sucked in a sharp breath. He glanced at the brandy snifter. One glass, surely? Even though it was only midday.

He didn't want to become that sort of man.

"Very well. Obtain livery for the footmen. And if that is all, Mrs. Fountain, you are dismissed."

"Thank you, Lord Lavay."

He watched her go. The swift way she moved and the line of her—slim shoulders, slender waist swelling into what appeared to be a neat little arse, a sliver of pale skin between what he suspected was a turned lace collar of her dove-colored dress—reminded him of a little songbird.

She stopped and pivoted, as if she knew his gaze had been transferred momentarily to her derriere.

He lifted his eyes swiftly but unapologetically.

For a confusing instant their gazes met and held.

She cleared her throat. "If you will allow me to ask—"

He sighed gustily. "It seems she has more questions," he said with theatrically taxed patience and outward flung hands to the room at large.

"Do forgive me," she persisted, apparently inured to theatrics. She was nothing if not persistent. "The footmen, Lord Lavay . . . what color would you like to dress them in?"

"You'd like me to choose a *color*?"

"Color*s*," she revised. "Plural."

He raised a hand irritably, prepared to wave her away dismissively.

His hand froze midair when his eye caught the bouquet of lavender and hyacinth.

It was just. . . . these were the things . . . hothouse flowers, the intricate turns in the legs of his chairs, the heft of a beautifully crafted silver spoon. Ormolu and Gonçalo alves, marble from Carrera, Sevres porcelain, Savonnerie carpets. Grace notes, emblematic of privilege and a way of life that stretched back centuries. He would be damned if everything that made him who he was, everything his ancestors had fought and died for, would be lost, even though it had been violently taken from them. He would not be the one to allow it to vanish.

And why quibble, when he always knew what he wanted?

"Blue, Mrs. Fountain. A rich, deep shade. Picture a clear midnight sky over Pennyroyal Green. Perhaps silver trim, for a bit of dash."

They were the colors of his family livery at Les Pierres d'Argent.

He said this almost impatiently. As if this should have been the most obvious thing in the world.

"Blue and silver . . . it will be like stars in a midnight sky." She almost breathed it. As if she was enchanted by this vision.

He rather liked how the notion lit up her face and made her eyes dreamy. Imagine a woman who was easy to please.

"If you wish," he said shortly.

The light in her face faded when realization set in. "It's a very particular color, my lord."

"I'm a very particular man. That will be all, Mrs. Fountain."

THAT NIGHT, ELISE plopped down on the bed next to Jack and looped her arm around him.

"What did you learn today at the vicarage, Jack?"

"When I hang from the bell rope, nothing happens. I don't weigh enough. So Liam has to hold onto my legs while I'm up there to get the bell to go. And then when he did hang on my legs, my trousers came off."

Like every little boy his age, his trousers were usually buttoned to his jacket, so she would probably need to do some buttonhole repairs.

"Well, I suppose there's a physics lesson somewhere in there," she said dubiously, imagining with some alarm the two of them swinging from the bell like a huge clapper.

"I got my trousers back on."

"Clearly."

"You have to kick out to get the bell to swing,"

he said authoritatively. "The vicar said something about force and mass and vocity. I need to grow faster, Mama," he said plaintively. "Oh, and I learned Greek, a lot of prefixes. *Ab*- means 'against.' *Pre*- means 'before.' "

The vicar had gone to Oxford and had had a rigorous classical education. It was evident that he wasn't going to spare his students the same thing.

"Well, that's all well and good then, if you learned something as useful as that today. And it will be, my love, mark my words. And the word is 'velocity,' Jack."

"Velocity," he repeated dutifully. "There were seed cakes with lunch from Mrs. Sylvaine. This was "pre" the bell ringing. I was 'ab' the marmalade, though. Henny made the seed cakes. I like Henny, she's funny."

Jack was usually in favor of anyone he found funny.

"I like Henny, too," she said cautiously. Henny was an alarmingly—or disarmingly, however one wished to view it—earthy and energetic maid who had arrived in Pennyroyal Green with the vicar's now wife, the former countess, actress, and courtesan Evie Duggan. Jack would probably learn as many colorful words from Henny as he'd learn from Liam or Seamus.

Speaking of colorful words: bloody hell. She didn't know *how* she was going to manage the midnight blue and silver livery she was now required to produce.

She sighed. Miss Marietta Endicott had admonished her about her reach exceeding her grasp, about the pitfalls of pride and boldness. She had accomplished wondrous things with difficult pupils; she had spoken up when she'd felt strongly about something. She'd succeeded so often. When she failed, she failed spectacularly.

"Mama, will you read the one about the lion with the thorn in its paw?"

"Here, why don't we read it together? You know it as well as I do."

She pulled the book of Aesop's fables from the little selection of well-worn, much-loved books on the desk and handed it over to Jack, who fanned it open.

Jack was always greatly sympathetic to the poor grouchy lion who turned out to be grouchy because he had a thorn in his paw, and greatly impressed by Androcles, who was brave enough to take it out and was then saved by the lion.

"I wish I had a lion."

"We'd have trouble finding things for it to eat. I think it's more likely the lion would have *you*."

Jack giggled. "He'd eat you first! You're bigger! And slower."

She ignored this insult. Because damned if an epiphany hadn't sounded, clear as a church bell, in her head.

I do have a lion.

Well, she supposed it was less an epiphany than something that had been coming into focus bit by bit.

Lord Lavay was in pain.

Fairly severe pain.

It was probably why he moved slowly, and why he'd rung for her to pick up a quill pen of all things: it hurt to bend. His hand must have been injured—he favored it, she'd noticed—and it probably made it difficult for him to write. Who knew what else was injured beneath his clothes? And the taut skin, the shadows beneath his eyes, the whiteness around his mouth . . . why hadn't she seen it? He was too proud to show it. He obviously didn't want a head fogged by laudanum, and he hadn't touched the refilled brandy, because he probably didn't want to be drunk, either.

This was a man who was accustomed to being in control. Of himself, life, and everything around him.

She supposed she hadn't fully seen it because he was beautiful and fascinating and frightening and very, very difficult. He'd been an object to manage, an object of beauty. Not a person.

She shifted restlessly, imagining what he must be enduring.

She was ashamed of herself.

But men . . . Men were such *fools* that way.

She blew out a long shuddery breath, resigned.

Damnation. And this was what her father, a doctor, had bequeathed to her. She never could bear anyone's pain. She never could stand by without doing something about it, if it was in her power to do it.

It was up to her to be as brave as Androcles.

"And what does this story teach us?" She always asked this of Jack. She was talking a bit to herself at the same time.

"We should always help. Even dangerous lions. We should always be kind."

"We should always help," she agreed and gave him a squeeze. "Even lions. And we should always be kind."

Even when being kind was terrifying. Even when being kind didn't guarantee that you wouldn't be eaten by a lion.

Figuratively speaking, of course.

What would Lavay be like without the thorn in his paw?

"Sing a song about the lion, Mama."

"Oh, very well. Let's see . . ." She threw her head back and thought for a moment.

The song changed a little bit every time.

There once was a lion and his paw was sore, oh!
And if you came near oh how he'd growl and roar, oh!
But guess who arrived to pull out his thorn?
The bravest and kindest man ever was born.
Ohhhhh Androcles! He helped that poor lion as bold
    as you please,
And now they're the very best of friends
and the lion saved
Androcles in the end . . .

Not her best work. A bit awkward rhyming "end" and "friends." But Jack's lids were already closed, his absurdly luxurious and precious long lashes shivering on the curve of his cheek, and his faint smile was fading.

Good Lord, to be able to fall asleep like children did. Instantly and with such sacklike abandon.

"Good night, Mama. I love you, Mama," he slurred, already half in dreamworld.

"Good night, Jack. I love you, Jack."

She waited until his breathing was even, and she kissed that velvety skin between his eyes.

She leaned back against the wall, slumping in a way she'd never allow anyone to see, and swiped her hands wearily over her face. Then she sighed and gave a short laugh. Half despair, half amusement.

In the little mirror on Jack's wall, she could see her bed, the blankets turned down.

And because she had learned to take her pleasures where she could, she allowed herself a moment of indulgence and superimposed Lavay there, the white sheets slipping from a body warm from sleep, the gold glints of the start of a beard on his chin. Not in any of her wildest dreams could she have conjured such . . . casual magnificence. He wore his beauty as if it was of no consequence. As if it were simply something that served him and king and country. As if it were not a weapon that could stun armies into submission, if all those armies were comprised of women.

In the air now, tentatively, and then with more certainty, with a single finger, she slowly traced the outline of him as she saw him in her mind's eye: the sloping curve of that vast shoulder, the chest etched in hard quadrants of muscles. She could feel her body reacting, stirring in a way it hadn't for so long, and in a way she didn't feel she had a right to.

Edward had certainly not looked like that underneath his clothes.

She'd also seen a pink slash over Lavay's skin, and she did wonder how much of that beautiful body it traversed, and how deep it went, and she felt her own stomach muscles contract at the thought.

She took a long breath, blew it out gustily.

Life might not precisely be spiked on all sides anymore, but suddenly the tension of being a woman, and being alive, and being young, and longing to be seen as beautiful and charming made her feel three times larger and the box three times smaller and the torment three times more intense, because Lavay was . . . well . . .

"Dear God, if this is your idea of punishment for my sins, I must congratulate you on your originality."

She liked to think God had a sense of humor. Despite everything.

And she would like about five minutes of amnesty from the need to be brave.

And perhaps another five minutes of leaning against a hard chest, and hearing a kind voice, a deep voice, a voice she trusted implicitly, murmur against her hair that everything would be all right.

Jack had his dreams, she had hers.

She climbed into bed and slid beneath her

blankets, prepared to dream about just that. She shoved her feet down, then yanked them back with a yelp when they met something sharp.

She turned up her lamp and threw the blankets back, and investigated.

Chestnuts in their hulls. Spiked all around. At least five of them.

The staff, of a certainty, had done it.

She plucked them one at a time with a sigh.

"Oh, honestly," she said crossly, It wasn't so much the attempt at sabotage as how unimaginative it was.

Chapter 7

THE NEXT DAY, SHE realized the prevailing sound of her new life was jingling.

The keys she kept on her hip, which now and again startled her, and sometimes made her feel like a jailer, and other times made her feel like a prisoner who hears the jailer happening by.

She personally roused her staff before dawn. which was not among a housekeeper's usual duties, but she'd decided they would take meals together. After instructing Mary to tend to Lord Lavay's fire, she gathered them for a communal breakfast of buttered bread served with an inordinate selection of preserves—

—and toasted chestnuts.

She'd personally toasted them even earlier and arranged them neatly in a little china bowl.

She didn't say a word about them, unless "Mmm, delicious," counted as she helped herself. She simply coolly watched faces—Dolly's unblinking and impassive and Kitty's eyes downcast and Mary's gaze darting between Elise and Dolly and back again, and Ramsey and James still too bleary-eyed to care, slurping down cheap black tea. She would buy better tea.

"I'd like each of you to go through every room in the house and do precisely what you did to the prince's study. Clean it until everything squeaks and blinds the eye. Beginning with the drawing room in which guests are received. Windows included."

"That will take at least a week to move the furniture and roll the carpets and . . . and if it rains we canna beat the carpets . . ." Dolly expounded.

"It will take as long as it takes," Elise said pleasantly. "And I will inspect every room that you declare finished, and I will decide if and when you are finished. Begin now, please."

And so her day began to the promising rhythm of beaten carpets, which she heard through a partially open window in the kitchen.

Afterwards, she roused Jack, scrubbed his face, and sent him off with a kiss and jam and bread and apple tart to the vicarage, along with Liam and Meggie Plum, who worked at the Pig & Thistle. Her entire life was an intricate relay.

She fished through the keys on her immense key ring and began to explore the cabinets where the linen and silver and china were kept, as well as the dearer foods, like sugar.

In the linen cabinet she found a stack of fine linen sheets gone ivory and buttery soft with age and laundering, now musty. She wondered if they belonged to Lavay, and if he'd had them sent.

She touched one, and as surely as if it opened a portal in time, she was transported to yesterday morning, and sheets spilling from a vast shoulder and drowsy gold-brown eyes and—

She yanked her hand away immediately.

Perhaps she ought to be allowed to touch only sackcloth or bristly things.

Although Lord Lavay was a bit like sackcloth in human form, given that every encounter brought with it fresh punishments to endure.

And bristly things only made her think of the gold glints of his whiskers.

Her heart lurched when she considered what she intended to do today, and the likelihood of his responding with anything like gratitude.

She drew in a long breath.

She knew, quite simply, it was the right thing to do. Perhaps the only thing to do, for the sanity of everyone in the house.

She'd already put the coffee on. After dropping a few isinglass chips into the pot, she pulled down a china cup, shook her paper of powdered willow bark into it, and poured over it the rest of the boiling water in the kettle. It would need to steep for a half hour at least.

Time to see to the silver.

She pried open one large shining case of silver, which creaked like a sarcophagus.

Which was all well and good, she decided; the sound could wake the dead and betray any attempted thievery.

Inside was an exquisitely simple set of tableware, the handles engraved with filigree initials and the most delicate imaginable fleur-de-lys—

knives and forks and dessert and table and serving spoons and ladles, marrow scoops and grape
shears, asparagus and sugar tongs, and a half
dozen different types and sizes of forks and skew-
ers, the purpose of which she could only guess. She
imagined they'd all been accessory to generations'
worth of laughter, arguments, cold silences, hang-
overs, romances. She half smiled.

The last time she'd seen her parents had been
over breakfast on the day she'd told them the news
about Jack. Her father had been aiming a forkful
of scrambled eggs at his mouth, but he'd missed it
and stabbed it into his cheek instead, sending egg
shrapnel flying everywhere.

But her mother had very, very slowly and very,
very carefully lowered her fork, the forks the family
had used daily for as long as Elise remembered, and
laid it back down beside her plate, as if doing that
could restore everything back to the way it should be.

Elise squared her shoulders and gave her head
a toss, as if shifting a burden she was bearing.

The rest of the silver collection was comprised
of voluptuous tureens of varying sizes and vin-
tages, a punchbowl, several teapots, and serving trays and platters. *All* of it wanted polishing.
And by the time they'd finished polishing it, they
would need to start over at the beginning.

She'd begun to feel like Sisyphus.

Elise dutifully counted and noted each and
every piece.

She sifted through her great wad of keys until
she found the one that opened the china closet.

Plain, everyday plates and saucers and cups were stacked on shelves in the kitchen, but the truly fine things were locked away.

She yanked open the door handle, and something small and soft swung violently out at her and thumped her forehead.

Something hanging from a string.

She shrieked and swatted at it, doing her best not to whimper like a child, and leaped back with her hand clapped over her heart.

When it didn't seem to want to attack her, she peered at it.

A dead mouse had been tied by its tail to a length of twine, which was affixed to the door frame.

It continued to twist and swing to and fro like a macabre little pendulum.

Once she knew precisely what it was, she was furious.

"For the love of God. The least they could have done was fashion a little noose for it. I would have found it infinitely more sinister."

She gave the twine a yank, and it broke free. "I hope you met a more or less natural demise, Mr. Mouse, before you wound up at the end of a rope," she said grimly. She transported the late mouse across the kitchen and laid it down gently on a scrap of sacking one of the maids had been using to scrub. They certainly didn't need mice in the storeroom, anyway. Perhaps they ought to get a cat. Jack would like that.

She'd been raised in the country, and barn cats routinely deposited gifts of dead mice in all manner of surprising places. She didn't precisely cherish them, but it was certainly nothing alarming. The schoolteacher in her was growing increasingly furious at the servants' lack of . . . well, ingenuity.

How had they gotten into the locked porcelain cabinet? They must have gotten hold of the keys before she'd arrived.

And now that her heart had slowed to its usual pace, she began inspecting the porcelain.

Some of it was exquisite—a few pieces of delicately painted Sevres, pieces enough to support a small dinner party, but most of the china was merely serviceable. She wondered if any of it belonged to Lavay.

And then she saw the robin's-egg blue sauceboat, painted in pale blooms, and she just knew it was his.

Her bell suddenly jangled.

She gave a jerk, and the sauceboat jumped right out of her grasp. She dove for it, then spent a horrifying three seconds juggling it from hand to hand before she managed to successfully grasp it to her bosom, a full year shaved from her life.

How ironic that the bell, and the man on the other end of it, could make her do what a swinging mouse couldn't: nearly jump out of her skin.

With great delicacy, she lowered the sauceboat back into its pride of place in the cupboard, which she quickly locked. Then she locked the linen cupboard and the silver, but not before ducking to review her reflection in the side of a gracious silver tureen.

Yes, every hair in place.

And she did look well in dove gray.

Not that it mattered. Not that it mattered at all.

She arranged the tea and tart and coffee on a tray and squared her shoulders like someone heading into battle.

"THANK YOU FOR arriving so quickly, Mrs. Fountain."

"I should dislike for you to need to ring twice, Lord Lavay."

He threw her a quick narrow-eyed look.

She gave him only studied innocence in return.

She knew a minute pang of disappointment that she would not be bringing an apple tart and coffee to him in his chambers. He was already dressed and booted and apparently roaming the perimeters of his study.

From her vantage point now she could see the underside of his hard jaw and a line of whiskers he'd missed with his razor. It seemed terribly wrong that someone so proud should walk about not knowing he'd missed a row of whiskers.

Clearly he was right-handed. She could see now that his right hand was the one he favored. It must have been injured.

Her resolve redoubled. But the tray in her hands was heavier than she'd anticipated, and combined with her nerves, it began to rattle just a bit . . .

"I wished to give you a revised budget before you go into town to do the marketing today, Mrs. Fountain. A cart and horse are available to you for that purpose."

He extended a folded sheet of foolscap, and she took it.

"And I had grown so fond of the first budget, my lord."

"Then I suggest you have it framed as a memento. Perhaps embroidered onto a pillow."

She would have laughed in other circumstances, if her nerves weren't currently stretched tauter than violin strings, if he'd been someone else, and perhaps a bit less testy.

"You will not find livery in it," he added, a challenging glint in his eye.

"Of course not, my lord," she said soothingly.

His eyes flicked to the tray she was holding.

"I recognize the coffee and the apple tart. What is that?" He eyed the steaming cup grimly. "I didn't call for that."

"No. You didn't. It's . . . it's a cup of tea."

Good heavens, her voice sounded frayed.

"You are not in my will, Mrs. Fountain, so poisoning me seems rather pointless. Unless someone has paid you to do it. If so, perhaps we can negotiate."

Again, almost witty.

"My salary is sufficient, thank you, and I know a dozen ways to poison you effectively, but this willow bark tea won't finish you off. At least not at this strength."

He stared at the red-brown liquid. It did bear an unfortunate resemblance to diluted blood, at least in this light.

"Why have you brought me such a thing?" he said gruffly.

She drew in a breath, gathered courage, and said:

"It's for pain."

He went as rigid as a pike driven into the ground.

And then something that might have been guilt flickered across his face, as though he'd been caught in the act of a crime.

The usual hauteur returned.

"I do not need—"

She sucked in another audible, fortifying, very impatient breath, which clearly astonished him, judging by the launch of his eyebrows. She settled the tray down on the table, and everything clanked. "If you'll pardon my insult to your vanity, Lord Lavay, you haven't been sleeping well, and it shows." She pointed beneath her eyes. "You've hollows here. You cannot bend without pain, and so you ring for your housekeeper to fetch up quill pens. And you cannot write properly with your right hand, so your correspondence has begun to heap up. I do not know precisely what happened to you, but I suspect being attacked hurts rather a lot, and continues to hurt for some time after that. Unless, that is, one is made of stone. I beg forgiveness for the presumption, but my father is a doctor. I recognize pain."

A wondrous cavalcade of emotions chased each other across his face as she spoke. Astonishment gave way to indignation, stubborn pride had its moment, a hint of amusement, fury, a cold, cold disdain that boded ill for her future here.

He opened his mouth.

She braced for something scathing.

He closed his mouth again and stared at her. Right through her, or so it seemed.

He was so utterly tense that she suddenly had an inkling of what he might look like poised for attack, and she thought she might have lost another year from her life just then.

And then he sighed.

It sounded like surrender.

Something like relief began to tentatively creep in to shoo away her nerves.

She was shaking a little from the risk she'd taken, and she hoped it didn't show.

"Contrary to rumor and to my own chagrin, I am indeed made of flesh and bone," he admitted. "More's the pity." His mouth quirked at the corner.

Chagrin. God, but the word was beautiful the way he said it. *Chagreen.* His voice was quiet, too. Lilting, almost amused. Not his usual precise arrogance, as if every word had been carved from a diamond. She suspected it was a relief for him to admit to pain.

"I do not know what you have heard, Mrs. Fountain. But I am not a young man anymore— not a very young man, anyhow," he said with a rueful upward flick of his brow, acknowledging his own vanity. "And I do not recover in a day or two, as before, like that." He snapped his fingers.

"It is difficult to recover fully when the pain won't allow you to properly sleep . . . or properly bend. Or properly write. Or, I suspect, ride a horse. And however will you waltz again or reel? Or leave this . . . 'godforsaken corner of Sussex'?"

He was watching her with great bemusement.

She could see that he thought he ought to be angry but quite simply was not.

"Mrs. Fountain, I can find no fault with your priorities."

She suspected he might actually be teasing her.

"Surely the credit belongs to you, as you were merely exercising your faultless instincts when you hired me."

He snorted at this. "Clever, Mrs. Fountain. The trouble with clever people is that they often assume that no one else is as clever as they are."

Which sounded like a warning. Then again, it wasn't one she hadn't heard before.

She mutely lifted the cup of tea and extended it to him.

And then, in resignation, he took it from her, lifted it to his mouth, and paused, peering at her from over the brim of the cup.

"Any last words?" she risked.

The corner of his mouth twitched. He raised the cup to her. "*À votre santé*, Mrs. Fountain."

He took a sip.

Rolled it around in his mouth thoughtfully, as if sampling a wine, and swallowed, then made a smacking noise. "Presumptuous. Cheeky. Managing. Meddling. With notes of *une je-sais-tout*."

"You forgot fearless."

"Ah, yes. An oversight, of course. Thank you. Trust Madame Je-sais-tout to point it out."

A "je-sais-tout" was a know-all. But the words lacked rancor.

He *was* really rather amusing, in a dry and

prickly way that reminded her, strangely, of herself.

She smiled at him, tentatively.

He didn't return the smile. But she liked that faintly troubled way he looked at her when she smiled perhaps a little too much. As if he was peering at something in the distance with a spyglass and it was slowly coming into focus, and whatever he saw was unexpected and disturbingly pleasant.

"Shall I leave the tea with you, Lord Lavay?"

"You may leave it," he said abruptly, his usual dismissive hauteur restored, and he turned his back on her. "And you may leave me now."

ARGH. *YOU MAY leave me now.*

She didn't know if she'd ever get accustomed to being dismissed so abruptly. Her ears rang from it, as if suffering through the echo of a slammed door. She surreptitiously dragged her hand across the top of the brown chair on the way out, for luck, and because the velvet was such a pleasure, and she took her pleasures where she could.

On her way down the stairs again she paused, exhaled resignedly, and unfolded the budget and quickly scanned it.

And at first it seemed identical to the original.

And then she saw it:

Flowers.

One shilling.

And she threw her head back, and grinned and gave a triumphant little hop.

Chapter 8

✣

Philippe bolted the willow bark tea, which tasted exactly like licking a tree.

He rewarded himself for this with the apple tart, chased it down with coffee, leaned back in his chair, and waited to die.

He didn't really think his new housekeeper intended to poison him; after all, she'd come recommended by the Redmond family, and he was an excellent judge of character, on the whole.

Then again.

It was just that he'd learned that death could come at any time, in any form: it came for his aunt at the age of ninety, expiring at a crowded family gathering and tipping with a sound like dropped lumber out of the very brown velvet chair Mrs. Fountain seemed to favor; it could come brutally and unjustly, at the guillotine, like it had for his father, brother, cousins, and friends; or violently and suddenly, at the hands of cutthroats in London. Why not, then, at the hands of a housekeeper with eyes as soft and dark and deep as the hearts of pansies—no, perhaps a deep purple orchid—and a smile that made a point of her chin and lit her face and made him want to turn toward her, the way one turned toward a lamp in a dark room or the hearth in a cold one.

It occurred to him that if she were the last person on earth he saw before he met his maker, he wouldn't complain overmuch to his maker. That thought amused him bleakly.

Thirty minutes later he was still alive.

And he felt significantly better.

Mrs. Fountain was right: the pain got its talons into him and made everything more difficult.

It had taken a good deal of courage to force willow bark tea upon him.

It had been quite the risk, too.

He frowned, wondering how he truly felt about it.

But mostly it had been kind.

Often kindness and courage were tantamount to the same thing.

No. Kindness was softer.

He turned to confront again the stack of correspondence representing his present, past, and possibly future. He would need to write to his grandfather first. The man wasn't getting any younger. The healing slash across Philippe's right palm made writing a struggle, and when he tried to write with his left hand, the result looked as though he'd either been staggering drunk, or he'd delegated the task to a three-year-old.

He exhaled, feeling another bit of the tight coil that seemed to have wrapped him since he'd arrived in Pennyroyal Green unwind.

Because he'd just thought of an excellent excuse to ring for Mrs. Fountain.

A *use* for Mrs. Fountain, he revised in his head immediately.

An excellent *use* for Mrs. Fountain.

MRS. FOUNTAIN WAS in the kitchen, about to settle into a noonday meal with her staff.

She moved toward the table, where Mary had laid out sliced bread and cheese and cold chicken. A fresh pot of tea awaited them, and all the plain, everyday plates and saucers were set out neatly.

Elise pulled out her chair to settle in with a sigh. "James and Ramsey, I should like you to attend to polishing the silver. It will be a few days' work, that, but—"

A long, juicy flatulent sound erupted from beneath her.

She froze.

And then scorching heat rushed into her face.

Surely *she* wasn't actually *capable* of making such a sound? Then again, nerves could play havoc with all manner of things. This much she'd learned from her father the doctor.

She looked across the table at James and Ramsey, whose eyes were red, bulging, and brimming with water from the effort not to laugh.

The maids were looking down, but their shoulders were shaking like leaves in a high wind. Stifled hilarity, no doubt.

Elise sighed and reached beneath her to retrieve a sheep's bladder that had been inflated and thrust beneath the chair cushion.

She gingerly placed the thing on the table. "My son will enjoy this, thank you. It's his very favorite sound. You may laugh now, James, before your eyes pop from your head."

James spluttered out his held breath, with a sound rather like a deflating sheep's bladder itself.

"I'd like to clarify something, which will save all of us a good deal of time," she said gently. "I am not alarmed by flatulence, or by mice, or by chestnuts. Challenge only makes me more cheerful. Insubordination makes me very angry, indeed. And good, hard work earns my appreciation and flexibility. If you object to doing the jobs you are paid to do, you may tender your notice now. But you will leave without references. I. Am. Going. Nowhere."

One of her students had once said, "You give me the shudders, you do, Mrs. Fountain, when you stare so and don't blink." She possessed the gift of channeling the considerable force of her personality into a stare, and she aimed it at each of the servants in turn, an attempt to persuade them that she could see deep into their guilty, yearning, dark little hearts.

Her heart was, in fact, hammering. If her entire staff walked away right now—and servants were capricious that way—they could easily have her over a barrel. She simply could not imagine telling Lavay that the entire staff had defected virtually the moment she'd arrived. Not even any of the failed housekeepers had managed to drive the servants from the house like some domestic pied piper.

"Mrs. Fountain," Dolly began as she leaned toward Elise and reached out to lay a large hand on her arm. Elise stared at it until Dolly slowly, gingerly retracted it, folding it into her other hand instead. "'is lordship will be here another month or so. Ye can double yer wages in five-card loo in a week or two and not lift a finger, or only just. Why ruin yer pretty figure and hands wi' lye and labor?" This was all delivered in a sort of confiding wheedle. "'Tis a fine life we've got 'ere, and we dinna care to change it. We're good company, ain't we?"

Much nodding all around. This much, at least, they seemed able to agree upon.

"Why don't ye be a good lass and join us, like? I bet ye're a bit of a larf when ye want to be. It's been a fine arrangement."

The unspoken words being *until you came along*.

"Dolly's very good at five-card loo, too," James admitted. "Wins and wins. Except when she loses. But ye wouldn't want to see her when she hasn't had her cheroot."

"I likes me pleasures," Dolly said piously. "And some of me pleasures come dear."

"Do you all feel this way?" Elise said this somberly, but her heart was racing, and she was thinking furiously.

Apparently nobody wanted to commit to so much as a nod.

"Because," Elise mused, "it would be a pity to lose all of you now, especially since I spoke to Lord Lavay about outfitting James and Ramsey in livery."

James's hand froze in the midst of buttering bread.

"Livery?" he breathed. He and Ramsey exchanged meaningful, hopeful looks.

"Oh, yes. For there will be a grand party soon, with many elegant guests, and he agreed the two of you would look ever so impressive in livery. We also decided midnight blue would suit best." Elise crossed her fingers in her lap.

"I always fancied meself in blue," Ramsey mused. He rotated the coffeepot to admire his reflection, turning his head this way and that.

"And his lordship may very well require the services of a valet, and perhaps even a messenger to take correspondence all the way to London or to friends nearby. Provided either of you know enough about the care of a gentleman's wardrobe, or how to sit a horse."

She was extemporizing wildly, but the footmen had caught the whiff of glamour, and they liked it. They were both already sitting straighter.

"I can do both," they said, almost simultaneously.

"If this is true, then you will share those kinds of duties. And"—she turned to Mary and Kitty—"when Lord Lavay holds a ball, many of the ladies there will need assistance in the withdrawing room, and one never knows when a fine lady may require a new lady's maid or house-keeper. Imagine the beautiful gowns that may be handed down to you, the traveling . . . possibly even to France! . . . The higher wages, the pensions, the handsome young men you're bound to meet. Why, the position you're in now at *this very moment* is actually bursting with potential for the ambitious or clever woman. Life is best played as a long game. *Not* as five-card loo."

This sounded very sage, but she wasn't certain she believed it. She herself had taken more than one risk. But she was used to holding entire rooms rapt with persuasion and lectures. Albeit rooms full of girls age eight through twelve, but certain aspects of human behavior and need never really changed. Everyone wanted to belong. Everyone wanted to have value. Everyone wanted to know where they stood.

Not everyone wanted to work.

Dolly Farmer had crossed her arms over her breasts, and she was regarding Elise with cynical amusement, as if she knew precisely what *Elise's* game was.

The bell jangled and Elise gave a start and put a hand over her heart.

For the love of God, one day that was going to be second nature.

She didn't know whether to look forward to that day with enthusiasm or bleakness.

She was honest enough with herself to admit that there was a pinpoint prick of delicious excitement in the pit of her stomach. She smoothed her hands down over her skirts as she leaped to her feet.

"By the evening meal, I will require you to tell me what your plans are so that I may tell Lord Lavay. I should note that I anticipate that applicants for your position will line up outside the door, given Lord Lavay's stature and . . . and . . . legend. I can think of three even now I'd be quite willing to hire."

And with that, she dashed up the stairs and came to an abrupt halt to review the condition of her hair (smooth, ruthlessly pinned) in a mirrored sconce.

And then, on impulse, she all but tiptoed the rest of the way to Lavay's study.

She paused in the hallway and peered in. Because she wanted to pretend as if this was the first time she'd ever seen him. To catch him unguarded, perhaps, to ascertain for herself whether his unusual glamour had been simply due to her own newness and nerves, and whether she would get used to him bit by bit.

His back was turned to her.

Damnation.

She could write an entire song about the way his vast shoulders filled his coat and then magically narrowed to a taut waist. And so many things rhymed with "Lavay." *I could walk up to him and slide my arms around his waist, and my face would fit just so, in that space between his shoulder blades,* she thought. *I wonder what he smells like. I bet it's a bit like pressing your face against a granite wall. A delicious, dangerous, man-scented granite wall.*

And these were the kinds of thoughts that no doubt showed on her face when he surprised her by turning precisely the way a normal person would turn, rather swiftly.

She schooled her features to stillness a beat too late.

There was a funny little moment of silence.

As if he'd needed to adjust to her presence, too.

"Mrs. Fountain. I wondered if you might be willing to do something for me that falls somewhat outside the scope of your usual housekeeping duties."

Oh . . . no. Could he really mean . . .

She swallowed.

"Outside the scope of . . ." she repeated faintly, her imagination rifling through a dozen possibilities, all of them, thanks to her recent feverish imaginings, staggeringly improper.

"I'm wondering whether to interpret your expression as hope or trepidation, Mrs. Fountain."

His voice was a hush. If he'd been any other person, she might have described his tone as suppressed hilarity.

"You may interpret it as patient acquiescence," she said serenely. Or she tried. Her voice was pitched about an octave higher than usual.

"And yet patient acquiescence is so seldom accompanied by a blush," he pointed out.

Please don't let him be charming on top of it all. I couldn't bear it.

"And if I were asked to describe you," he relentlessly expounded, "I doubt 'patient' and 'acquiescent' would be among the first adjectives I'd choose."

She didn't know whether to worry or to feel flattered that he'd actually formed an opinion of her and didn't view her as purely functional as, for instance, the clock on the mantel or a barouche. *Which words* would *you use*? The old, glib, saucy, less careful Elise, the one not employed on a trial basis for a fortnight by a surly aristocrat, might have said them, because she wanted to know. And it was like seizing someone's arm as part of a reel. It could be an exhilarating dance, a flirtation.

It could also be quite the trap.

The memory of that sobered her quickly.

"If you find me pinker than usual, my lord, it may well be because I lit the stoves in the kitchen in preparation for baking, so it's a trifle warm. And I took the stairs at a run, as I should dislike for you to need to ring twice."

"Ah. I see. Apple tarts and acquiescence. I compliment you again on your priorities, Mrs. Fountain."

"Your priorities are my priorities, sir."

"Indeed."

There passed a strange little silence filled with nothing more than mutual, inappropriate, palpable enjoyment of the moment and each other.

"Are you perchance feeling a bit better, Lord Lavay?" she ventured softly.

"I am, Mrs. Fountain. Why? Are you concerned I will now turn into one of those frisky, bum-pinching sort of lords?" He asked this very gravely.

"I was unaware that lords came in that variety," she said even more gravely. "But my reflexes are excellent, and as you'll recall, I'm fearless. So no. I'm not concerned."

So much for not flirting. Because she most certainly was. In a reel, if someone extended an arm, one took it. It was the polite thing to do.

"Ah, yes, of course. Fearless. Thank you for reminding me, Madame Je-sais-tout."

You're the only thing that still frightens me. In so many ways.

Forever, probably.

She knew again the delicious little frisson of fear that came with walking the edge of something she knew better than to cross. She had forgotten what this was like. How a man could heighten every moment, remind you of the *point* of possessing sight and smell, let alone skin and nerve endings and a heart. That a man could so easily make your heart sing like a bloody lark or plummet like a stone.

This man could probably seduce by crooking a finger.

He was a prince.

She was a housekeeper.

It meant nothing, of course.

That little lift became a plummet, just like that.

"How did you find the taste of the willow bark tea, Lord Lavay?"

"Vile. But then, I've eaten weevils baked into biscuits on board ship, so 'vile' is a matter of perspective."

"I feel compelled to point out you've left no room in the budget for weevils."

"A shame. They taste a bit like mustard."

She laughed.

He blinked, as if she'd flicked something sparkly into his eyes, and again that faintly troubled expression flickered over his face. He turned away abruptly, took a restless step or two away.

"I'd hoped you would be willing to help me respond to some of these letters. Since my injury, writing is something of a painful exercise"—he held up his hand—"and some matters cannot go unaddressed forever. Some are, in fact, quite urgent."

"I'd be happy to help, of course."

"You may write in English, if that will go more swiftly. My correspondents will be able to read it perfectly well."

He pulled out the familiar brown chair with his left hand and gestured to it with a tilt of his head and an arch of his eyebrows. She settled in with a sigh.

Ah, brown chair, my old friend, we meet again.

The foolscap, quill, ink, and sand were already waiting for her.

He turned toward the window again, apparently the source of all his inspiration and reverie.

Chapter 9

"*Dear grand-père,*" he began.

He shot her a look over his shoulder to see that she was writing.

"*Dear grand-père,*" she repeated dutifully.

"*I hope this letter finds you still in robust health. I remain amazed at how quickly news can travel and through what channels. My deepest apologies for the delay in responding. I am so sorry to worry you, and thank you for your concern. I fear there is some truth in what you've heard—*"

"Mrs. Fountain, are you keeping up?" he demanded.

"*. . . truth . . . in . . . what . . . you've . . . heard . . .*" she confirmed.

"*—but I am alive and well enough in a town called Pennyroyal Green, in Sussex, brought here by my dear friend the Earl of Ardmay, whom you have met. You called him "a genial ruffian," as I recall. I will return to Paris as soon as I am able to travel comfortably. If you have noticed a difference in my handwriting, it is because I am dictating this letter to my assistant.*"

She scribbled away diligently and availed herself of more ink.

One curl escaped its pin and hovered about her eyebrow.

He didn't tell her.

He did pause to peer over her shoulder. Such beautiful copperplate handwriting made distinctive by impatient, bold, darker upward strokes, emphatic tall spikes on some letters and voluptuous loops on the others.

When he breathed in, he discovered Mrs. Fountain used a subtle floral soap, the scent of which was clearly set free by the heat from the stove in the kitchen and her dash up the stairs and perhaps that intriguing blush earlier.

He saw his own shadow cast over the foolscap.

She'd gone very still while he hovered.

"Everything is spelled correctly." Her voice was a bit thready. "If that is your concern."

How long had it been since he'd been this close to a woman? Too long, clearly, which would explain the almost violent surge of sensual pleasure and the impulse to touch his tongue to that pale spot between her collar and nape. He knew from experience that spot was an excellent place to start a seduction.

He took two steps back. His head swam a little, as if he'd momentarily stepped into and then out of an opium den.

"Please read what you've written back to me," he said shortly.

She did, quickly, the way she did everything.

He raised an impressed eyebrow. "This might work after all. All right, then . . ."

He took a deep breath. His grandfather would want to know it all.

"It was the dark of the moon, and there were six of them, grand-père. They appeared out of the night near the Horsleydown Stairs on the Thames. I was in London at the behest of the king, who'd assigned me the work. I suspect their motive was to stop me from doing what I had been paid to do, which was to stop them from doing what they wanted to do. I know I drew blood more than once—I could feel my blade sink into one mongrel's cursed gut, and God willing he crawled off somewhere to die while I—" "Mrs. Fountain, why are you not writing?"

She was absolutely frozen. Her face was nearly as white as the feather on the quill, and she was staring at him with abject horror.

"Mrs. Fountain?" he said impatiently.

"S-six of them?"

"Yes. My grandfather enjoys stories of *action* and *valor*." He gave these words an ironic flair.

She brightened. "Oh! So there weren't really six of them?"

"No. As I said, there were six of them," he said slowly, as if she was a slow child. "Please pay attention, Mrs. Fountain."

She opened her mouth a little. A tiny dry sound emerged.

And then she got the words out.

"But . . . you're still alive."

He smiled very faintly. "I'm beginning to think my gravestone should read, 'This time there were seven of them.'"

She stared at him as if he'd just attacked *her*.

"That was meant to be amusing, Mrs. Fountain. You may laugh."

Her mouth curved in an unconvincing and wholly dutiful way. "But . . . how did you know there were six? If it was the dark of the moon? *Was* it the dark of the moon?"

"You may assume everything I tell you to write is true."

In truth, Philippe didn't know how he'd been able to count. But he was certain there had been six. His vision became almost faceted, more precise, when he was in combat. He remembered all of it. A flash of every face, the wink of blades, the grunts of blows taken and given, the stench of unwashed men, the moment he'd realized he'd taken a blow that could very well prove mortal. That should have been mortal. If any of those men had been half as skilled as he with a sword, he would have been dead.

And if a certain Redmond hadn't appeared out of the night like a hallucination surrounded by his own deadly men, Lavay would have died like a dog on the Horsleydown Stairs.

"When I'm in combat, sometimes my vision seems . . . more acute. I know there were six of them as surely as I know the sun will rise tomorrow, and that you will ask me another question when I prefer to remain unbothered, and as surely as I know that you will not produce midnight blue livery for the footmen before the month is out."

He'd said it to get her spine straight and the color back into her cheeks, and it worked almost instantly.

"'When you're in combat,'" she repeated ironically. She was, in fact, still studying him, as if to ascertain he wasn't a ghost. "You say that the way I might say, 'when I do the weekly shopping.'"

But her eyes were troubled. It was strangely a relief to be looked at the way she was looking at him. As if for a blessed moment his entire spirit had stretched out on a feather mattress, and he hadn't known until then just how weary he'd been. He supposed his existence had become rather tenuous and deadly, and yet somehow, for all of that, mundane.

"Will the subject matter prove too much of a challenge for your delicate sensibilities, Mrs. Fountain?" he said abruptly, shortly. "Mind you, this is for the entertainment of my grandfather, who is nearly seventy years old, and he's always had a bit of a bloodthirsty streak."

"Please do continue," she said quickly. "My sensibilities are as cast iron."

He doubted this greatly, but he blew out a breath and gathered his thoughts.

"But as you know, grand-père, when a Lavay is given a fighting chance against his enemies and not

slaughtered like a pig in a cowardly and unjust way, a Lavay will always prevail."

He could hear the steely clang in his own voice, as if he was telling it directly to his grandfather, who did indeed love tales of valor.

"*Slaughtered . . . like . . . a . . . pig . . .*" Mrs. Fountain repeated tautly, scribbling away.

"*Thank you for news of Les Pierres d'Argent. I, too, think of it often. It was so much a part of my boyhood, and so much a part of who I became, that the loss of it is as another . . .*" He paused to clear his throat. "*. . . another death. I often wake from dreaming of it with a smile on my face. But it is a death I, as you say, hope to resurrect.*"

"*. . . another . . . death. . . .*"

"*A fever took me as I recovered from my injuries, and I saw Father, as he was the day before he was taken away, so proud and defiant and bold. It gave me courage, and I knew I must live for his sake, and for the sake of maman and Marie-Helene, and for . . .*"

"Mrs. Fountain," he said sharply.

She had gone still again.

She cleared her throat, but she didn't lift her face. "I'm sorry, Lord Lavay. Will you kindly repeat the last sentence?"

"*. . . It gave me courage, and I knew I must live for his sake, and for the sake of maman and Marie-Helene, and for you, so that no one we have loved will have died in vain.*"

"*. . . died . . . in . . . vain . . .*" she repeated softly.

He paused. It was always difficult to write to his

grandfather, because so much had transpired, and there was no way ever to say enough. He could only hope he knew his grandson well enough.

"*I kiss you on both cheeks, grand-père, and send much love. Please do not worry about your rent, for I will arrange for funds to be made available to you as soon as possible. One day our home will be restored to us. It has been too long, but we will be reunited in this lifetime soon.*"

He stopped speaking.

She stopped writing.

A hush of a sort fell, as though he'd uttered an incantation that had turned them into statues. Philippe stared out the Sussex window and saw a weathered and leaning wooden pasture fence in the distance. If he squinted, he could imagine it was the long, low wall surrounding the garden of his childhood home, Les Pierres d'Argent. The silver stones.

It had been seized by the rabble during the revolution, part of the momentum of bloodlust against the Bourbons and anyone related to them. They might as well have ripped off his arm. His family members, the ones not captured and executed for the grave crime of simply being of an old and wealthy family who had perhaps enjoyed too much power in France, had been forced to scatter like insects with the few possessions they could carry or smuggle out of France. And only now were they trickling back home. Some would never return.

"I will sign it," he said crisply.

He swiveled toward Mrs. Fountain abruptly, just in time to watch a fascinating expression flee from her face.

She gave a start and imitated his briskness.

"Very well. Would you like me to post it, or to send a footman into town to post it?"

"Perhaps I should read it again to see if there is something else I wish to have said. I can manage the word 'Philippe' without disgracing myself, no doubt. Shall we continue?"

"As you wish."

She smoothed another sheet of foolscap before her.

Another curl had gotten away. She noticed this one and swiped at it, tucking it behind an ear.

"Les Pierres d'Argent was your home?"

"Yes," he said shortly. "Please listen, Mrs. Fountain."

"Dear Monsieur LeGrande,
I apologize for the delay in responding to you regarding the sale of Les Pierres d'Argent. While the irony of needing to purchase the home taken from my family does not escape me, and doubtless you recognize it as well, I understand why you are compelled to offer it for sale. It is kind of you to inform me that you have received a very attractive offer for it, and I thank you. I . . ."

He stopped abruptly here, as if the next word was about to hurt. He cleared his throat.

". . . humbly . . ."

He said nothing for quite some time.

". . . humbly," she prompted very delicately.

"Yes, yes," he said testily.

". . . *humbly request your patience, as I anticipate being able to offer handsomely for it as soon as . . . as soon as . . . my nuptials are official.*"

She went still.

The quill might as well have been a feather-topped brick. She couldn't quite seem to make it move to form the word *"nuptials."*

"No," he said swiftly, and turned toward her. "End it with *'handsomely for it.'* "

She dropped her head abruptly.

". . . *for it,*" she repeated dutifully. Her cheeks felt warm again.

He stopped speaking.

"Will that be all?"

"Perhaps one more, Mrs. Fountain, if you would be so kind."

"As you wish," she said quietly.

The only sound was the crackle of the sheet of foolscap as she smoothed it out.

"*Dearest Marie-Helene,*

Thank you for your letter. It is indeed heartbreaking to learn that your ball gowns are of last season's vintage, and that you feel ashamed to show your face in polite society . . ."

". . . *polite society . . .*" Elise repeated.

". . . *particularly since Lady Montrose has four new gowns and also a riding habit. I would hope that you would recall your heritage, which means that YOU—*"

"Please do underline that word, Mrs. Fountain."

". . . *are polite society, and should behave as such,*

*which means holding your head high in the face of a
new riding habit. And . . .*

He peered over her shoulder at the original letter
and nudged it closer to Elise with his forefinger.

"What is that word, Mrs. Fountain? It appears
to have been blurred by bitter tears."

"'Coldhearted,' I believe," she said.

"And that one?"

"'Indifference.'"

"Ah, so I thought. And so we go on."

*"If you would be so kind as to tell me whether the
roof is leaking, whether the livestock lives, whether
your horse is starving, whether there is enough food
on the table, and whether the servants have defected or
remain, my cold, indifferent heart should be gladdened.
With love, your brother,"*

Elise stopped writing and tilted her head, imagining the beautiful Marie-Helene, beautiful and
spoiled and frantic, who would read this letter and
stomp her foot and perhaps completely miss the fact
that the entire letter was a sardonic masterpiece.

" . . . and I shall read it and then sign it, Mrs.
Fountain. I will ring when I should like them
posted."

"Very well."

She sprinkled sand over the text of it with the
gravity of someone trickling new earth into a
grave. He was silent. She could feel him watching
her intently. Or perhaps it was just that her skin,
her entire being, for that matter, felt acutely sensi-
tized every time his eyes landed on her.

"That will be all for now, I think, Mrs. Fountain. You may go."

She stood almost unsteadily and curtsied absentmindedly, her gaze colliding with his.

Then holding for a moment.

His face was steely and impassive.

She wondered if what she was thinking showed on her face, because she didn't think she could hide it. She hadn't been a servant long enough.

HE WATCHED HER leave and was surprised at the impulse to catch her by the elbow before she disappeared from sight.

He turned and looked at those three letters. More remained. But at least these three letters would stem the flow of need and concern and demand for a little while longer. But he could feel the familiar pressure building up in him. Time passed too swiftly. And there never seemed to be enough money. He was like Tantalus, always reaching for something just out of reach.

He drew the one to his grandfather toward him. He was confident his grandfather wouldn't share a word of it with Marie-Helene, which was as it should be.

He frowned down at it faintly.

This one, unfortunately, would need to be rewritten.

Because a word was already blurred almost beyond recognition.

Very like a tear had dropped upon it.

He pressed his thumb very gently against the word, as tenderly as if he were brushing it from her cheek. It was indeed damp.

He lifted it to find the word "home" imprinted there in Mrs. Fountain's handwriting.

ELISE INSTINCTIVELY PLACED her hand on the banister and let it guide her down the stairs, rather than take them at her usual dash. Somehow the smooth wood helped ground her careening emotions, a bit like a lightning rod might.

She rather wished she *was* a clock or a barouche, and not a woman. Because then she wouldn't be pulled this way by charm, that way by pathos, moved when she wanted to be made of stone, when she couldn't *possibly* be more significant to him than a clock or barouche, because servants were meant to be just that impassive. Oh, to be able to simply plant one's feet wide and adopt a steely stare and coolly shoulder everything the world chose to heap upon you, just like Lord Lavay.

"You may *go*," she mocked cheekily in a stern baritone whisper. An attempt to cheer herself up. He would always be able to summon or banish her, just like that. She was never going to like it. But she would simply have to endure it.

Just as she would have to endure the word "nuptials" and the eventuality of them, and why on earth should it matter in the least to her? He was only here temporarily, after all. Men like that married for money and for heirs, and bred more men just like that, who employed housekeepers, and so forth. That was nature's way.

She tossed her head with a sniff.

She slowed, savoring the silken glide of the fine wood beneath her hand.

It was just . . .

She stopped.

The break in his voice when he'd said the word "home."

That little break was very like a crack in his facade through which light poured.

How she longed to see through to the other side.

And she had felt, in that moment, her own heart crack a little for him.

She'd begun to suspect "steely and impassive" was in fact the opposite of "coldhearted and indifferent."

She recalled his face when she'd offered him the willow bark tea. He'd actually looked guilty today at the very notion of being in pain.

As if he hadn't the right to it. As if he was *supposed* to be impervious.

She was a believer in counting her blessings, and it was a blessing that she would be able to take out her stormy emotions on the baking of apple tarts this afternoon.

She sniffed and dashed at her eyes.

Thank *God* he hadn't seen her shed a tear. At least she had that to be grateful for.

Chapter 10

❦

AN HOUR LATER, ELISE brought the rolling pin down with a satisfying *thud* and leaned with all her weight on the dough, rolling it, flattening it. She seized up a handful of flour and let it sift down through her fingers like fairy dust, then gave the dough another vigorous flattening.

She'd patrolled the efforts of her staff first pleased to discover all of them vigorously laboring, Dolly Farmer included. They hadn't simply leaped into motion when she'd appeared. They'd been moving furniture, sweeping floors, polishing, rolling rugs and taking them outside to be beaten, all under their own volition.

She'd sent them in to re-beat the rugs in one room when she'd detected a dusty spot beneath the leg of one chair. She hadn't, not really, but she'd learned the efficacy of keeping her staff on guard. She'd also pointed out a patch of dust on a strip of molding.

"I suspect you're just a bit out of practice," she'd said sweetly. "Unlike, doubtless, the other servants lining up to apply for your positions. A prince of the House of Bourbon should not suffer one bit of dust."

She was probably testing her luck quite a bit, but there was no denying that Lord Lavay's influence was useful. Not to mention versatile. She could wield his name in all manner of ways. As a teacher, she'd learned to use whatever tools had been at her disposal to get her students to do whatever she'd wanted them to do.

A sheet of light entered the kitchen through the rain, and inspiration poured in along with it.

She might not be allowed to throw things in a fit of pique, but she could certainly sing.

Oh, you'd better not get in the way
Of the dour Lord Philippe Lavay,
He'll throw a vase or cup or two
Or he might decide to run you through!
He fought with dozens and dozens of men
And he'd happily do it all again
So you'd better run away from him
Before he gets you, too!
Ohhhhh. . . .
*you'd better not get in the way of the wayy—*accccck!

She whirled, brandishing the rolling pin, when she saw something move in the corner of her eye.

And the floor seemed to drop out from beneath her when she saw it was the man himself.

In the horrible moment that followed, her life flashed before her eyes.

Silence rang, and a cloud of flour hovered,

sinister as London smog. Much of it, she feared,
sifted down over her hair.

"Pray, do not leave me in suspense. How does
the rest of the song go, Mrs. Fountain?" He said
this idly. Almost a purr. That delicious accent that
could so easily caress or menace.

He was leaning against the door frame, filling
her escape route entirely. His arms were folded
across his chest, his face stony and impassive.

The rest of the song? She'd lost her ability to
speak, let alone sing. She held the rolling pin up
like Poseidon holding a trident.

"Lord Lavay . . ." she managed faintly. "I . . ."

She *what*?

"That is, indeed, my name. And how very convenient that so many things rhyme with it."

It truly was, in fact, quite convenient, but she
wasn't about to agree at the moment.

She nodded.

Why had she *nodded*?

Oh, God. Her face was scorching.

His face was strangely taut, as if he was holding
back something.

"Lay down your weapon, if you will, Mrs.
Fountain."

"My weap—oh." She gently, soundlessly put the
rolling pin down and, needing something to do with
her hands, folded them tightly and faced Lavay.

"Here is my concern," he said gravely, and her
heart sank and sank. "There are many facets to
me, you see, Mrs. Fountain. You've captured

my warriorlike qualities quite well, but I am renowned for other qualities, too. For instance, you haven't yet used the word 'charms,' which rhymes so beautifully with 'arms.'"

She froze.

And then delight surged through her.

"Not to mention 'cause for alarm,'" she risked. Because God help her, she couldn't help herself.

He regarded her thoughtfully, and something about that look traveled up her spine like a trailed finger.

"Am I?" he said silkily.

Dear God, yes. But not in the way he ought to be. Heat had begun at the back of her neck.

"You've a lovely singing voice," he said abruptly.

Now she *knew* for certain he was teasing her.

He smiled. Slowly, to allow her to fully appreciate it, to give it time to snake around her heart and stop her breath. It spread, wickedly, delightedly, and it made him look twenty years younger. His beauty *hurt* in a delicious way.

And the smile felt like a benediction.

It occurred to her that there was very little she wouldn't do to earn those kinds of smiles.

"You look *lovely* when you smile," she breathed.

Dear God! She hadn't meant to say that aloud!

What's worse, she'd sounded incredulous.

She put her hand up to her mouth, as if she could belatedly stuff the words back into it.

He laughed.

That's what he'd been trying to suppress. It was

an enormous laugh, as wonderful as sunlight after
storm. It echoed in the kitchen, and sounded free
and natural. And this, she decided, was precisely
what the house needed to cleanse the corners and
freshen the air. Lots of this kind of laughter. Even
if it was at her expense.

" . . . *And I haven't done it for a while,*" he sang in
a baritone lilt.

Her jaw dropped.

And then she laughed and brought her hands
together in a clap that sent up a cloud of flour. She
coughed and spluttered, but beneath that she could
hear him laughing again, and the sound trailed off
into a happy sigh, and he shook his head to and fro.
As if she was an endless source of amusement.

"If you would kindly send up apple tarts and
willow bark tea when you have finished with the
baking, Mrs. Fountain. My purpose for coming
down the stairs can wait. Oh, and you've flour on
your . . ." He waved an index finger to and fro in
the general area of his left breast.

Wicked, wicked man.

And then he strolled off singing,

*Ooohhhh, you'd better not get in the way
of the powerful Lord Philippe Lavay—*

"I think 'powerful' works better there, don't
you, Mrs. Fountain?" he called over his shoulder.

*He'll have an apple tart or two
Right before he runs you through!*

She thought she saw him gesture the "running through" with an invisible sword.

The willow bark tea must certainly be working.

And as she watched him go, she fought a suspicion, a radiant, unnerving suspicion, that the reason he had come all the way down the stairs and into the kitchen . . . was to see her. Just to see her.

She went still for a moment and stared at the place where he'd disappeared. She knew many underservants in large homes never even got a glimpse of the master of the house, so separate were their worlds, even beneath the same roof. And often masters of the house never learned the names of the underservants, let alone saw them or noticed them. Most masters of the house dealt only with a butler or steward.

Servants were meant to be acquiescent and un-obtrusive and obedient.

If he was assessing her on those criteria, she had already failed.

She gave her head a toss.

"What ruddy nonsense, Elise," she told herself firmly. "He came down to the kitchen because he *can*. You've restored mobility to the man with willow bark tea, and now he'll simply be everywhere when you don't expect it, like chestnuts in the bed and mice swinging from porcelain closets, just to keep you on your guard."

The mice reminded her of her impending confrontation with the servants during which they would tell her whether they were staying on, which perversely improved her mood. As she'd told the servants, challenge only made her more cheerful.

And the anticipation of seeing Jack in just an hour or so shifted everything back into perspective. No one, not even the appeal of Lavay, was a match for a mother determined to care for her child.

ELISE STOOD AT the kitchen door, her eye fixed on the area of the downs between the house and the vicarage, and her heart leaped when two figures, one small and running, as usual, the other taller and running after him, waving his arms in a vain attempt to get the smaller one to slow down, came into view.

"Mama!"

"Good evening, Jack, my love!"

He crashed into her thighs, laughing, and flung his arms around her in a hug.

"Whoops!" He laughed. "Mama, we've something for you."

Seamus came panting up behind him, came to a halt, bowed, then put a hand over his heart and recited:

Roses are red,
Violets are rare
Mrs. Fountain would look splendid with both in her
  hair.
But all we have are lilies, so there.

He and Jack presented flowers. Indeed, lilies.

She took them and curtsied, laughing. Jack's lily was rather more crushed than Seamus's.

Who, bless his fickle rogue's heart, was like balm after Lavay. Seamus didn't fascinate or enrage or move or toss her emotions about like fall leaves in a windstorm, or occupy a good part of her mind for the whole of the day. But he did flatter, and he was certainly easy to look at.

Surely, for some women, Seamus was temptation incarnate.

His eyes were green, and they were sparkling at her now.

"Lilies *and* a small ruffian delivered unto me. Could a woman be any luckier? Good heavens, Jack, did you get jelly on your collar?"

"No, it's blood, Mama!" he said cheerfully.

Elise clutched at the door frame in shock that was only a little feigned.

"Dinna ye worry, Mrs. Fountain. They wrestled a bit and Jack's elbow caught Liam in the nose."

"They were wrestling? I wasn't aware this was part of the curriculum."

"It's what boys do, Mrs. Fountain. One moment they're doing their lessons, the next it's warfare. Adam, er, Reverend Sylvaine, and I managed to part them. They're still the best of friends."

"It's mostly Liam's blood," Jack said cheerily. "The vicar made us stand in the corner and think about violins, and why they are not the answer."

"Violin . . . oh, I think you mean 'viol*ence*,' Jack, darling. Violins are the little musical instruments you play like this." She mimed drawing a bow across the strings. " 'Violence,' with the short *e* sound, means fisticuffs and wrestling and the like." She mimed putting up her fists. "And he's right. It's nev—well, seldom the answer."

Because an image of six men coming at Philippe Lavay in the dark of the moon rushed at her, and inwardly she inserted herself into the scene, throwing her fists at all of them before they could get anywhere near him. No one who had a smile like his should ever be subjected to violence. The very idea knotted her stomach.

Where the devil had *that* untoward thought come from?

"Oh." Jack scrunched his nose. "Well, I thought about violins while I was in the corner. Dunno what Liam thought about. Seamus plays the violin. He's going to play the violin in the Christmas pantomime."

"Fiddle," Seamus said modestly. He hoisted an invisible fiddle to his shoulder and mimed vigorous playing, concluding with a flourish.

"I'm not surprised."

" . . . that I'm a man of many talents?" He smiled. "Violence may not be the answer, Mrs. Fountain, but fiddles often are."

"Mama makes up songs, Seamus." Jack was leaning against her now.

Elise felt herself blushing again. "Jack," she said warningly.

"Do ye now, Mrs. Fountain? Come down to the Pig & Thistle on yer night out, and join in the singing. We've a tin flute player, and a drummer, and someone who claims he knows all of the verses to the 'Ballad of Colin Eversea.' Everyone comes, the vicar, Mrs. Endicott, the Eversea boys. If you bring the little one, we'll swear to only sing the decent verses. If there are any left."

"That's a kind invitation, Mr. Duggan. Perhaps one day I'll join all of you. For now, thank you for bringing Jack home. Here are four jam tarts for your trouble."

She thrust out the cloth-wrapped bundle, and he handed off to her the cloth she'd wrapped his tarts in yesterday.

"Oh, it's no trouble. 'Tis naught but a pleasure, Mrs. Fountain. Until tomorrow."

He bowed and turned, sauntering off, and a high, clear, lilting Irish tenor rose into the air over the green.

Oh, if ye thought ye'd never see
the end of Colin Eversea, then come along with me,
lads, come along with me!

She watched him go, smiling faintly, and wondered vaguely if Seamus Duggan was . . . courting . . . her?

Surely not. When plenty of young women who hadn't any children would fling themselves into his arms with less provocation or incentive than a bouquet of flowers.

Poor, poor foolish young women. If only they knew.

She liked to think that Edward had essentially inoculated her against men like Seamus.

Or any men who possessed formidable, suspect

charm, really. She'd been susceptible once before. Surely she possessed formidable resistance now?

She hovered in the doorway awhile longer, watching Seamus become smaller and smaller as she thought about another man entirely.

Just to be safe, she would send up James or Ramsey with willow bark tea and an apple tart later.

AN HOUR LATER, after she'd gotten Jack fed, they all gathered around the long kitchen table like a tribunal.

It felt to Elise like she was the one on trial.

"We've some conditions," Dolly drawled, after they'd all silently filled their plates with stew and bread that wasn't, as it turned out, intolerable.

"I'd like to point out, Dolly, that you are not entitled to any conditions, but if you have reasonable suggestions or requests, I'd be happy to consider them, and, if necessary, convey them to Lord Lavay, who would be happy to discuss them with you."

Dolly Farmer looked at her with that same cynical amusement she always employed. Perhaps skillful five-card loo players knew when someone else was bluffing.

Elise decided that, regardless of her skills as a washerwoman or scrubwoman, she wouldn't mind in the least if Dolly was struck by lightning.

The others, on the other hand, had encountered Lord Lavay in his throwing moods, and his name still carried a whiff of a threat. It wasn't something they wished to repeat.

"Well, then," Elise said pleasantly. "What may I tell Lord Lavay about his staff?"

"We shall stay on, Mrs. Fountain," Dolly Farmer said magnanimously, and rather sweetly. "I think you'll be a right *pleasure* to work for."

Elise narrowed her eyes at Dolly.

Who looked innocently back at her. And beamed and batted her eyelashes.

Perhaps she meant it. One would probably never know with the likes of Dolly Farmer.

Ramsey cleared his throat.

"*But* . . . our condition is that we should like livery."

Elise nodded. "Very well. You shall have it inside a fortnight."

"And we would like one evening a week to play five-card loo."

"If Lord Lavay doesn't require your services, you may play five-card loo one evening a week. If there are guests in the house, then the game is rescinded, which means you will not be allowed to play. If I see evidence of it when you ought to be working, you will be immediately sacked."

"Fair enough," James said cheerily, and stuffed half a slice of bread into his mouth. "You're a right good baker, Mrs. Fountain."

"Thank you, James," she said regally. "I know."

Chapter 11

AFTER DEVOURING AN UNOBJECTIONABLE beef stew mopped up with a fine slice of bread washed down with a glass of wine from a bottle donated from the Earl of Ardmay's cellars, Lavay rang for Mrs. Fountain, almost as a reflex. The way some men would have a pleasant snifter of brandy or a cigar after dinner.

He knew a certain amount of impatience before she arrived. He had an agenda.

But when she did arrive, he briefly forgot why he'd rung for her. It was just that it was such a pleasure to look at her, particularly after she'd clearly taken the stairs at a run and her cheeks were pink and her hair wasn't anywhere near as tidy as she thought.

"Ah, good evening, Mrs. Fountain. I should like to say that it was very kind of you to inflict the willow bark tea upon me. Or rather, it was three parts kindness, one part desperation to make me something other than insufferable."

Her eyes flew wide in alarm, but then he could see that she decided he was teasing.

"I'll add 'how to tame a prince' to my heirloom recipes."

"Splendid. You taught the girls at Miss Endicott's Academy? A variety of subjects, I would imagine."

"Yes." She was clearly suddenly wary.

"And you enjoyed your position?"

"Yes."

"Ah. My loquacious new housekeeper is suddenly taciturn. Why are you now a housekeeper, Mrs. Fountain, and not a teacher?"

She hesitated, then said, "I thought we conducted our interview on the day I was hired, Lord Lavay."

"Mrs. Fountain, why don't you have a seat and indulge my curiosity, if you will."

He said it pleasantly, but it was the sort of tone that clearly brooked no argument.

She sat down in the chair as if she were mounting the steps to the guillotine.

He sat down opposite her. The firelight turned her fair skin a glowing amber, and her eyes were softer and shadowier.

"I said something out of turn," she admitted softly.

"Shocking."

That made her smile, and that was better.

He was a little concerned that if she'd said *I committed a murder*, he would have found a way to rationalize her current position. Perhaps merely keep her away from the meat cleavers, that sort of thing.

He shrugged with one shoulder. "In some places, such a thing is more welcome than others. One must choose one's moment, of course, and one's opponent. And do you see, I can shrug now with less pain. You have restored my vocabulary to me, Mrs. Fountain, with your willow bark tea and speaking out of turn."

"I'm glad to hear it, sir."

"And now I must ask you to rewrite the letter to my grandfather."

She looked astonished again. "Was it unsatisfactory?"

He was amused at how doubtful she sounded. Clearly Mrs. Fountain was rarely found unsatisfactory.

"Someone wept upon it."

It was stealthy. He'd deliberately ambushed her.

She froze.

And then she looked up at him with something like a plea in her eyes, as if she'd been caught in the act of a crime.

He loved that she hadn't denied it.

They locked gazes for a moment.

"Where *is* your home, Mrs. Fountain?" he asked softly.

"Northumberland." She said it almost numbly. Still surprised by the ambush.

"Ah."

The big, healthy fire gave a hearty pop.

"Home becomes a part of you, doesn't it?"

She seemed to be breathing through some sort of pain.

"Yes." The word was thick.

"Les Pierres d'Argent was my home," he mused softly. "We've a number of homes, my family. But this was the home I knew and loved. It has belonged to my family for nearly two centuries. I know every tree as if they were playmates with whom I was raised. After a manner of speaking, they are. I fell out of more than one of them."

She smiled faintly. But she was still tense. Her hands had vanished beneath the table, and he suspected they were folded together in a knot.

"I know every flower in the garden. I know every stone in the walkways and walls. I scraped knees, caught fish, climbed, took a whipping for stealing a tart meant for dinner, fought and played and laughed with my brother and sister and cousins. I learned how to be a man there. The voices of my family, all the laughter and tears, who we are, are in the timbers of it, in the stones. It is as much a part of me as . . . this." He raised his hand. "And it was taken from us. Those of us who could scattered like insects to new countries. Taking only what we could. Things like . . . sauceboats. Silver spoons."

She was imagining it, and her eyes looked hunted.

He found the notion of making her suffer in any way very distasteful. But for some reason, he wanted her to know.

"I'm sorry," she said softly. "I took only a hairbrush with me."

He nodded shortly but didn't ask any questions.

"You miss your home, Mrs. Fountain."

Another pause. "Yes."

So tentative, that word, and he was certain it hid multitudes.

"When will you go for a visit?"

"I cannot."

She'd gone pale with tension.

"You are allowed time off from your position, Mrs. Fountain. Provided you last beyond a fortnight and outfit the footmen in livery."

That ought to have brought a smile.

She tried for one. "I . . . cannot."

He sensed he ought not press.

And yet.

"Why? Did you say something out of turn?"

This made her smile in fact. "In a manner of speaking."

But her eyes were imploring him not to ask any more questions.

He relented.

"If you would be so kind as to copy this letter word for word again? I should like to take it to be mailed tomorrow."

"Of course, sir."

With apparent relief, she bent her head and applied herself to the foolscap and ink. In all likelihood happy not to show her face to him.

"I don't need to return home. I'm quite fine on my own," she said suddenly, after a moment.

"Of course you are," he said lightly.

I thought I told you I didn't like liars, Mrs. Fountain.

He settled onto the settee with Marcus Aurelius. One of the benefits of his convalescence was that he was able to read to his heart's desire. He'd much rather be out galloping a horse on the green, of course, but that day would come again soon, and meanwhile he could improve his already satisfactory brain.

He turned the page and didn't read a word of it, and watched the firelight amber her cheeks, and turned another page and didn't read a word of that, and watched her tongue dart out to touch her top lip as she dipped the quill in the ink again, and he turned another page and glanced down at it, when the quiet was interrupted by a sharp rap on the door frame.

"Messenger for you, sir. Seems rather press—"

The messenger was the same granite-faced person who had pushed past Elise and hadn't wanted tea, and he pushed past Ramsey into the room now.

Lavay, she noticed, didn't even blink. As if he was expecting the man.

The messenger was an interesting man, Elise thought, glancing up, then reflexively ducking again so as to seem as unobtrusive as possible. He didn't radiate any particular self-importance or station, but neither was he subservient or humble; his face was expressionless—she would not have been able to identify him in a crowded room after this evening, she was certain. But single-minded intensity of purpose accompanied him into the room.

Lavay rose to his feet.

The man held a missive out to Lavay, bowed, saluted, turned and was gone.

Lavay broke the seal.

He looked up. "Mrs. Fountain, have you finished with the letter?" His voice was abstracted and dismissive.

"Yes, sir."

"That will be all this evening, thank you."

And just like that, after he'd fished around and unearthed her deepest pain based on a teardrop on a letter, she was dismissed with the usual head-spinning abruptness.

But oddly, he had shared with her a peculiar moment of absolute peace, so singular and distinct that she realized that nothing had been peaceful about the last six years of her life, no matter what she tried to tell herself. His silent understanding, their complicity, had flowed into all those fissures that ached like cracks in skin.

She'd seen his face when he'd read the message from the messenger. It had gone cold, abstracted, intent as a predator's.

She'd felt a clutch in her gut that she recognized, unnervingly, as concern.

She was forgotten.

But some things, she suspected, were more important than her pride.

Chapter 12

Elise got through the following day without a single jingle from Lord Lavay, who had closeted himself with the Earl of Ardmay for the afternoon. In all likelihood, something to do with that message brought last night. Something about it struck her as ominous, as portentous as the great lingering masses of rain clouds now hovering between the kitchen door and the vicarage.

Those clouds would likely contribute to a magnificent sunset, given half a chance, if the rain didn't fall.

She stood on the steps outside the kitchen door, her eyes aimed, as usual, toward the vicarage like a hunting dog's. She would not exhale until she saw the two figures, small as birds on the green in the distance at first.

They increased in size.

When they came into view as people rather than dark specks, her heart launched heavenward.

And when he saw her, Jack began to run, and Seamus, bless him, did again, too, to try to keep up.

"We know you like these, Mama, so we brought more," Jack huffed.

Jack had a fistful of daisies and some roses that had once sported considerably more petals, but which had been balded on the trip from the vicarage to home.

Seamus gave him a nudge.

"It was Seamus's idea."

"Was it now? Thank you, Mr. Duggan. Thank you, Jack. "

"I'm going to be a sheep, Mama!"

"When you grow up? Instead of a bell ringer?"

"In the Christmas pantomime. *Baaaaaa! Baaaaaa!*"

He bent over and waggled his hindquarters.

"Very convincing. Excellent casting decision on the part of . . ."

"Mrs. Sneath." Seamus's face darkened, and his voice deepened as if he'd said *Beelzebub*.

Elise knew Mrs. Sneath. She was the redoubtable head of the Society for the Protection of the Sussex Poor, and she worked closely with the vicar. She was the sort of woman who would never let the Seamus Duggans of the world get away with anything, let alone get near all the dewy young women who volunteered for charity work.

And Mrs. Sneath was an *accomplisher*. If something needed to be done, she would make sure it was.

And . . . a pantomime would need costumes.

Hope and inspiration violently surged through Elise.

"There will be girls, too, Mama! The younger

girls from Miss Endicott's will be in it. They will be angels."

"I wondered if I might have a word with Mr. Duggan while you run upstairs, Jack." She said it in such a rush that Seamus's eyes went wide. "Go and tell Kitty and Mary and James and Ramsey about your day. They would love to hear about the sheep and angels."

Nearly the entire staff had fallen in love with Jack. Kitty and Mary treated him like a favorite pet, and James and Ramsey were jocular and silly with him. Jack gave Dolly a wide berth, however, with that instinct children and animals have for something that might not be quite right.

"All right, Mama. Are there tarts in the kitchen?"

"Yes, but no tarts before din—"

He was already off like a shot.

She whirled back to Seamus. "Forgive me for being brief, Mr. Duggan—"

" . . . as I've said to more than one young lady."

She blinked. Good heavens, he was incorrigible. She recovered with aplomb.

"—but will the ladies of the Society for the Protection of the Sussex Poor be sewing costumes for the pantomime?"

"Yes. Sheep, shepherds, and the like. A baby Jesus. Angel dresses. The reverend got hold of some music he'd like me to play. Singing and the like. A few hymns, 'While Shepherds Watched Their Flocks at Night.' Like that."

"I'm in a bit of a pickle, Mr. Duggan. I need two

footman uniforms. Coats, waistcoats, stockings, the works, on down to the shoes. Inside a fortnight. Well before Boxing Day."

This gave Seamus a moment's pause.

"Well, now, the baby Jesus was special indeed," he said gently, "but I don't think even he had footmen, Mrs. Fountain."

"What are the wise men if not . . . holy footmen, of a sort?"

Seamus tilted his head. "Ah, ye poor lass. Ye really are in a pickle if ye're spouting nonsense like that."

"The wise men are kings! And kings have footmen!" She blurted it. Divine inspiration, that.

Seamus liked it. "*Now* you've given me a bit more to work with."

"They have to be midnight blue. Trimmed in silver."

"You don't want much, do you, Mrs. Fountain?"

"And stockings. Silk stockings."

"Shoes?"

Seamus was clearly thinking now.

"And shoes."

"If I could persuade the ladies of the Society for the Protection of the Sussex Poor to add footmen to the Christmas pantomime, I'll need something in return from you, Mrs. Fountain, and it won't be apple tarts."

Oh, God.

"Come to the Pig & Thistle on your next two evenings off," he added swiftly.

"Is that all?"

He gave a short laugh. "It should be enough," he said confidently. "Disappointed, dove?" He winked. "The pleasure of pulling one over on Mrs. Sneath is more than enough reward. If I can manage it."

INSURRECTION WAS ALLEGEDLY afoot.

The Crown's messenger had brought to Lavay a few curt lines scrawled on foolscap, a date, a meeting place, the names of men whom he needed to meet and track, the names of people with whom he would work, men he knew, including the Earl of Ardmay.

It was, of course, dangerous. He was to infiltrate their ranks by positioning himself as a French national still bitter about the outcome of the war.

That much wouldn't prove too much of a challenge.

And the money . . . oh, the money they offered would solve nearly everything.

The trouble was Lavay knew he was currently in no way physically equipped to do it. He had his vanity, but he was no fool, and he would never endanger the men with whom he worked.

He had a month to decide.

And this decision essentially stood between him and everything he wanted.

The Earl of Ardmay had received a similar message, and they had talked it through yesterday, while reminiscing about some past adventures and skirting the true conversation they needed to have: whether or not they would accept the assignment.

Or whether Philippe would do it without the earl.

Because Philippe's intuition told him that his friend was reluctant, despite the rewards promised, because of his wife and baby. There was just too much to lose now. Having lost nearly everything he loved, Philippe would never blame him.

He absently flexed his hand, which was still stiff, as was much of the rest of his body, though the willow bark tea did help. This did nothing for his temper.

And perhaps because he was feeling masochistic, he fished about in his stack of correspondence and slit open Marie-Helene's most recent letter.

And his internal barometer shot upward.

Almost as a reflex now, he rang the bell violently.

And when Mrs. Fountain arrived, for a moment he just looked dumbly at her, his mood elevating already, as if she were a shot of brandy.

Her dresses were all simple and somber, and though they fit beautifully, they were clearly designed with economy in mind. She ought to wear more colors. Vivid ones. Deep ones. Soft fabrics that draped the lines of her and moved like liquid, because she was lithe. He wondered how she might look in a ball gown. Or if she'd ever worn a ball gown.

"Red," he muttered.

"I beg your pardon?"

"I . . . er, that is, I'd like you to help me with a response to a letter."

She paused and studied him. "Would you like me to throw the vase for you, sir?"

His mouth quirked at the corner. "If you would be so kind."

She picked it up and quite deliberately and gently placed it at the far end of the mantel, well out of his reach.

"Excellent aim," he said dryly.

"Thank you."

"The letter is in response to my sister," he explained tautly.

"Ah," she said.

The pure understanding in that syllable was balm.

She settled into the brown chair, and he watched her, amused, as she slid back into it with a suppressed sigh. Mrs. Fountain was a sensual creature.

It took one to know one.

He began almost before she could pick up the quill.

"Dearest Marie-Helene. Whilst my fondest wish is that you will rot in hell—"

"Dearest Marie-Helene," she repeated firmly as she wrote, *"I hope this letter finds you enjoying continued good health and happiness."*

"—with regards to your latest request for money to supplement the gowns from last season, I am pleased to tell you where to stuff it."

"With regards to your latest request for money, I request your patience and economy, and would beg you to recall that you look beautiful in everything and to hold your head high always and remember your lineage.

And as to your inquiry about the reasons I am dawdling in Sussex, it is hardly your concern how or where I spend my time.

And as to your inquiry regarding the reasons I am dawdling in Sussex, I thank you for your concern and assure you we will meet again soon . . ."

She stopped writing and looked up at him limpidly.

He glared blackly at her.

"Is that what you meant to say, sir?"

"Yes. Damn you, Mrs. Fountain."

He leaned over and slipped the quill from her fingers and scrawled his name at the bottom. As if he were done with Marie-Helene forever.

And then he sighed a long-suffering sigh.

"Lord Lavay . . ."

"Are you about to ask a question, Madame Je-sais-tout?" he said testily. "And here I thought you knew everything."

She didn't even blink. "Does Marie-Helene know you were . . . shall we say accosted . . . in London? And that you are in Sussex because you are recovering?"

"Of course not," he said dismissively.

"Why not?"

"My responsibility to Marie-Helene is twofold, Mrs. Fountain: to protect her from such ugly realities, and to ensure she is equipped to make a magnificent marriage and never want for a thing."

Something wistful and lovely flickered over Mrs. Fountain's face, a surge of emotion he couldn't quite identify, but on the whole, women as a species were irritating him at the moment.

"Wasn't the revolution one long ugly reality?" she asked.

This brought him up short.

"Yes," he said curtly, after a moment.

She paused, thoughtfully, plucking up the quill again and tapping the feather end of it against her lips.

White quill against those red lips. Mesmerizing.

"Did Marie-Helene not lose a father and a brother, too? And perhaps friends and other relatives?"

He narrowed his eyes at her again.

And then at last he heaved a long, long sigh and swiped his hands down his face.

"That is why," he said wearily, "I don't want her to know what happened to me. She has been through enough. And watching her experience the other things . . . when I could not stop them, or protect her from them . . ."

They regarded each other wordlessly.

What have you been through, Mrs. Fountain, to understand such things? he wanted to ask then.

"Whereas you have been frolicking in meadows for the past decade," she pointed out.

"It is my responsibility, Mrs. Fountain," he said again, slowly, as if she was an idiot child. "What

I've been doing to uphold them is none of her concern, either."

"Have you considered she might be concerned about you? That her tone may be anxious because she misses you? And perhaps she is stronger than you know?"

"Pah," he shrugged with one shoulder. "She is a young girl. She is spoiled, and should remain so."

But he was less angry now.

He hadn't told a soul any of this before, and something in the mere articulation of it lightened him, as if one more layer of weight had been lifted from his chest, freeing his breathing.

"How old is she?" Mrs. Fountain pressed.

"Eighteen."

"A grown woman."

"A grown woman who ought to be married by now, but for a dowry befitting her family name. And her dowry is my responsibility. I will not see my sister a spinster, or married to someone below her station."

His voice escalated until that last word echoed in the room.

The unspoken, throbbing word, of course, was that Mrs. Fountain was *well* below their station.

But there was nothing English people understood better than "station."

"She is old enough to make a few decisions of her own," Elise pressed gently.

"She has not been raised to 'make decisions,' Mrs. Fountain." He said this dryly.

"If she is anything like you . . ."

He straightened to his full height.

And gave a humorless laugh. "Even you may not be rash enough to finish that sentence," he warned grimly.

Her spine straightened and her chin went up. " . . . if she is anything like you, she is a survivor," Mrs. Fountain said. "May I just say this? Women are often more resilient than men credit us with. And often much stronger than you know. And that is all I will say."

"For now," Philippe said grimly.

She gave a one-shouldered shrug. She was clearly trying not to laugh. The cheek of her.

He studied her a moment in silence. "Do you perhaps speak from experience, Mrs. Fountain?"

She simply regarded him evenly. Which was answer enough.

He paced again.

And then he turned and began haltingly. Because for some reason he wanted her to know.

"I am not angry at her. I am angry at myself. I am angry at fate. I am angry at this"—he thrust his healing hand into the air—"and I am angry at the limbo that prevents me from earning the money I need to *buy back my own home* and provide my sister with a dowry and every bloody ball gown her heart desires. I am angry that my family was smashed to smithereens by revolution and I am left to pick up the pieces. The best cure for anger is constructive action, Mrs. Fountain. The time is ticking away from me. I can marry well and swiftly, or I can accept another assignment from the crown, or I can, feasibly, do both. But I need to decide which it will be before the winter is over, because Les Pierres d'Argent will be sold out from under me if I do not."

She took this impassioned speech in.

"So . . . you can hurl yourself back into danger because that is lucrative, or you can . . ."

"Hurl myself into matrimony."

It was another word that seemed to ring portentously. More like a tolling, really, than a joyous ring of the church bell, as accomplished by two small boys, one dangling from the other.

"Was that why the king's messenger was here?"

"Yes. The Crown has . . . work for me."

"And by work, I suppose you mean something involving weapons."

"I'm prized for my charm, as well, Mrs. Fountain. And my skill with languages."

"None of which would mean a thing to His Majesty's men if you did not also know how to wield a sword. I expect you're wanted to do something dangerous again."

To her surprise and his, he smiled. She was so tart and astute and bracing. "Oh, you better not get in the way of the powerful Lord Philippe Lavay . . ." he sang softly, teasing her. "Ah, I long for the days when my charm was all that was necessary to keep a roof over my head."

It ought to have made her smile.

But she was studying him thoughtfully, and something darkened her expression.

She was clearly deciding whether to speak.

He sighed. "Say what you wish to say, Mrs. Fountain," he ordered.

"Where . . . precisely does it hurt? Besides your hand?" she ventured.

His eyebrows shot up.

"I'm sorry . . . is that too indelicate a question?"

"Is 'everywhere' too indelicate an answer?"

"Is it true? I'm terribly sorry if it is."

"Thank you," he said finally. Simply.

Because it was so very clear that she meant it. There was nothing accusatory or fawning or hysterical in her.

He held up his hand in a silent gesture. "Here is what is troubling me the most, as you know. Or rather, it's the most inconvenient."

"May I . . . see it? As I said, I am a doctor's daughter. I know a thing or two about injuries."

"Are you trying to make me battle worthy in order to save me from matrimony, Mrs. Fountain?"

He realized his breath was held while he waited for her glib answer.

Something flickered in her eyes then. It was like watching clouds rush across the face of the sun.

"I think both conditions will require the use of your hands, Lord Lavay."

He laughed, surprised. And thoroughly delighted.

And he settled into the chair opposite her and extended his hand as though she were a gypsy reader who could read his future in it.

She took it with grave gentleness and a bit gingerly, as if it were a sleeping baby hedgehog and not a hand.

She studied it for a moment, so seriously it made him smile.

What a luxury it was to surrender himself to someone for a moment. Her hands were soft and cool, but not the silky, tended kinds of hands his female relatives and all the beautiful women with whom he'd danced or made love possessed. It was a hand you could trust with precious things, with serious things.

It had been so long since a beautiful woman had simply touched his hand. Without wanting or expecting a thing.

This realization surprised him, too. It wasn't an entirely comfortable conclusion, and he wasn't certain every man would reach it. It was more of an intangible thing. Some magical formula comprised of the lovely softness and angles of her features, combined with the way she moved, the way her skin took the light, the depthless eyes that lit like stars when she smiled, that crackling wit she wielded so very strategically, the things she hid.

It occurred to him that surely whatever his hand had to reveal should have been revealed by now.

But she hadn't relinquished it.

And suddenly the air around them seemed close and velvety, as if they were beneath a dome, separate from the rest of the world.

A peculiar peace stole over him. He could not recall ever experiencing a similar sensation.

He wouldn't know what to call it. Perhaps "rightness."

"Who stitched the wound?" Her voice was a hush, too, as if his hand was a patient who was resting, and they both ought not disturb it.

"A . . . I shall describe him as a samaritan . . . who fortuitously happened to be at the same place I was at and came to my assistance. And I was then given into the care of someone who was, rightly so, more concerned about me bleeding to death than the aesthetic appeal of my hand. There was a good deal of me to attend to, you see. Cut open and so forth."

"You do say such things so casually. 'Bleeding to death,'" she quoted dryly.

"Do you wish I wouldn't?"

She shrugged with one shoulder, which amused him. It was contagious, apparently.

"They nearly gutted me like a fish. But I am quick like a cat, so I rolled before they had my liver on the tip of a sword, like a pickle on a fork."

Her head shot up again and she stared at him in wondering horror.

He grinned like a naughty boy. "Consider it a test of your fortitude, Mrs. Fountain, and your ingenuity—how not to blanch when I say such things. Though it is gratifying to know my survival is of interest to you."

She dropped her gaze immediately.

He realized he kept saying these things to see how she would respond.

There was naught but silence for a few minutes.

"Part of what is troubling you is that you should have had more stitches, and stitches that were closer together. Like . . . lettering on an embroidered pillow. It would allow for freer movement of your hand."

"What would you embroider upon me, Mrs. Fountain?"

"Caveat emptor," she said, sounding entirely serious.

He laughed.

He thought perhaps he would like to spend the rest of the day sitting here across from Mrs. Fountain, waiting for one of her curls to escape, while she looked up at him with those dark eyes that were three parts sympathetic, one part wary, and one part wicked, sensual humor that she tried very hard to squelch.

Because he suspected this last part comprised most of her.

This was the part he desperately wanted to tempt out of hiding.

He touched that pink slash across his cheekbone. "Given that my face is my fortune, I suppose it's fortunate that the rest of me took the brunt."

She quirked her mouth. If he was fishing for a

compliment, he was destined for disappointment. "Where else are you injured?"

He made no move to remove his hand from the soft little cradle of hers.

She made no move to give it up.

The moment had officially shifted into something for which neither of them possessed a compass.

He gestured with his other hand. "There's a slash from here . . ." He pointed to a space in the low center of his chest and watched her eyes follow it. ". . . to . . ." He drew his finger slowly down, down down to a spot her eyes couldn't follow. ". . . here."

Her gaze stopped and lingered on his chest.

Then she slowly raised her head. Their gazes met. Collided, more accurately.

He wondered if his pupils were as large as Mrs. Fountain's pupils currently were.

"And everything gets so very . . . stiff . . . you see," he added. Somberly.

She visibly drew in a breath.

"I know how to address the stiffness," she said gravely.

His eyes widened. An interesting sensation had begun to trace his spine. That delicious whisper of desire that could so easily be fanned into a conflagration.

"Do you? I am all ears, Mrs. Fountain." His voice was a hush.

She hesitated again. She bit her lip thoughtfully and leaned forward just a very little.

"Well, you first need to warm it . . ."

And then her hand came up and covered his with her other hand, making a little sandwich of it. As if it were a creature she needed to capture and release into the wild.

" . . . to loosen the muscles around it."

He couldn't speak.

It was very like she'd just laid down a card in a daring wager.

"Ah," he said softly, hearing the tautness in his voice. "Is that so?"

"Stretching it will help. In fact, you must stretch it if you'd ever like to wrap it around a sword again."

Were those glints in her eyes actual glints, or a reflection of the lamplight?

"And as my sword is of significant length and girth, and I am a renowned swordsman, this is of grave concern to me." He kept his voice soft and so, so serious, too. They might as well have been at a funeral.

The air was officially full of illicit sparks. A bit like the air before a thunderstorm.

"And then, once it's warm, Lord Lavay, you need to rub it . . . like so . . . to loosen the muscles."

She took her thumbs and pressed them into the palm of his hand, and kneaded.

Once.

Twice.

He sighed at length, a sigh he seemed to have held for years. "Mother of God, that feels good."

She froze.

He could almost hear an inaudible shattering sound. As if some sort of spell had been broken.

"If only I had something warm to cover the rest of my poor, wounded body in order to keep it limber, Mrs. Fountain."

Her eyes flew open in alarm.

She practically thrust his hand back at him.

He'd officially shocked her.

Or she'd shocked herself.

He wasn't *un*shocked, for that matter.

His impulse was to rescue her, regardless.

"Thank you," he said briskly. "That will help, when I had begun to think nothing would."

"I'm glad," she said just as briskly. "You will be able to rub it for yourself, with your other hand, and I think you will find that things improve rapidly."

"I've become accustomed to rubbing it for myself with my other hand."

She froze.

And that was when he witnessed one of the mightiest struggles he'd ever witnessed. The corner of one side of her mouth turned up, and then it seemed to drag up the other corner.

But she ducked her head before he could see the smile. She took a few deep breaths.

When she lifted it again, she was somber and composed. If considerably pinker. He had a pleasant vision of her staggering down the stairs, roaring with laughter when she reached the bottom so he wouldn't hear.

"Shall I post the letter to your sister tomorrow, Lord Lavay?"

"Thank you, Fountain. Please do take it with you."

She shot to her feet so quickly that she nearly tipped the brown chair.

"I'd best return to the kitchen now. I think something is burning."

That was putting it mildly. He was tempted to say *my loins*, but then he might never see her again.

She was out of the room so quickly that she nearly created a wind.

He watched her go.

And he looked at the doorway long after she was gone, then gave himself a good shake when he realized what he was doing.

He frowned and looked around the room. He'd best light another lamp. The room seemed dimmer now, somehow.

He stared at his hand, gave it a flex. It felt strange somehow to have it back. Oddly, it felt as though it now belonged to her.

Chapter 13

ELISE WASN'T LAUGHING.

In fact, if she'd had a vase to hurl on her way back down the stairs, she would have done it, reveling in the smithereens.

"Why, why, why, why?" she implored the ceiling with a wide-armed gesture that was wholly Lavay. She was muttering again. "Why make me a woman, why make him a man, why make him charming, why make it such a pleasure to touch him, why must it feel as though I'm touching a flame, why must I be tempted like this? I'm just a frivolous way to pass the time for him until he marries magnificently or gets himself killed, and I do. Not. Want. To. Care. I am *not* that weak. I need nobody but Jack."

Having clarified her desires to whatever celestial beings might be listening, she felt somewhat bolstered.

Which would she prefer? That he thrust himself back into danger or into the arms of some woman appropriate to his station?

Was it evil to prefer the former?

She gave a helpless little laugh at her own expense. The trouble was . . . when she'd touched him, he'd been both chaos and peace. Nothing had ever felt more right. Nothing had ever been more wrong.

And ah, what a pleasure it was to touch him. The heat of his skin, the rough elegance of his hands, scarred and callused through use. What kindling it would add to her dreams any nights she might find it too difficult to sleep.

Because she did know what a man's hands could do, given free reign of a woman's body.

The memory of that was just the sobering cold splash of water in her face that she needed.

She stopped and took a deep breath as her seesawing emotions came to rest upon some sort of equilibrium. But she felt a bit like Lavay, moving stiffly, holding herself still, so as not to jar the wound.

She thought she now understood the rather picayune budget. The man took care of everyone and everything around him, except, it seemed, himself.

She glanced down at the letter she was clutching. The one addressed to Marie-Helene.

She went still, and thought for a moment.

She decided it needed a couple more sentences, which she could easily accomplish in her rooms.

And she decided she would make sure Lavay had something warm to cover his poor, wounded body.

"BAAAA!" JACK SAID by way of greeting that evening. And butted her with finger horns. "I met an angel today—well, she's going to be an angel—named Colette."

"Well, baaa to you, too. We're all going to be angels one day, Jack, my love."

"All save me," Seamus said, still breathing a trifle hard from running, as usual, after Jack.

"You're not dead yet, Mr. Duggan. Whatever news you bring me today might play a role in your admission to Heaven. Jack, go and see Kitty and Mary about having a tart before—"

He was up the stairs in a flash.

"We're fresh out of flowers over at the vicarage, but I brought news instead," Seamus said immediately.

She closed her eyes and clasped her hands in prayer.

"The wise men will have footmen. Mrs. Sneath was quite taken with the idea—thinks it will add a dash of elegance, and she has a son who's a merchant who will donate the fabric, braid and all. She quite liked bragging about him, and how I might amount to something some day if I—well, suffice it to say, Mrs. Fountain, I suffered a good deal on your behalf."

"Oh." Elise exhaled and sat down hard on the steps in relief. "I suppose they'll need to keep their own shoes. But the stockings . . . I mean, thank you, Seamus."

"Postlethwaite's Emporium has silk stockings. For ladies. Possibly for men, too."

She could only imagine how he knew that.

And she could hardly eke out enough money from Lavay's budget for silk stockings for the footmen, no matter how she trimmed or maneuvered. They both knew how dear they were.

"Tell Mrs. Sneath I'll send Ramsey and James over for a fitting. I'll help with the sewing on my half night out. And my spare time will be at her disposal for the next few months if she'll allow me to keep the footman costumes."

"As you wish, Mrs. Fountain," he said, backing away.

"*And* I'll see you at the Pig & Thistle next week."

She made so bold as to blow him a kiss, which he made a great show of trying and failing to catch, and he then pretended to chase after as though it were a butterfly, across the downs and all the way back to the vicarage.

LAVAY WAS PORING over the map of the London docks when the footman rapped at the door.

His head shot up.

He glared.

The man really *was* unprepossessing. Which one was this? James? Ramsey?

Livery would improve him, but he hadn't heard anything about it since, and he simply couldn't imagine how Mrs. Fountain would achieve such a thing. He sighed, resigned.

"Yes?"

"I've brought something to you, sir."

Whoever he was held in his arms something that looked like a baggy pillow.

"What the devil is that?"

"Mrs. Fountain sends it up, sir. This is a stocking sewn shut, and it is filled with seed. It has been heated on the hearth, and you can drape it across sore muscles, like so. She said you . . ." He paused and looked upward as if he'd been given something to recite. ". . . needed something warm to cover 'your poor, wounded body.' "

The strapping footman draped it over his own neck and turned this way and that, demonstrating. Then he extended it to Lavay.

Philippe's hand reached out slowly.

He was strangely reluctant to take it, because he recognized it for the message it was meant to be. A peculiar little hot spot of shame burned in his gut. He felt . . . *spurned*, of all things.

Which was absurd, and *patently* not a familiar sensation for him, particularly at the hands of a woman. Let alone a servant. And why he should feel spurned when in fact the gesture was . . .

He finally took it from Ramsey.

"Tell Mrs. Fountain . . ."

"Yes, sir?"

He quirked his mouth wryly. "Tell Mrs. Fountain it was a very kind thing to do."

AND BECAUSE ELISE was a woman of her word, and because the reverend and Mrs. Sylvaine had kindly offered to fetch her in their horse and cart,

she went to the pub on her night off, after Mary
and Kitty had promised to look in on Jack period-
ically until Elise arrived home, well before midnight.

A wave of light and sound and merriment
washed over them as they pushed the pub door
open. Ironically, it was a bit like entering the
vicarage—the church and the pub shared the
same clientele, after all. And like a church, its an-
cient timbers seemed to have absorbed a bit of everyone and everything that had passed through:
smoke from fires and cigars both rank and rare,
spilled ale, the savory smell of centuries' worth of
roasted haunches and meat pies. The chairs and
tables were battered but sturdy and burnished by
centuries of handling and shifting bums.

A table had been reserved for the popular Reverend Sylvaine next to the fire, and she settled in
with the reverend and his wife amidst the laughter, clinking glasses, uprising voices, and stomp-
ing feet, all of it in response to the musicians in
the corner, who were making a beautiful racket.

Seamus was in the throes of a jig when they entered, tossing his head, his bow arm a blur. He
brought it to a melodramatic finish with a final
vigorous head toss and thrusting his fiddle and
bow up in the air, like an acrobat landing.

A delighted cheer went up, and everyone
shouted requests. Seamus pointed his bow at
someone in the crowd, and they called out a request that Elise couldn't quite hear.

But when the song began, she recognized it instantly.

Seamus's voice rose above the noise, which soon became a hush, in thrall to his singing.

What's this dull town to me?
Robin's not near;
What was't I wish'd to see?
What wish'd to hear?
Where all the joy and mirth,
Made this town Heav'n on earth,
Oh! they've all fled wi' thee,
Robin Adair

Robin Adair. Ironically, quite syllabically similar to Philippe Lavay. And now, through all the rest of the verses, that was all she could hear.

"I think I need a bit of fresh air," she said abruptly to the vicar and his wife, and before they could say anything, she shoved her chair back swiftly, wound her way through the crowd, pushed open the door, and leaned up against the side of the Pig & Thistle in the merciful, vast silence.

And breathed in.

And breathed out.

The sky was midnight blue. The stars were silver. And her breath made little white ghosts.

The door swung open a few minutes later, and she gave a start.

Whoever it was hovered a moment in the dark.

"It's a midnight blue sky, Mrs. Fountain."

It was Seamus.

She smiled. "The livery will be absolutely beautiful. Thank you again, Mr. Duggan. I was just out here trying to think of how I will obtain silk stockings for two very tall footmen. They're so very dear."

Seamus leaned against the wall near her, fiddle dangling from his hand.

"Oh, I'm not certain that's the reason ye're out here. 'Tis a lively crowd in there. Good friends, good music, the best ale in all of England. And yet ye still look lonely, Mrs. Fountain, and ye're out here with the stars."

She sighed. "You do play very well, Mr. Duggan."

"Aye," he agreed without vanity. "Were ye moved?"

"Oh, perhaps. But probably not for the reasons you hoped."

That emerged even more acerbically than she'd intended.

There was a silence.

"There's more to me than people think, Mrs. Fountain." He said it quietly.

Imagine her bruising Seamus Duggan's dignity.

She was hurting feelings left and right these days, she suspected.

Saying the wrong thing, doing the wrong thing. Touching the wrong hands and the like. She'd never viewed herself as a vixen, and she didn't like it.

"I suppose people can only draw conclusions based on what they *see*, Mr. Duggan. And the most recent thing anyone saw was you stealing a kiss from Miss Annie Wimpole."

He laughed. "What is life but not a great buffet of little pleasures to be stolen?"

"I think men get away with stealing those pleasures more frequently than women do."

He gave a little grunt of a laugh, a rueful one. "Aye, lass, you're likely right."

"Mr. Duggan, I believe the only reason you're interested in me is that you're certain I'm not interested in you."

"Nay, that's not the only reason," he said shrewdly, but he didn't expound and he didn't sound the least insulted. His voice softened. "Who has your heart, Mrs. Fountain? Because if there's one thing I recognize, it's a woman who has given hers away with naught to show for it in return."

She was shocked.

She didn't need a life full of men who pointed out uncomfortable truths to her.

Her silence was probably incriminating, but she could think of nothing glib to say.

But surely she hadn't "given her heart away," of all things. What an absurdly poetic way to put it; trust a sentimental Irishman full of ale to say it.

Still, all she could think of was how lovely it would be to linger outside the pub and look up at the stars whilst standing next to Lord Lavay, maybe leaning a bit into that vast chest that was

simply made for leaning, and feeling it rumble as
he sang along to pub songs.

It was as fanciful and hopeless a yearning as any
woman had ever had, and she hadn't the right to it.

But there was something amiss when a feeling
was so large and uncontainable that she preferred
to be outside with it, alone among the stars, than
inside, where the room was alive with sound and
merriment and people who were more appropriate to . . . what was the word . . . ? Ah, yes. "Station." Of course.

"You could do worse than me," Seamus said.
Sounding perfectly serious.

"A lot worse," she agreed generously. It wasn't
altogether complimentary.

He laughed at that and turned to go back inside.
"I'll see Reverend Sylvaine takes ye home if ye'd
like."

"I'll stay a bit longer," she said stoutly.

And she did.

WITH MRS. FOUNTAIN at the helm, day by day,
room by room, Alder House became cleaner,
brighter, more comfortable. More like a *home*.
Meals improved. Morale improved. The weather
improved. Lavay's health improved.

Lavay's mood did not improve.

Or rather it metamorphosed into restlessness.
Now, thanks to Mrs. Fountain's willow bark tea
and her admonishment to rub it himself, walking
and bending were both a bit easier, and he took to

·roaming the halls of the house, peering out windows, startling the chambermaids at their work. On days when it wasn't pissing down rain, he ventured into the garden. He once walked nearly as far as Postlethwaite's Emporium, but he paid for it when he returned home. He was *winded*, of all things—he who had always been so effortlessly fit—and nearly everything on him throbbed, and not in a thrilling way. He was forced to lie still and rest, which infuriated him, but fury made him tense, so he forced himself to relax, and to breathe in and out, evenly.

If he was patient, he might be on a horse before the winter was out. But patience was almost a skill he needed to learn, as deliberately as he'd once learned fencing or chess. Nothing about his life had required it of him in recent years. For so long it had been all ceaseless, instantaneous reaction and defense.

He somehow rarely encountered Mrs. Fountain in his restless wanderings. Perhaps she'd acquired an instinct for dodging him.

He could have invented an excuse to see her. He paid her to answer to a bell, after all. But three times daily she sent up footmen with willow bark tea, and he accepted it as humbly as if each cup were a chastisement.

The two of them, he and Mrs. Fountain, were almost like two people who were recovering from an embarrassment, as if she'd caught him picking his nose, or scratching some intimate place. He still felt a little raw, for reasons he couldn't quite identify.

And as he held himself still but not too still, and forced himself to improve his mind with Marcus Aurelius, he was all too aware of the two pieces of correspondence requiring his attention. His penmanship was still far from flawless, thanks to his stiff hand. Both pieces of correspondence represented decisions that would determine the rest of his life. And neither would wait forever for him to make up his mind.

He'd sailed the high seas, survived the rabble during the revolution, and fought off six cutthroats in London.

Never in his wildest dreams had he thought he would ever need to muster nerve to ring for a housekeeper.

ELISE WAS ALL too aware of how inert her bell had been lately. But it wasn't the silence of endings. The silence was alive with tension. It was a bit like the wait between skirmishes in a battle—or perhaps more accurately, the rest between movements in a symphony, a melodramatic metaphor she allowed herself when she lay awake at night, attempting to count sheep and instead holding her own hand and pretending it was Lavay's, to her own helpless chagrin. Or *chagreen*.

Tonight she promised herself she would do no such thing.

She decided this temporary silence presented

the perfect opportunity to tamp down all her fancies and solidify her control so that the next time he rang—for he would ring again, she was certain of it—her heart, let alone the rest of her, wouldn't so much as twinge.

And besides, she had more mundane things to worry about at the moment. For instance, how the devil was she going to obtain silk stockings for the footmen? All the livery now required was finishing touches, and James and Ramsey looked thrillingly elegant in it.

Alone in her room—Jack was tucked into bed— she freed her hair from its pins and placed them all neatly in a bowl on the little desk. Then she took up her ivory-backed hairbrush, a gift from her mother on her fourteenth birthday.

One hundred strokes nightly before plaiting her hair. The receipt for apple tarts, for simples and tisanes and soaps and milks for the complexion. The need for and pleasure in beauty, the ability to find it in the humble, the everyday. Her mother had taught her all of this. They were so alike in many ways, from the big, dark eyes to their quick minds.

Now that she was a mother, it seemed inconceivable that her own could ever have loved her if she shunned her now. *Nothing* Jack ever did would stop her from loving him, even if he ended up being sent to the gallows, God forbid, in which case, she'd do everything in her power to make sure he'd disappear from them in a puff of smoke a la Colin Eversea and live on as a folk hero.

She ran her thumb lightly over the initials engraved on the back of her brush. ELF. Elise Louise Fountain.

She'd once thought her parents' love was just as permanent as those initials.

Intervening years buffered the wound like layers of cotton wool, but when she was weary, she felt it, the way an old injury aches when it rains.

She did own another brush. But this one was, as she'd told Lord Lavay, one of the few things she'd seized when she'd been told to leave her parents' home for good. It had been so precious to her, a gift that made her feel loved and grown up.

And she knew how to get those silk stockings now.

Because she'd learned that when she was at her lowest, there was pleasure in making other people happy, and she could make James and Ramsey happy.

But mostly she could make Lord Lavay happy, which was really all she wanted to do, if she was being honest with herself. And she was usually unfailingly, ruthlessly honest with herself.

"Are you at one hundred, Mama?" Jack called, familiar with the nightly routine.

"One hundred. I'll be right in with a story."

"The one about the lion!"

"Naturally," she said.

THE NEXT DAY, Mr. Postlethwaite was arranging a selection of lady's combs in what he hoped was the most enticing fashion when the bell jangled on the shop door.

He swiveled to beam at Elise.

"Well, good morning to you, Mrs. Fountain. Are you bringing more letters to post?"

"I have a proposition for you, Mr. Postlethwaite."

"Ah, so seldom are my days enlivened by propositions from comely young ladies anymore. Please go on."

"Would it be possible to trade this for a pair of silk stockings? Silk stockings for men, that is?"

She produced her hairbrush.

To his credit, Mr. Postlethwaite didn't even blink. He took it and hefted it, turned it this way and that, studying it with a merchant's eye.

"Ah, it's lovely, Mrs. Fountain. The initials on it . . . they are yours?"

"Yes."

"ELF. Whimsical, really."

"I suppose. Do you think someone would buy it even with the initials on it?"

"Oh, certainly. Eventually. It's a lovely brush, and the initials are unobtrusive enough. I'd be happy to effect a trade. Go and choose your stockings, Mrs. Fountain."

Chapter 14

T HE FOLLOWING MORNING, PHILIPPE woke with a start. Again, he thought he heard heated whispering outside his door.

And then came, unsurprisingly, a tap.

He yawned. "Enter," he rasped.

The door swung open. To his shock, a masculine voice said, "I am at your service, sir, if you would like assistance with dressing."

Lavay propped himself upright and stared. He rubbed his fists in his eyes and took another look.

Surely he was *dreaming* he was back at Les Pierres d'Argent. Because standing before him was a tall, proper, elegant footman . . .

. . . and he was dressed in midnight blue.

Trimmed in silver braid.

Philippe slid out of bed and circled him as if he were an apparition.

He slowly reached out a finger and gave him a tiny poke.

The man didn't budge or so much as blink.

"Who the devil *are* you?" he finally asked.

"I'm Ramsey, sir. Your footman, sir."

"You're one of the pair of footmen that came with *this* house?"

"Yes, sir."

"Why are you here?"

"I won the coin toss, sir."

"The . . ."

"Mrs. Fountain was unable to decide which of us to send to attend upon you, as we both, as she said, 'suited.' We tossed a ha'pence, sir. Lion side up, and here I am."

Philippe stood back and studied him. He shook his head to and fro slowly. He was an absolute vision in well-cut livery, a striped waistcoat, pale silk stockings, and shoes that were polished to mirror brilliance.

Lavay gave a short, wondering laugh.

"Well, you're *magnifique*, Ramsey."

"Thank you, sir. I think."

"You do thank me," Philippe confirmed. "It means you look magnificent."

Ramsey didn't twitch a brow or alter his expression. He was impassive and regal. His posture was as straight as a mizzenmast. He was every inch the sort of footman Philippe had known his entire life.

And wonder poured through him like sunlight.

"And thank you, sir, for being so kind as to think of myself and James. Mrs. Fountain told us it was your idea."

A clever strategic move on Mrs. Fountain's part.

"Mrs. Fountain may have made suggestions, to which I agreed. Never forget how very fortunate you are that she is in charge of the house, Ramsey. She is a . . . she is a miracle."

"Of course, sir. She runs a very tight ship."

Lavay smiled. He suddenly felt made of light.

"Please tell me how I may be of service, my lord."

"Well . . . how are you with a razor, Ramsey?"

"I could shave a baby's bottom and leave nary a nick."

"Well, then, you ought to be able to shave me, I suppose."

"But of course, sir. And might I suggest the nankeen trousers today, if you intend to go out? The weather is inclement, sir."

"I thank you for the suggestion. But right after we've made me presentable, Ramsey, there's something I'd like you to do."

ELISE WAS WAITING in the kitchen with bated breath for Ramsey's return, but she hadn't expected him to return at a run.

"Quickly, Mrs. Fountain! There's no time to lose! Lord Lavay wants you to fetch the vase from your room and bring it to him immediately!"

"The *what*? But what did he say about—"

"Go, Mrs. Fountain! Go!"

Well, all right, then.

Her cheeks were hot with disappointment. Perhaps he hated the livery so much that he felt the need to throw something, and his sense of economy resigned him to throwing something humble, rather than invaluable.

With a heavy heart, she scaled the stairs to her little room.

And came to a sharp halt.

The brown velvet chair was situated right beneath the window, next to the little writing table. The previous occupant of that space, the pedestrian wooden chair, had apparently been whisked away.

She approached it slowly, as if it were perhaps a hallucination.

Very like, in other words, Lavay had approached the footman earlier.

She circled it at first, then reached out and dragged her hand across its luxurious, now familiar, nap.

"What are *you* doing here?" she asked it.

The chair remained inscrutable.

She gave a short, wondering laugh and closed her eyes as joy poured through her, warm and soft and brilliant. Then she brought her hands up to her face and down again.

She seized the little vase, though now she thought it was a ploy.

She pivoted on her heel and wandered in a daze down the stairs to the kitchen, where things were as usual and none of the furniture seemed to have migrated to where it didn't belong. Then she paused to review her hair in the nearest reflective object, which was the coffeepot, and bolted with unseemly haste for the stairs.

She remembered to adopt a more dignified pace as she approached, so that she managed to look entirely composed when she arrived, clutching the vase.

And her heart of course gave an appallingly eager little leap when she saw him. He hadn't gotten uglier in the intervening days.

"A footman woke me this morning, Fountain," Lavay said without preamble. As if it had been only yesterday since they'd last spoken, instead of a number of very awkward days.

"Very good, sir."

"He offered to shave and dress me."

"Did you take him up on that offer?"

"What do you think of my chin, Fountain?"

"It's very shiny."

That slow smile of his began, the one that wound around her like a golden net, and she smiled, too, helpless not to.

They basked for a moment in each other's happiness.

"How did you do it, Fountain?" he said on an awestruck hush.

"Ingenuity, sir."

He laughed, delighted.

She saw an interloper chair in the place she usually sat, retrieved from the second, smaller sitting room. This chair was a shade of rum, and it, too, looked quite soft though she'd never quite tested it.

"Lord Lavay, the brown velvet chair is in my quarters. Do you know why?"

"Is it? Puzzling, indeed. Perhaps it missed you and your caresses. Perhaps it walked up there all on its own."

He used his fingers to walk across the desk, presumably demonstrating the chair walking up the stairs.

"My *caresses*?"

Her face all but burst into flame. Of course he'd noticed her touching the chair. He noticed *everything*. Just as he was likely noticing her flaming face now.

He made his fingers walk across the table again. "You see? A week or so ago I could not do that comfortably. Soon I will be stabbing cutthroats with alacrity once more."

She clearly looked horrified, because he became serious instantly.

"I am giving you the chair, Fountain. You gave me footmen, and you have made me feel more at home than I have in so long. I will give you a chair. A fair exchange, *n'est-ce pas*? It is my wish as your employer that you should accept my gift. It has been in my family for generations. It was, in fact, once temporarily a throne."

Oh, good God. Now she felt a little faint.

"It was a *throne*?"

"For heaven's sake, no, Fountain." He sounded pained. "And I thought you were clever. Only two generations, and I believe my aunt Louise-Anne died in it. She was ninety, closed her eyes, died, and tipped out of it during a game of faro, or so family legend has it."

She laughed again. "But I can't keep your chair! It's an heirloom!"

She could in fact finance a few years of her life and Jack's with that chair.

"It certainly is. *Your* heirloom now. But if you doubt me, I shall call it and see if it comes to me. If it does not, then it belongs to you."

She gave a short, breathless laugh and shook her head. "I . . . I don't know what to say."

"Say 'Thank you, Lord Lavay.'"

She breathed in deeply and exhaled. "Thank you, Lord Lavay."

He smiled at her approvingly.

"Perhaps you will fall in love with this one, too." He gestured broadly to the chair that had taken the brown one's place.

The word "love" throbbed in the air so obviously that it might as well have been a heart, especially since all her senses were acutely heightened, anyway.

They both looked momentarily nonplussed.

He hurriedly added, "I wondered if you would be so kind as to sit in this new chair and take a letter for me, Mrs. Fountain."

"It would be my pleasure."

She settled into the new chair—also quite comfortable—and wriggled in until the back cupped her back. Then she took up the quill.

He strode to the center of the room, prepared to orate.

"Very well. It is to a young lady, so your best penmanship, please, Mrs. Fountain."

"I have no other kind of penmanship, Lord Lavay."

"Of course not, Fountain. And we begin." *"Dearest Alexa."*

She dashed off the words.

"It has been too long, and as you suggest hopefully in your letter, I am indeed indestructible and all the essential parts of me remain intact. How could you question whether I'd like to see you, when you know your very presence is like spring in the midst of winter, and so forth? I hear you laughing even now, but how could I resist hyperbole when I know how it entertains you?"

"Mrs. Fountain? Why are you not writing?"

"Oh! Forgive me." *". . . entertains you . . ."*

It was just . . . who was this Alexa? And why was his prose suddenly so sparkling?

It certainly sounded rather too enthusiastic to be another sister.

"It is as lovely to be known as it is to survive an attack in London that would have killed most men. Deep is my regret that our paths did not cross when you were last in Pennyroyal Green, and I should rend my garments if you did not pass this way again before I return to Paris."

He paused.

"Do you think 'rending my garments' is a bit much, Mrs. Fountain?"

"Not if you don't mind breaking the hearts of your new footmen-valets, who think you have beautiful clothing."

"Lady Prideux finds me amusing, Mrs. Fountain. It is my responsibility to perpetuate that illusion."

She froze.

The quill hovered over the foolscap, not touching it, like a bird frozen in flight.

And then she lowered it very, very carefully.

She was unusually still.

As if she was enduring some sort of twinge or pain.

"I notice you raised no objection to the word 'illusion.' I'm hurt, Mrs. Fountain, truly. In some circles I am in fact considered charming."

He was teasing. Gently.

Her expression, stunned and blank, was puzzling.

She cleared her throat. "Lady Prideux?" she said faintly. She didn't look at him. Her gaze was aimed steadfastly at the foolscap.

"Our families have been friends since I was born. They emerged from the revolution a trifle more intact than my family, in terms of both family members and fortune."

He said this shortly. Because tension was gathering in the room, and he wasn't certain why.

"Ah," she said finally. And gave a strange, short little laugh.

She finally did look up at him. Staring at him as if she was seeing him for the first time, or rather, seeing him clearly for the first time.

She didn't appear to be breathing.

And why on earth had she gone so white?

"Have you said all you wish to say to . . . Lady Prideux . . . Lord Lavay?"

"No," he said, bemused, and a bit gently. "I have not. There is a bit more. If you would, Mrs. Fountain? Or have you chairs to caress?"

"Of course."

She squared her shoulders, as if he'd asked her to lift the table instead of a quill, then bent to the task.

"I hope to hold an assembly in the home I am renting, my dear Alexandra, and if you should return, I most certainly will. Nothing gives me more pleasure to imagine dancing with you again, and the possibility of kissing your hand would warm the winter.

I remain your,"

" . . . and then I shall sign it, as I usually do."

She was silent, motionless, gone stiff and formal, and the light had gone out of her face. The joy of the previous few moments might never have happened. He was bewildered.

"If you have said what you intend to say, Lord Lavay, I shall post the letter."

"I will take it to be posted tomorrow, Mrs. Fountain. It will do me good to walk as far as Postlethwaite's."

"Very well."

She still hadn't moved. As if she was waiting out some great pain.

"Is aught troubling you, Mrs. Fountain? Do you think the line about 'hand kissing' too florid?"

"No. If you have no further need for me . . ."

She stood abruptly and turned to leave as if the

room were on fire. She was nearly to the door, and
he felt something akin to panic.

"If I were to kiss you, for instance, you would
never forget it."

He all but flung the words at her like a net.

She froze midstride.

It was as if he'd shot her in the back with a dart.

Then she spun so quickly that her skirts continued to sway after she'd stopped.

She looked utterly stricken.

Hardly flattering.

"Mrs. Fountain, you've gone white. Am I so
very repulsive, then? I thought my new scar made
me look rakish."

But his words emerged awkwardly. It was a jest
meant to disguise a serious question, but it had
failed at the task miserably.

She gave her head a little shake.

"You ought not tease me that way." Her voice
was peculiarly hoarse.

She tried for a smile.

It slid from her face like raspberry jelly.

He stepped toward her abruptly, concerned.

She stepped back.

"Tease you?" he said softly, urgently.

He realized he was burning her with a stare
when she dropped her eyes.

He regretted it instantly, because he wanted to
study the effect of his words there, because what
he'd just witnessed had probably been more thrilling than it ought to have been.

And if he was honest with himself, he'd said those words for a reason.

The silence was filled with confusion.

And she was suffering. He wasn't certain why. He only knew that he couldn't bear it.

"Mrs. Fountain," he said gently. "I sometimes forget that I am French and others are not. The English are perhaps more reticent. We speak of such things as if it were the weather."

She looked up at him, searching his face as if for the truth of this.

"But not typically to housekeepers." She said this gently, as if she were pointing something out to a child.

And yet there was the faintest hint of a question in her words.

He went utterly still.

His mind blanked in astonishment.

And all at once he was wholly abashed.

Then flooded with admiration.

Damned if she hadn't skewered him with truth.

She was not a toy. She was not a game. She did not exist to ease his moods. She was not a woman of his world, for whom flirtation was merely a second language. For whom gifts were all but meaningless.

But she *was* a woman. With feelings of her own, no doubt secrets of her own, and right now she was suffering.

Was it . . . because of him?

Or perhaps his vanity suggested this.

The notion elated him in a way he was afraid to examine.

But it made him gravely unhappy to distress her.

"Perhaps I have forgotten my place," he said gruffly at last.

She drew in what sounded like a bracing breath. "I won't forget mine," she said.

At the moment, they seemed like the worst words he'd ever heard.

He could feel the beginnings of a flush on the back of his neck. Of *all things*.

When was the last time he'd blushed?

Perhaps when he was fourteen years old.

"Forgive me if I carelessly caused offense," he said stiffly.

"Oh, there is of course nothing to forgive," she said hurriedly, graciously, and gave him an actual smile. The sort that made an impish point of her chin and revealed dimples and turned her eyes into stars. "One cannot help being French."

The smile was gone too soon.

His regret made him realize he'd begun to crave that smile a bit too much.

It was better than laudanum. Than brandy. Than the vile willow bark tea.

And she was always so much more comfortable easing his distress than allowing her own to be eased.

Since "humbled" was another unfamiliar condition for him, he remained silent and thoughtful.

At a loss, for perhaps the first time in . . . he could not recall.

"If you've no further requirements at the moment, my lord, I must oversee the apple tarts or they will burn. And just to remind you, tonight is my evening off."

"Please do leave. Nothing is more important than those apple tarts. Enjoy your evening, Mrs. Fountain."

But he could hear that his voice had gone peculiarly thick.

He didn't know why his feelings should be hurt.

She curtsied and hurried past him.

He watched her go, rotating as if he'd been a weathervane and she the wind. Just that helpless.

Chapter 15

THE NEXT DAY BEGAN very early and innocently enough, apart from the glowering skies and the intermittent torrential downpour that would keep Jack inside and underfoot in the servants quarters. No one minded his presence, though, since he was like a lively breath of spring, and in great danger of being spoiled by everyone. Elise and the servants had reached a civil, even collegial, rhythm to their days—truly, everyone enjoyed being in a spotless house featuring strategically placed vases of flowers here and there. The footmen were quite decorative, as well.

They now all breakfasted together along with Jack.

Even Dolly had been . . . sweet.

Treacle sweet.

Elise decided to forgo suspicion and congratulated herself on winning her over.

Jack, perhaps with the instinct small children and animals have for people, generally went mute around Dolly and eyed her with big, wary eyes, which got warier when she smiled.

Fortunately it was Dolly's half day off, and she wasn't about to forgo it, rainstorm or no.

She pushed her empty plate away from her and thumped out a muffled belch with one fist to her sternum. "I'll just get me cloak and go then, Mrs. Fountain."

"You won't want to go out in this, Dolly, will you?" Elise scooped Lord Lavay's coffee into a pot and shook his tea into a cup, too. "Perhaps you can have an extra entire day later?"

"Oh, it willna be like this all day, Mrs. Fountain. Me sister will be taking me out, ye see, for a visit, and she'll be waiting."

Elise stood on her toes and peered out the window. She could just make out a cart and horse waiting at the far end of the drive, with what appeared to be a very large driver bundled in heaps of clothing. One would have to be mad or desperate to go out in this weather. It was close to being dangerous for everyone.

She frowned faintly.

They all scattered to see to their duties—Kitty and Mary to clean the kitchen, the footman to see to the fires—and Elise decided it would be a fine time to make more headway on polishing the silver. She sifted through her keys and paused.

The cabinet containing the fine porcelain appeared to be ever so slightly ajar.

She leaped for it and yanked the door wide open. She peered inside, her heart in her throat, a suspicion burning.

Suspicion was sickeningly confirmed: the little blue sauceboat was missing.

Fury hazed her vision.

She whirled and listened. Dolly hadn't reappeared on the servant's stairs. Usually one could hear her footsteps coming from a significant distance away.

Dolly might be big, but Elise was faster.

"Jack, stay here in the kitchen!" she ordered as she shut the cabinet. And then she bolted down the passageway and ran like the devil through the house.

She intercepted Dolly hastening her way out the front door.

Dolly was swathed in a vast cloak.

And interestingly, carrying a valise that appeared to be bulging.

Elise leaped in front of her and barred the exit.

"Ye'll want to move, Mrs. Fountain," Dolly drawled. "Me sister will get drenched out there."

"Why are you carrying a valise, Dolly?"

Dolly remained rooted to the spot. The hand not holding the valise was tucked beneath her cloak.

"I dinna think that be yer business, Mrs. Fountain," she said pleasantly, which only served to make it sound sinister.

"Show me what is in your hand, Dolly."

Dolly remained as rooted as a boulder.

"*Now.*" Elise spat the word like a bullet from a gun.

Dolly's hand shot out, her eyes wide, looking as surprised as if she'd been a puppet and someone had yanked her strings.

Gripped in her fist was the blue Sevres sauce-boat.

The sense of betrayal was immense. How, how, how could she have been so foolish as to trust Dolly?

Elise's temper was sizzling dangerously. She'd given her trust before and regretted it deeply, and she would be damned if it would be trampled upon like this again.

"Why are you holding that sauceboat? Were you about to use it to put out a cheroot on your little jaunt with your 'sister'?" Her voice was low and menacing.

The silence was deafening.

Elise was smaller than Dolly, but her anger radiated from her like the fur on a furious cat. She felt three sizes larger and twenty times meaner.

Dolly remained silent.

"How did you get into the cabinet, Dolly?"

"Ach, ye poor dear, ye think ye're so kind and clever, and ye're such an *amateur*. Ye wi' yer sweet-ness and kindness and thank-yous. One thump with me fist at the corner and it popped right open."

Elise blinked. "I thought we reached an agree-ment." Beneath the fury, she was surprised to find that her feelings and pride were hurt.

"'Tis better to be quick than kind, Mrs. Foun-tain. Now, if ye'll *kindly* step aside."

"Listen to me, you *fraud*. You are as of now released without references. I care not what becomes of you. You are fortunate I won't ensure you are hanged for theft."

Dolly finally, appropriately, blanched, which was not a pretty sight.

The first appropriate thing she'd done since Elise had arrived.

"'Tis just one thing. That rich cove has so *many* things and I've—"

"You've what? A job? A roof over your head? Food in your belly? A sense of entitlement? No gratitude? How *dare* you. How *dare* you. The 'he' of which you speak is a prince of the House of Bourbon, who shed blood for this country and his own so that the likes of you can remain safe and enjoy, as you say, 'your little pleasures.' He is a remark . . ." Elise felt her voice crack. ". . . remarkable, kind, and just man, and he is the one currently keeping you alive. The thing you hold is one of the few things left of his possessions when his home was *stolen* from him. And now you would steal from him again? You've been treated a sight better than most servants ever are, and you repay him with thievery. Which you then, astonishingly, attempt to justify."

It was such an assault of passionate eloquence that Dolly stood blinking, stunned, as if she'd been sprayed with shrapnel.

A fraught little silence ensued.

"What will 'e do?" Dolly murmured nastily. "Chase after me?"

Elise had never been so tempted to strike someone.

"He doesn't need to run in order to shoot you, and if he should wish to shoot you, I'd lie to the magistrate and say it was in self-defense. That you had gone mad and attacked him, because surely you must be mad to think I wouldn't eventually discover your thievery. You've always struck me as the sort who would eventually meet her end at the end of a rope."

Dolly was now scorching red.

"You're one to judge, ain't ye, Mrs. Fountain," she hissed. "I've 'eard a thing or two about ye, so's I have. Let ye who be without sin—"

Elise stepped forward abruptly and put her face up to Dolly. So close she could see the hair in her nostrils and the color of her eyes and the tiny broken veins fanning from either side of her flaring nostrils. She could smell the woman's sour breath, which was coming rapidly now.

"Spend a lot of time in church, do you, Dolly?" Elise said it very quietly, but apparently she managed to sound sinister. "I *dare* you to finish that sentence."

Dolly's throat moved when she swallowed.

"If you can tell me from whom *I* stole, and who I injured, then you may keep your position."

Dolly remained wordless.

"I thought not. Give me the sauceboat."

Dolly lifted her hand, prepared to throw it, but Elise was faster and snatched it from her.

"Drop that valise and get out of this house. NOW. You'll find any belongings you left behind in the road tomorrow morning."

Dolly spat toward Elise's feet, missed, dropped the valise, and stormed her way out of the house, slamming the door behind her.

Elise seized the valise to search later, whirled on her heel, prepared to storm off, and staggered to a halt.

Lord Lavay was standing at the end of the hall-way.

He was watching her.

His expression was very nearly . . . wonderment.

As if something was dawning on him.

He must have heard her passionately defend that blue sauceboat as if it had been Lord Lavay himself being spirited out of the house by a ham-handed Dolly Farmer.

They mutely regarded each other. The expression in his eyes nearly buckled her knees, so soft yet fierce it was.

"Thank you for defending my honor, Mrs. Fountain. You looked for a moment there ready to do murder," he said softly. "And I should know, as I'm quite familiar with the look. Pirates frequently sport it."

She tried to smile. She couldn't quite do it.

If I were to kiss you . . .

She held his sauceboat out to him wordlessly. Tenderly. As if it were, indeed, a kiss.

He strode slowly over to her and took it from her just as gently, almost ceremoniously, his fingertips brushing hers.

He looked down at it for some time without speaking.

Very like he didn't want her to see his expression, either.

"She was wrong, Mrs. Fountain. It's better to be kind than to be quick. Please don't lose heart."

"I won't. But I think we need a new lock for the porcelain cabinet."

He looked up. "I'll find room in the budget."

She smiled at that.

"I fear she was the cook, Lord Lavay."

He shrugged with one shoulder. "I'll eat bread and cheese if necessary. Or dine out with the Earl and Countess of Ardmay."

"It won't be necessary," she rushed to assure him. "A man can't live on apple tarts alone. I can cook adequately until we find another. And I'll have your coffee brought up to you. My apologies for the delay in bringing it to you this morning, if that's what brought you down."

"I can survive a few minutes more without coffee. And fear not. These things happen, Fountain. I've sacked many a man in my day. None so large as Dolly Farmer, however."

She smiled at him.

He turned to return to his study, and over his shoulder called, "Oh, and congratulations. The job is officially yours."

ALL THE WAY up the stairs, down the hall, and back to his study, Philippe was savoring in his mind's eye the expression on Mrs. Fountain's face when she'd defended him.

He could not recall ever before seeing quite the same expression on a woman's face. That tender ferocity. Moments of peril had much the same effect as alcohol: they shook loose truths.

He held the sauceboat tenderly, as if escorting a prisoner of war to safety.

He came to an almost skidding halt, just as a small boy he'd never seen in his life did as well. They were approaching each other from opposite directions.

They perused each other silently, nonplussed and warily, from a distance of about twelve feet.

"You must be the giant," the boy said finally.

"The *giant*?"

The house likely had its share of ghosts, given that it was a century or so old, but he hadn't yet encountered any of them. This one wasn't transparent. He had what appeared to be crumbs clinging to the corner of his mouth. In all likelihood apple tart.

Philippe approached slowly, as if the boy were a feral animal with sharp teeth rather than a child.

He stood and looked down.

The boy stood his ground, his eyes huge.

"Please don't eat me."

"I'm not hungry," Philippe found himself saying inanely.

Did he work in the kitchens? What was he doing running amuck on this floor of the house?

"You can eat Liam," Jack offered, as smoothly as a courtier maneuvering palace politics. "He can run faster than me, but there's more of him. For now," Jack vowed. "I'll be bigger."

"You really ought not betray your mate. It's a matter of honor, young man." This was somehow a reflex, too.

"Honor?" Jack repeated, testing the word and clearly liking it.

"Yes. It means to be proud to do what is right. And a true man is loyal to his compatriots."

He couldn't shake the dreamlike quality of the dark hallway. And there was something about the boy . . . it was like a word at the tip of his tongue that he couldn't quite reach.

"Are compatries like apple tarts?"

"'Com-pa-tri-ots' is a word that means 'friends' and 'comrades in arms.' The men who look out for you when you go into battle. And every day in life, too."

Why had he launched into a lecture as naturally as if it were something he did always?

"I wish I had a lion," the boy said suddenly.

"Of course. Everybody does."

"And a horse."

"Naturally."

He'd happened into a conversational labyrinth without a compass, clearly.

Jack brightened. "Do you eat little girls instead,

then? I know where you can find *loads* of them.
Over at Miss Endicott's Academy. They're usually
cleaner."

"I'm partial to apple tarts. I have not yet eaten
a person. I *have* eaten a weevil." He said this as if
playing a trump.

"Ewwww!"

A gratifying reaction.

"When I'm a little bigger, I'll be able to ring the
church bell by myself with no help at all."

"An admirable ambition."

"I like apple tarts, too," the boy confided. "Have
you slept in a hammock?"

"Have I wha—yes. I have." He'd begun to rather
look forward to where this conversation would
next lead. It was a bit like fencing, but much less
dangerous. "I was a sailor on a great ship. I slept
in a bunk, which is simply a very hard bed. But
my men slept in hammocks."

"My mama says sailors sleep in hammocks."

"Your mama . . ."

"She told me not to bounce on the bed or I
would sleep in a hammock."

The back of Philippe's neck prickled portentously. His mama . . .

"What do you think giants eat?" the boy asked.

"Whatever they want to eat, I should imagine."
Philippe heard his voice go remote, a little colder
now, because a realization was beginning to solidify.

The boy giggled.

Lavay did smile reflexively at that, because one

would have to be made of stone to not smile in the face of a child's giggle.

And as Mrs. Fountain had pointed out, he was most assuredly not made of stone.

Oh, most assuredly not.

"I'm not a giant, young man. I'm merely very tall. You will be one day, too."

"Do you think so?"

"It's inevitable."

Children were merely young humans, and he didn't believe in speaking down to them.

"Because I think I need to get a little taller to get up a beanstalk. That would be grand."

"Has someone given you magic beans, then?"

"Ohhhh!" Jack breathed. "Do you know the story, too? My mama named me for Jack. She sings a song about Jack before we go to sleep."

Philippe closed his eyes briefly as realization sank in, peculiarly sharp, like an arrow.

The soft dark eyes, the curls, the dark slashes of brows.

The little dimple in his chin.

A peculiar cold knot solidified in Philippe's gut. It felt like betrayal.

He could not for the life of him have said why.

He heard the frantic clicking and skidding of the slippers on the marbled hallways, the huff of her breath. "Jack, where have you—"

Elise came to a halt when she saw two men, one very small, one very tall.

Young Jack's face went brilliant.

"Mama! I found the giant!"

"So I see." Her voice was cheerful, if wary.

"This young gentleman says he's your son," Lavay said.

"He is indeed, and a luckier mother never lived."

Jack glowed up at her, and she dropped her hands like epaulets on his shoulders and gripped him tightly. Two against the giant.

"Jack, I am pleased to present you to Lord Lavay, who owns this beautiful house that I look after, but I am disappointed that you disobeyed me. We live at the top of the house, and this part belongs to Lord Lavay, and it's impolite to intrude. Have you made your bow to him?"

"No, Mama. Sorry, Mama. I was looking for you, and here he was. It was an accident, Mama."

"Do make your bow now, if you please." She lifted her hands from his shoulders.

Jack bowed so low that his forehead nearly touched his knees.

"A handsome bow, Master Jack. Thank you," Lord Lavay said gravely.

Jack glowed, then began to fidget happily.

She dropped her hands back onto his shoulders and he went still, leaning against her.

"Please go and return to your room now, my love, while I speak with Lord Lavay. Do you know the way?"

"Follow the cupids on the banister, the wallpaper with the pattern a bit like pretty eyes, go all the way down the stairs, wait for the smell of apple tarts and then go into the kitchen, down the hall and up the stairs."

It was like he was describing the vast distance between their social stations.

"You are quite correct and very clever, Jack."

"All right, Mama. Good-bye, Giant Lord Lavay."

"Until we meet again, Soon to be Tall Master Jack," he said gravely.

Jack laughed and turned, poised to bolt.

"Walk!" she admonished.

He adopted a mockingly sedate pace that made her smile after him.

They watched him until he was out of sight.

Or rather, she watched him.

Lavay watched her.

Her expression stole his breath.

"I was unaware you had a son," he said softly, as if hesitating to wake her from a beautiful sleep.

Her attention returned to him abruptly.

She looked worried. "I apologize if you feel I excluded this information, my lord. I didn't think it would interest you or that it would be a condition of my employment."

"It is not," he said shortly.

Another silence.

"I'm terribly sorry if he troubled you."

"He did not."

He feared he sounded quite brusque.

"He is charming," he added.

And then they stood regarding each other in silence, in the now well-lit and dusted hallway.

The air was so aswarm with unspoken things that he felt he could reach up a hand to swat them. There were questions he had every right to ask, given that he was her employer, and he was arrogant enough to do it. Then again, he had no right to wonder about them, because she was his housekeeper for a house he intended to live in after he could gracefully waltz again, and in his hierarchy of concerns she ought to rank a step or two above the furniture.

But it was even more damning and awkward that he didn't ask the questions.

"He's a handsome child."

"He's beautiful," she said instantly, in a rush, and then flushed, because it sounded like a correction.

There was a silence.

He smiled faintly. "Yes," he said gently. "That is the word I was thinking. Thank you, Madame Je-sais-tout."

"Thank you," she said faintly, which is what she ought to have said the first time.

Her face was pink.

"Will there be apple tarts soon?"

"Yes, of course. I will go see to them."

They could always take refuge in apple tarts, it seemed.

Chapter 16

Husband.

He'd of course been contemplating becoming one, but now he thought it was a surprisingly distasteful word.

Made even more distasteful with the addition of another word: *her*.

As in *her* husband.

He returned to his study, settled his sauceboat on the desk, and paced—how gratifying to be able to pace again—as he repeated the word in his head, as if it were a purgative or a hair shirt. Was that the reason she kept the best of herself back?

Because she was *Mrs*. Fountain, and surely there must be a husband somewhere? Housekeepers were often given the honorific of "Mrs.," even if unmarried. But there was, after all, a son.

Her. His. That was the point of pronouns, after all—to indicate ownership. Perhaps "ownership" was wrong. Perhaps "belonging" was a better word. A more painful word, in a way, because it implied choice. She'd chosen to belong to someone else.

He'd never been one to shy away from hard truths, because once he knew the truth, he could do something about it.

And so, as if to flagellate himself, this is what "belonging" meant: some man knew what it was like to see that shining black hair spread out over a white pillow, and knew what it felt like to feel her bare limbs tangled with his, and to hear her laugh in the dark. Someone woke next to her every morning and knew whether she sprang from bed cheerful or grumpy and needing coffee or tea—or was it chocolate?—to start her day.

He didn't know. He didn't know. So many things he didn't know. All the mundane things seemed absolutely the most important of all, suddenly.

And he hadn't realized until now that he wanted to know them.

This made him pace to the window and yank back the curtains as if they were poised to leap and attack him. He glowered accusingly out at the day.

If there was a child, there was a man, because of course she was not, after all, the Madonna, exquisitely run household and flawless apple tarts notwithstanding.

Then again . . . the man in question *might* be dead.

He was absurdly buoyed by this hope, and suddenly the day was beautiful again and he fancied he could hear birds singing, even from this distance.

"Pah!" he said to himself, and shrugged and pushed away from the window.

And *all* of this was ridiculous: the strange pressure in his chest that felt like someone was in there trying to pry apart his rib cage, the histrionics involving the curtains, the wishing fatherlessness on that sweet child, that thirst to know, know, know.

He was . . .

He was jealous.

That pedestrian word.

Ah. *So this is what the peasants feel like*, he told himself dryly.

He didn't like it. He didn't know what to do about it: he couldn't muffle it with laudanum or numb it with willow bark tea. He couldn't reason it out of existence. He couldn't shoot it or sail away from it.

It needled in a peculiar way.

He'd thought he was inured to all of that.

It seemed he'd simply been numb. But now that feelings had begun to recirculate, *this* was the one that decided to reassert itself? Were there no end to the torments to be rained upon the House of Lavay?

She now knew so many things about him, yet she had never once mentioned what was clearly the most precious thing in the world to her.

He snorted. "You're being ridiculous, Philippe!"

Perhaps it was just his vanity that was wounded. Perhaps he had come to think of Mrs. Fountain as something that belonged to him.

He was probably bored. Surely in other circum-

stances a man of his station would not be so dis-
rupted by his housekeeper, albeit a . . . comely one?
Comely servants abounded in houses everywhere,
tempting heirs and causing all manner of trouble.

He had been too long confined and too long out
of the context of his real world, where beautiful,
charming women abounded, none of whom made
his pulse hammer uncomfortably or tempted him
to throw things in a fit of jealous pique, like a
scorned mistress.

It was time to hold that ball.

And like a reflex or a lifeline, he rang the bell.

"THANK YOU FOR coming," he said inanely when
she arrived in his study.

"Yes. Of course. It's what I typically do when
you ring the bell."

She was jesting, or trying to. But it sounded
nearly as stilted as his greeting. Suddenly they
were strangers.

He felt as gauche as a boy. He fumbled for what
to say next.

"Again, I'm so sorry you had to witness the . . .
unfortunate incident with Dolly Farmer," she ventured into the awkward silence. "I searched her
valise. She stole nothing else."

"I'm not sorry I witnessed it. I now understand
a bit more about the miracle you've wrought with
the staff. I don't think I fully grasped the nature
of the challenge."

"It was noth—"

He gave his head a rough shake. "It was every-thing. You see . . . for most of my life, in every house I've ever lived in, I never even saw most of the servants. You noticed them only when they failed to work properly. They were like . . . oh, the circulatory system of a house. That would make you, I suppose, the heart."

It was out of his mouth before he could stop himself, and for a second the words all but throbbed like an actual heart.

Her eyes widened in astonishment.

"As I said earlier, I've sacked men before, but I'm not certain I've ever sacked one as big as Dolly," he added hurriedly, very nearly flustered.

She smiled at that, mercifully. But only briefly. She couldn't sustain it amidst the tension of what remained unspoken. They were both still skirting the real reason he'd rung for her, and they knew it.

He cleared his throat. "I think I understand now where you get your courage, Mrs. Fountain," he said gently. "Mothers are fierce."

And there it was.

She went still. Bracing herself, apparently.

"Your son . . . Jack, his name is?" he said softly.

"John. But we've come to like 'Jack' better."

"After the boy with the magic beans."

"Yes," she said shortly. She inhaled at length, as if gathering strength, then exhaled. "Lord Lavay—I apologize again if he troubled you. He wasn't meant to go . . . perhaps I should have told you about . . . I never meant for him to—"

"Elise."

She fell silent.

As surprised by the use of her name as by his tone. Intimate. Impatient. Warm.

They let the word ring there, both of them quietly marveling at it.

She smiled softly at him, in gratitude.

It was easier to think about balls, and beautiful women, and Alexandra, and flirtation and debauchery, when Elise wasn't standing in front of him. Those things seemed superfluous and not part of his real world anymore, when in truth sanity dictated that he ought to feel the other way around.

And yet he always felt so much better when she was standing near.

"His manners are lovely, even if he is a bit loquacious," he teased gently. "A clever child, clearly. Takes after his mother."

She glowed. "Thank you. I do try. He usually spends his days at the vicarage. Reverend Sylvaine gives some time to his tutelage along with Liam Plum, a local boy, and some of the other boys of limited means. Between us, with luck, he will not grow up to be either a heathen or stupid. I hope one day he'll find a profession he loves. His current ambition in life is to ring the church bell."

"He also wants a lion. And a horse."

"Yes, well."

"He's welcome in all of the house, truly. I do like children, you know. They have that combination of honesty, innocence, savagery, and wit all tied together with unpredictability common to all my favorite people."

She laughed again, delighted.

He could stand here all day saying things to make her laugh.

"If the weather remains this inclement, send him in to me and I'll use the globe"—he gave it a spin with one finger—"to teach him about geography, if he'd like. For I, like you, enjoy imparting information, and I've been to many places. Or we could . . . string up a hammock. On clearer days."

She smiled again. "The offer is too kind, but I know Jack would love it. Thank you."

He simply nodded.

The question he wanted to ask, and the one she knew he wanted to ask, swung silently in the air, almost as tangible as a hammock.

He didn't want to say it aloud. It was a bit like taking a tentative first step on a sprained ankle.

He made it sound as casual as possible, but he knew they were both waiting for it, so it gave the words the false, jaunty air of a pantomime.

"The boy's father . . ."

Her face shuttered instantly.

Something was amiss, because it was clear she was deciding how to answer. Which meant he wasn't going to get the entire truth.

"He's gone," she said shortly.

"Gone?"

"Yes. Six years now."

Gone? Was "gone" a euphemism? Had he gone to the great beyond? London? Africa? Was she a widow?

Why was it so critical to know?

It wasn't. He didn't need to know.

And it ought not matter.

Get a hold of yourself, Lavay, he told himself.

"I see," he said, though he didn't. "Mrs. Fountain," he continued briskly, "I rang for you because I think the time has come to hold the ball we discussed earlier. Perhaps more accurately, an assembly featuring dancing, since a ball sounds a bit ambitious for the hall of this particular house. I suppose we'll have that insipid drink that pleases the ladies so—ratafia. Perhaps sandwiches and the other things people enjoy having at balls, too. Bring in some plants for drunks to vomit in and lovers to hide behind, that sort of thing. Some flowers and perhaps bunting, if it could be had. I imagine if you could outfit the footmen in livery, you can find bunting. A fortnight hence? There isn't a good deal to do in the country, so I imagine invitations will be welcome."

"A ball! Oh, that's wonderful news!" She sounded relieved the topic had changed.

He scowled.

She laughed. "Surely balls are happy occasions, my lord. The dancing, the music, the beautiful gowns, the company, the drunken revelry. I'm certain your staff is equal to the task. I've only attended country dances."

"I do like them," he admitted. "I excel at them, as a matter of fact."

"May I inquire as to the cause of your scowl?"

"I am concerned about my dancing."

There was silence.

"You are struggling not to laugh, Mrs. Fountain."

"I'm not!"

She was.

"I am a bit stiff, you see, and a bit out of practice, and I hesitate to bring shame upon my family by tottering about like an old man. I wondered if you would find it in your heart to assist me by practicing the waltz?"

It was utterly impulsive, yet the notion came to him as a gift.

His idle tone was in inverse proportion to how important her answer was to him.

The clock swung off several more seconds as she considered this, her head tipped a little.

"'Find it in my heart.' So very florid," she murmured.

He just waited, a peculiar pressure building in him. Probably because he was holding his breath.

Suddenly the fate of the world hinged on what she would say next.

"We've no music," she mused softly.

"You can make up a song about waltzing with Lord Lavay, who trod upon your feet today. Or we can count it off. We've certainly established that we both know how to count."

She laughed at that.

She drew in a long breath and exhaled. But said nothing.

"If you have other responsibilities to attend to now, Mrs. Fountain, of course you must excuse yourself. I simply wanted to make the best impression possible."

There. He'd just done what was right and fair. He'd given her an opportunity to bow out. To claim Jack, or apple tarts. And he'd delivered it with a small dose of guilt, because he knew she couldn't resist helping him.

She studied him a moment longer, her eyes soft and wary. Something sharp and bright flickered in there. Surrender? But it looked a bit like anger. A flare and gone.

And then she sank into a deep, slow curtsy.

He felt triumph surge through him, not unlike a welling of strings in a symphony overture. He'd never had a thought quite like that before in his entire life.

He bowed with the same elegant gravity.

He held out his hand, a brow arched, and her own hand reached out. He could have sworn time slowed painfully in order to torture him. Perhaps their hands would never meet. Perhaps she would snatch it back before he touched it.

And at last it was in his grasp. He closed his fingers over hers, gently but emphatically.

There was a stunned moment of stillness and silence when they finally met again, skin to skin.

And it wasn't until then that he was willing to

admit this entire waltzing nonsense was simply an excuse to touch her again.

He didn't know why. It didn't matter why. It only mattered that he held her hand, and he would have an excuse to lay his other hand on her waist, and soon she would be close enough to him to feel the heat from her body.

He settled his hand at her slender waist. He couldn't read the expression in her eyes, but her cheeks were already rosier.

Her hand came up to light on his shoulder, as delicate as a songbird.

"Shall we?"

She simply nodded.

And he eased them into a waltz.

"*One*, two, three, *one*, two, three, *one*, two, three, *one*, two, three, one . . ."

"Two . . ." was a murmur.

And then he forgot to count.

Because the silence itself sang. The soft, soft sound of their breathing, the rhythm of her breath as it lifted her rib cage beneath his hand, their feet sinking into the (freshly beaten) carpet were enough music. The flush in her cheeks. The heat in his own. She was so light that he felt as though he'd grown wings during his convalescence, rather than scars. He certainly couldn't recall ever feeling so weightless.

You've gone mad you've gone mad you've gone mad you've gone mad was the refrain in Elise's head, repeated in waltz time signature.

But she hadn't been able to resist touching him any more than she'd been able to resist drawing her next breath, and a large part of the reason was that she knew he simply wanted to touch her, too. How could she deny him? What harm could there be in just this moment? Those were the words every addict utters when he reaches for the next hookah full of opium, she imagined. His arm beneath the snug fit of his coat was thrillingly hard, the kind of arm that could hold up worlds. She was inches from that pillow of a cravat and that jaw she could draw with her eyes closed if asked, and his eyes were hot—too hot—on her. And his hand was warm and so very, very male, at her waist. She'd never felt more acutely female by contrast. And if she was to choose a glorious way to die—if her heart beat any more swiftly, there was a distinct possibility she would do just that at any minute—this moment could not be any more perfect.

A moment later he disappeared. Which is when she realized she'd closed her eyes. As if this had, indeed, been a dream.

At some point shortly thereafter she distantly became aware that the waltz had slowed, slowed to a lazy rotation, and when she could smell the starch of his shirt, she knew it was because they'd somehow shrunk the distance between them and they were not so much waltzing as perilously close to what amounted to a moving embrace. *This is wrong this is wrong this is wrong.*

"You appear to be waltzing successfully, Lord Lavay." Her voice was lulled.

Another three-quarter-time word occurred to her, and she really ought to remember it. *Housekeeper housekeeper housekeeper.*

No, she shouldn't flirt with him. No, she shouldn't dance with him. No, she should not be herself. She should suffer, just like Tantalus, too.

"But a bit stiffly, *oui*, like an elephant?" His voice was husky, too. And too intimate.

How she wanted to duck her head against his chest. To feel the rumble there when he spoke. To hear his heart beating. More three-quarter time: *This is wrong this is wrong this is wrong.*

"I understand elephants are graceful." Her voice was faint. "I once saw one in Covent Garden. He did tricks."

He laughed at that, soft and low, and the sound rippled through her body deliciously. The sweet tension of desire was rising in her, a pressure, like a river about to flood its banks, almost a fury. *I want you I want you I want you.*

Floods left disasters in their wakes.

No one knew that better than she did.

Every cell in her body cried out in protest when she stopped moving abruptly.

She forced herself to go as stiff as a starched shirt.

He nearly stumbled.

But he was composed quickly enough. His face was still and inscrutable.

"I think you'll comport yourself with dignity, Lord Lavay. Fortunate is the woman who waltzes with you at your party."

There was no reason to continue holding her hand. He relinquished it, like a pickpocket returning a purse to its rightful owner. His hand fell from her waist.

She took a step back, as if he'd been a trap rather than everything in the world she ever wanted. Her skin felt feverish and taut with anger and thwarted desire. She wanted to throw something. A vase. Or her body, right back into his arms.

So unfair so unfair so unfair. Her eyes burned. She was moved, her body aching and furious at the need to deprive herself of him but relieved she'd managed to do it.

He stood watching her.

His mouth tipped at the corner, ruefully. His eyes didn't smile.

"Thank you," he said gently. "It was generous of you. I shall feel more confident now."

She tried to speak. She couldn't just yet.

She just nodded.

And then she managed to clear her throat.

"Will that be all, Lord Lavay?"

"Yes," he said.

She began to move past him.

And Philippe watched as if in a dream as his hand reached out and closed ungently around her arm.

It was a reflex. It just seemed critical to hold

onto her, as if she would fly off, away from him, forever, like an untethered kite.

He turned her toward him.

She stared up at him. Astonished.

And then he saw a ferocity of yearning there, a pain and need bordering on fury.

It precisely mirrored his own.

He did not let her go.

The very silence rang.

And then he heard the sound of their breathing. Swift, astonished, in tandem.

"Philippe . . ."

He didn't know if it was a protest or a plea.

She'd said his name. His name.

And now he knew she thought of him that way, possibly alone in the dark, at the top of the stairs.

He pulled her into his body. And then his hand slid down her arm and glided as naturally as a river glides right to the sea, to the small of her back, where it fit as if she'd been carved by the Creator expressly for him.

And her face was lifting up as his came down.

Had he *ever* kissed anyone before?

He shuddered from the pleasure of it, from the glorious spike of newness that drove right down through his very being. The soft give of her mouth, tentative, at first, but not reluctant; finding the fit with his.

Surrendering.

Melting.

Oh, God.

His desire was serrated. He liked the little bit of fear of not knowing what would happen next, or what she would do or say, or what he even actually wanted. He liked feeling awkward, being utterly at sea. He liked wanting her so much that he trembled from it, and he liked holding himself back.

He kissed her because he wanted to kiss *her*. Not because he knew, or hoped, it would lead to something else.

He coaxed her lips open with his, and oh so gently tasted just slightly the hot, wet, velvet sweetness of her mouth.

Her hands slid up to latch around his neck . . .

. . . and somehow he was falling; no, he was floating. He wasn't memories or demands, he wasn't duty or revenge; he thought he was his purest self, perhaps for the first time ever. And the world was just the heat and forbidden sweet taste of this woman, the tentative curl of her tongue around his, the deepening sensual demand, the stirring of his cock. And she knew, she knew, what she did to him, and what he wanted, because she fit against him, moved purposefully against the bulge in his trousers.

He sucked in a sharp breath as she hit his bloodstream all at once, like a shot of raw liquor.

She wanted this. He could feel her desire humming in the tension of her body, in the jagged tempo of her breathing as his hands moved over her back. Her head dropped back to allow him to take the kiss deeper, and she began to meet his demands with her own.

He slid his hands slowly, slowly down over her buttocks and brought her harder up against him.

Her little gasp of pleasure was the most beautiful, most carnal sound he'd ever heard.

He moved his lips to her throat, and her hammering pulse met them.

Her skin was a wonder of cream satin.

He began to furl up the back of her dress with trembling hands.

She unlatched her hands, rested them on his chest, then slid them up and slowly curled them into his shirt.

And she took her mouth from his and ducked her head.

Stunned and dazed, he protested softly, "Elise . . ."

And then she gently, but quite adamantly, pushed him away.

He staggered a step back.

She took about four steps back, just beyond the reach of his arms.

They stood about four feet apart on the carpet.

He blew out a breath to steady his breathing, to attempt to slow his heart.

His erection would take a little longer to subside.

Stunned silence followed.

He'd lost all sense of time. They might have regarded each other for a minute or an hour across that safe expanse of carpet.

"I can't," she said softly at last.

It sounded like a plea.

He couldn't speak just yet.

"You must understand, Philippe, that I . . . I did not mean to give you the impression that I . . . that I am . . ."

"You didn't," he said, instantly absolving her from whatever her concerns were. "I took liberties. The fault is entirely mine."

He congratulated himself on being able to speak, though his voice was hoarse and his head was still spinning, as surely as if he was still waltzing.

He didn't ask her to explain. "I can't" could mean anything at all. Her son, her station, a man. Anything.

She gave a short nod.

She was still breathing swiftly, and this he at least found gratifying.

"Should I apologize?" he asked softly.

She shook her head abruptly, vigorously.

He knew a rush of gratification.

"But I shall anyhow. I apologize for any distress you are feeling now, Elise. Perhaps it's just . . . the waltz is considered very erotic."

She gave a short laugh. "It is, the way you do it."

He was so relieved to hear her laugh.

"Perhaps we were overcome. That is all."

"Yes. And perhaps you were being French again."

"Yes. This is the French version of the waltz, and I was being French."

"You are going to be the talk of the ball on Saturday, then. And exhausted on Sunday."

He laughed.

She laughed.

It was so painful to laugh, because this was perhaps the first time in his life he was laughing with a woman with whom he was in perfect sympathy and whom he would like to take to bed and thoroughly exhaust with every imaginable kind of lovemaking.

And see the next morning.

And see the morning after.

It seemed they'd exhausted all there was to say.

"Are you angry?" she ventured.

He was astonished.

"Am I *ang* . . . no. No. I'm not a beast, or a feudal lord who demands things of his servants, Mrs. Fountain. I am not angry. I will not make demands again."

Although the question *did* make him a little angry.

He'd said all those words that erected the wall again. "Lord" and "servants" and "demands." Partially in jest. Partially because the very fact that those walls existed did anger him, because this was a woman he wanted in a way he could not recall wanting any other.

Her hand rose, as if she meant to touch him, to placate him.

Then she dropped it.

Right back into its place.

Because everything had a place, of course.

"It will be better after the ball," she said gently.

She was likely right.

This intensity of passion needed diluting. Surely it had banked to such a pitch due to proximity. And once he was surrounded again by his kind—the wealthy and well-bred, the effervescent sophisticated chatter, the skilled flirtation, the beautiful gowns, the bright eyes and kid gloves of the girls he ought to dance with and ought to kiss—perhaps he would be embarrassed by his yearning for a housekeeper.

But now she was so lovely that it was an ache in him. It felt so wrong to simply stand apart. When in two steps he could seize her in his arms again.

He knew he could persuade her. The skills in his romantic quiver could conquer any woman.

But he would never do that to her.

He straightened. "Of course," he said.

He thought her face darkened then, but perhaps it was just a reflection of the day's shifting shadows.

"Will that be all?" she asked.

"Yes, Mrs. Fountain. That will be all."

Chapter 17

Since longing and innuendo and thwarted desire had moved into the house and seemed to occupy every corner, it suddenly felt much too small, so Philippe decided to escape the bustle of assembly preparations and walk all the way to Postlethwaite's Emporium to see if any correspondence had arrived.

He'd hoped time would blur the memory of that kiss. Instead, from the moment she'd said "I can't" until now, it had grown more mythical.

"I can't" didn't necessarily mean she never would.

And he was so consumed with imagining this possibility that he was surprised to find himself at Postlethwaite's; he scarcely remembered the walk over. He paused, testing, listening to his body. He was winded, but only slightly. He was aching, but not intolerably. And yet he was both winded and aching as a result of a simple walk across the downs. If six cutthroats leaped out at him now, they'd leave behind a dead man. The realization tightened his every muscle again in a surge of impatience, and he gave the door a more aggressive push than he might have otherwise.

The bells affixed to it leaped and jangled frantically.

Inside he nearly needed to shield his eyes from the dazzling array of shawls and bonnets, gloves of every hue, ribbons and bows and trims, glittering combs and pins and fans and reticules, things that glittered and glowed and gleamed, all the kinds of things that made a feminine heart yearn. He smiled, somewhat grimly, thinking of Marie-Helene, and how she would exclaim over all of it. They were things she ought to have. The kinds of things he ought to be able to give her.

He turned his back on them abruptly, only to confront a spool of gleaming, claret red satin ribbon. His breath caught. He drifted toward it and caught the loose end, drew it slowly, languorously through his fingers, as if it were a strand of Elise's hair finally unleashed. It would glow in her hair. It was merely a shade darker than her soft, soft mouth.

He dropped it abruptly.

Where on earth was Mr. Postlethwaite? Perhaps he was upstairs, availing himself of the chamber pot.

Opposite all the delightful female ephemera were a few things for gentlemen: cravats, stockings, gloves, and the like. He had no need for any of those at the moment.

Another shelf contained a very small selection of toys.

He paused and smiled and reached out to pluck up a wooden lion. Its whimsical little face was encircled with a mane fashioned of dyed wool, a stiff little tail protruded from its behind, and its legs were jointed.

He played with it for a moment, arranging it on the shelf in a pouncing position. "*Rawwr*," he said very softly.

He pivoted when he heard a throat clear.

Postlethwaite was small, bespectacled, and, after he got one long, clearly educated look at Philippe, very nearly obsequious. The merchant could size up his customers in an instant, and he knew a lord when he saw one.

He bowed very low. "I am Mr. Postlethwaite, sir, at your service."

"Lord Lavay, Mr. Postlethwaite. Will you kindly see if any correspondence has arrived for Alder House?"

"Of course, my lord. Straightaway, my lord."

While Mr. Postlethwaite ducked into the back of his shop again, Philippe circulated idly again among the furbelows.

He paused in front of a case of combs and brushes. He knew so little about Elise. One of them was that she'd left home, a home she said she could not return to, with only a hairbrush.

One brush was tipped on its side, and he could read the initials on the back of it: ELF.

He frowned faintly.

A suspicion dawned.

Postlethwaite emerged with a few letters in his hand, and Philippe absently, wordlessly, reached out for them.

"Cunning little lion, isn't it, Lord Lavay? And are you by any chance looking for a gift for a young lady?"

Philippe only half heard him. One of the letters was addressed in a hand he vaguely recognized.

He absently slit it open:

Dearest Philippe,

What a comfort and delight it is to hear your voice, if only by letter, though your handwriting has become prettier than mine! I will be in Sussex again before your assembly to see to my sister and visit with my cousins Lord and Lady Archembault, who are visiting with Lord Willam and his family. My hand will dream of its kiss, and I can think of no finer thing than to waltz with you.

Warmest regards,
Alexandra

Guilt pricked at him. The woman might very well be his future, but at the moment the idea of kissing Alexandra's hand was jarring and farcical, and the very notion of it embarrassed him slightly, as if he were remembering something callow he'd done years ago, instead of just a short time ago. He half suspected that kissing Elise was the most genuine thing he'd ever done, and that everything in contrast seemed artifice.

Perhaps all he needed was to see Alexandra again.

He folded the letter and stuffed it into his coat pocket, all too aware that when he did, the muscles of his hand went taut.

"Yes, Mr. Postlethwaite. I believe I *am* looking for a gift. May I see the hairbrush, please?"

"Of course, my lord." Postlethwaite unlocked the case and reached in, handing it to Philippe as if it had been a rare antique. Lavay took it gently, as gently as Elise had handed him that blue Sevres sauceboat, and drew his thumb over the initials tenderly. "Interesting story about this one," Postlethwaite said. "A young lady traded it for two pairs of gentleman's silk stockings, of all things."

ELISE DROVE HER staff with relentless cheer. Enlisting the additional help of Henny, Evie's maid (and promising her a healthy portion of Dolly Farmer's salary), they set to work making Alder House ready for the festivities. The ballroom—really more of a large hall—was scrubbed and polished and cleaned to glittering opulence, the floors spotless and smooth and golden and nearly as bright as mirrors, the chandelier crystals buffed to icicle brilliance. A few potted plants had been obtained—she'd stretched the flower budget to get them; flowers had been acquired from local hothouses; and Seamus and a group of fellow musicians had been engaged to play in return for drinks and food and flirtation with the guests.

And she and Lord Lavay skirted each other, less in abashment, like the first time, than in the way one might be careful about getting too close to an open flame. It was a mercy. She herself felt as though the kiss had set her softly, permanently alight, and she was concerned it was obvious to everyone. She longed for a new word to describe the mixture of terror and elation she felt. *Terration*?

Elise reflected on the fact that up until she'd done the unthinkable and become, as Miss Marietta Endicott had said with some wry delicacy, *with child*, everyone would have thought her ordinary, if a little prone to speaking out of turn. But no: apparently she was destined to be tossed like flotsam and jetsam on a great stormy sea of *romance*, buffeted by feelings no mother of a six-year-old boy conceived out of wedlock ought to have, like joy and terror and lie-awake-in-the-dark-all-night lust. And then, awakening, wound in her sheets like some creature preparing to turn into a butterfly, sweaty from tossing and turning.

Because that kiss had not been a whim, or the frivolous impulse of the moment, or the stratagem of a practiced flirt, or simply because he was French. It had been a release of dammed longing and emotion, torturously sweet, erotic and terrifying all at once.

What she felt about Philippe bore as much resemblance to whatever she'd felt for Edward as an echo did to an actual voice. The anguish of that abandonment resounded still. What kind of woman would she be if she subjected her heart to that kind of risk again?

He of course didn't want her at the expense of everything else he wanted.

Nor would she be the mistress. *Ever.* Not for her sake, and not for Jack's.

She'd been provided with a list of guests to invite to the assembly—the Countess of Ardmay had advised Lord Lavay, naturally. Interestingly, it included all of the Everseas and all of the Redmonds currently present in Sussex—among other local personages who could be counted upon to enjoy themselves thoroughly and dance every dance and drink entertainingly to excess. She recognized most of the names. It was the sort of party she would never, in her current or former lives, be invited to attend. But she would see the glowing faces of women as they passed through the room they'd set aside for cloaks and for fixing trodden hems and coiffures. All women who would be free to dance with Lord Lavay.

And of course, the beautiful Lady Prideux was on the list.

Elise held that particular invitation in her hand as she would hold a snake.

And then she laughed, softly, in a sort of despair. Ironies abounded in her life, and Lady Prideux's role in Elise's seemed to have a second act.

And she thought of the expression on Philippe's face when he said "home."

She would do nearly anything, she thought, to make sure he had what he wanted.

It just couldn't be her.

And so she took a deep breath, and into the stack of other invitations it went for the footmen to deliver by hand.

"YOU LOOK *MANYAFEEK*, sir."

"If I look *magnifique*, my thanks to you, James. Congratulations again on winning the coin toss."

Philippe's mirror told him that he did, indeed, look *magnifique*, in a crisp, stark black coat and trousers, and a conservatively tied, spotless cravat billowing up out of a pewter-colored waistcoat. His face was ruthlessly shaved to a polish.

And thusly his footman-valet launched him back into his real habitat.

Philippe took the stairs slowly. The orchestra Mrs. Fountain had secured was playing a jaunty reel of sorts that gradually grew in volume, and the low hum of the mingled voices of his guests became more distinct, and as he reached the landing he took a long, deep breath. In came perfume and liquor, starch and bay rum, sweat, scandal. It was like that first hint of salt tang in the air before you actually see the ocean.

The scent of wealth.

The scent of his old life.

It was as second nature to him as the scent of the sea, and as peculiarly soothing. He knew precisely how to navigate it, and it had been too long since he'd done it.

He paused at the foot of the stairs, like a diver preparing to surface.

As a test, he tried to picture Alexandra, Lady Prideux, as he'd last seen her. He waited for . . . something. Something to lighten or stir in him. And his heart did seem at least a little gladdened by the idea of her, though it might simply be her association with happy memories. But he seized upon this with hope, because he had begun to fear that it would never stir for anyone or anything else but Elise Fountain.

HE WAS QUITE humbly surprised to feel proud of how splendid the house looked. The hall was awash with color and soft, dreamlike light, and everything and everyone seemed to glow. Smiles flashed brightly, silk and taffeta and the toes of boots gleamed, heels came down on the polished wood in the pleasing rhythm of a reel. He paused to savor it for a moment.

Alexandra was easy to see in the crowd.

She was impossible to miss; she'd always known how to dazzle. She had presence, but then, her very character was shaped by expectations she'd had since birth: that she would be lavished with attention. That people would court and enjoy and always welcome her.

And yet, if he recalled correctly, she wasn't entirely insufferable.

He wove through his guests toward her, casually, leisurely. Pausing to greet everyone, introduce himself, exchange a few words, to thank them for coming, to entreat them to have a wonderful time. Charming as effortlessly as he always had.

Alexandra watched his progress.

When he arrived, her smile was brilliant and genuine.

"You always surprise, Alexa. Just when I think I've grown accustomed to your beauty . . ." He mimed an arrow to the heart.

She laughed and tapped him lightly with her fan, letting it linger—an action very much equivalent to a child seizing a toy and declaring, "Mine!" And she hoped every woman there saw it.

She wore ice blue silk, nearly the identical shade of her eyes. She hadn't acquired the dress through ingenuity or barter. She'd acquired it through money, and she had a staggering amount of it. Her honey-colored hair was bound in an intricate network of narrow little braids that latticed across the back of her head, and were pinned with what appeared to be diamonds. The net effect was exquisite and had likely required the cooperation of four maids working in skilled tandem. He wondered if there was a sort of secret Tattersalls for such maids that only women were allowed to attend.

Two very deliberate, very fetching curls flanked her cheekbones.

There would never be any accidental curls for Lady Prideux.

Very little of what she did was accidental.

He pictured a spiral of escaped black hair against a pale cheek and felt instantly restless.

He cast a glance up the stairs, though in all likelihood Elise was in the kitchen, or perhaps in the withdrawing room, assisting women with torn hems and collapsing coiffures.

"You're looking very dashing, Philippe. You do only seem to improve with age. My father is saving a brandy for that very reason. I suspect he'll taste it on his deathbed and will die very happy indeed."

Philippe laughed. "I hope you don't intend to save me for your deathbed, Alexandra."

"I prefer not to delay gratification, when at all possible."

He recalled now how Alexandra had always possessed a preternatural confidence and liked to consider herself outrageous and modern. He'd once found it amusing; he'd indulged her, the way he'd indulge a kitten for climbing his pant leg. For some reason it now felt a bit like . . . being at a picnic during which the sun blazed relentlessly down. Wearing.

And if ever there was a virgin, it was Alexandra.

But Philippe knew he remained a prize. He was still a Bourbon, if a Bourbon more distant from the French court. And it was something Alexandra had always aspired to be.

"Such a splendid touch, your footmen wearing livery so similar to that of Les Pierres d'Argent, Philippe."

"Yes, it does make it feel more like . . . home."

He was surprised to realize that this was exactly true.

"Nothing is as magnificent as Les Pierres d'Argent, Philippe. I always imagined myself living there."

It was certainly an opportunity to say, *And one day soon perhaps you will.*

A few months ago, during this same conversation, he might have said it.

He couldn't quite force the necessary words, and so a funny little silence ticked by.

Her smile grew slightly strained.

"I did hope you'd share a waltz with me," he said instead.

"Surely there will be more than one waltz to share." She sounded a trifle uncertain now.

"Ah, but you must not be greedy, my dear Alexandra. I am the host and I am in demand, and surely you of all people know how delightful I can be. And surely one or two of the gentlemen here would cherish for a lifetime the memory of dancing with you?"

It returned to him so naturally, the flattery, the charm. He found himself hoping he couldn't manipulate her so easily with it.

She pouted a little, charmingly and entirely unconvincingly. "Very well."

"I shall, however, save the best for last, Alexandra."

Best not to let Alexandra become *too* sure of herself.

He bowed over her hand and went off in search of the Earl of Ardmay, because they needed to bring to a close a certain matter. And what the earl had to say would come to bear on whatever happened with Alexandra.

And even though he was a brilliant navigator, somehow his search for the earl led him to the lady's withdrawing room.

ELISE AND HER staff had transformed a small room near the ballroom into a cloak and lady's withdrawing room by hanging a large horizontal mirror and arraying chairs before it, then fashioning a closet of sorts by cleverly partitioning the corner near the door with a curtain. Elise began her evening here, greeting ladies who streamed in in their finery, accepting cloaks and shawls and pelisses to hang, while Kitty and Mary put finishing artistic touches on the sandwiches and tarts heaped on tables in the ballroom.

"Good evening, Mrs. Fountain," came a low voice from behind the curtain.

Her heart leaped and Elise whirled toward Philippe just as a guest was thrusting a shawl at her. The woman toppled forward, her destination the floor, arms flailing. Philippe lunged out and caught her before she landed on all fours.

He set her upright, and Elise gave her a warm smile.

"You won't want to miss the waltz," he confided to the woman. "They'll play it soon. Best run!"

The woman was so startled that she obeyed him and took off at a dash.

Elise was struggling not to laugh.

"You see, the women are already falling all over me."

She ignored this. "Good evening, Lord Lavay. You slipped in quite stealthily. You look very dashing."

He in fact looked heart-stoppingly, breath-stoppingly handsome.

"Don't I?" He smiled. "I believe I smell wonderful, too."

If he was going to smile at her like that, and say things like that, they would be off again, enjoying each other as if no one else in the world existed, and that would simply never do. She took an unconscious step back as if to make room for all the *feelings* he brought into the room with him. She reflexively thrust out an arm to accept another cloak handed over to her.

She strived for dispassionate distance. "Do you have a cloak for me to collect, Lord Lavay? Have you questions, or do you need assistance?"

"The hall looks beautiful. Thank you for your hard work."

"You are welcome."

"And I want to thank you again for your assistance with the waltz, as I shall embark upon it any number of times this evening with confidence. But I believe that you and I, Mrs. Fountain, are now engaged in something like a reel."

She sucked in a surprised breath.

Because she understood.

Meeting and parting. Meeting and parting. Meeting and parting.

Their eyes met.

And just like that, all at once they might as well have been the last two people in the world, even as cheerful assembly-goers milled around her.

Another cloak was extended to her.

She didn't see it.

The woman gave it a shake in an attempt to get her attention.

Elise snatched it from her. Then turned a warm smile on the startled woman.

"Do you intend to be French tonight?" she murmured to Lavay.

It was a parry of sorts.

"Isn't that what you wished for me, Mrs. Fountain?" he countered softly.

Something complex sizzled instantly between them.

Every reel eventually ended.

The notion of an ending jarred Elise back into awareness. She turned to find a veritable bouquet of arms holding shawls out to her. The owners of those arms might even have spoken to her. If they had, neither she nor Philippe had heard it.

She retrieved all of them. "Thank you, thank you, thank you," she said to the ladies. "You all look so very beautiful. Thank you."

The ladies then clustered about the mirror

to pat coiffures and shake out dresses crushed in carriages. Then they sailed out, wreathed in smiles and radiating anticipation.

Elise squared her shoulders. "Lord Lavay, your guests will find ratafia and fruit punch in the ballroom, sandwiches enough to feed an army, jam tarts that would impress any palate, I believe, and a fair enough orchestra that might play a little quickly unless you give the violinist enough to drink, but if you give him too much to drink, he might become maudlin and then fight. Ramsey and James will patrol the ballroom and help eject anyone who becomes too obnoxious, as well as monitor the state of the food and drink. You best hurry, or you will miss the first waltz."

"Thank you, Mrs. Fountain. Whatever would I do without you?"

"I assume the question is rhetorical."

He smiled at her, and her heart turned slowly over in supplication.

He made no move to go.

So she did what she knew she had to do: she turned her back on him and walked away, toward the mirror, in a great pretense of fussing with her hair.

As if she was releasing him back into his habitat.

PHILIPPE AT LAST restlessly made his way back to the ballroom, which now seemed duller and dimmer by contrast to the small cloakroom—or any room, really—that contained Elise Fountain.

He fortuitously found the Earl of Ardmay helping himself to ratafia with something less than
enthusiasm.

"Do you remember a ball nearly two years ago,
Flint, where I overheard a group of young women
speculating about the size of your . . . what was
it . . . 'masculine blessing'?"

Flint nearly spit out his ratafia.

"It's *best* spit out," Lavay sympathized. "I will
not object."

"Where I first danced with my wife. Of course."

"More accurately, *I* first danced with her. And
then you danced with her."

"Perverse creature that she is, Violet preferred me."

"Proof that destiny is on your side, my friend,
as no one else would have either of you."

"If destiny is a wheel, it was bound to turn in
my direction eventually. *And* yours. And speaking of destiny, Lavay . . ."

The pause, with its hint of reluctance and apology, was all that was necessary for Philippe to
know the truth.

"You don't have to say it, Flint. I know."

Philippe had been prepared for the answer, yet
it was no less unwelcome:

The earl didn't want to participate in the latest
assignment from the king.

"I'm sorry, old man. Truly." Flint knew exactly
what that money, and the assignment, meant to
Lavay. "A large part of me wants to do it, and not
just because of the money. The rest of me, the part

that never had a family, never wants to leave their side again."

"You don't have to explain." But Philippe said it abstractedly. He was still absorbing the impact of the decision.

"And I know how to keep us from starving, Lavay. Even prospering, eventually. We can join Jonathan Redmond's new investment group. Right now they're looking at cargos of Indian spices, teas and silks, and we can use the *Fortuna* for transport. We wouldn't have to crew the ship, but we can hire our own captain and crew. But potential profits are months away. I do know you need them sooner."

An understatement, to be sure. Monsieur Le-Grande would sell Les Pierres d'Argent if Philippe didn't have the funds inside a month.

Lavay almost unconsciously turned toward Alexandra. Who was occupied in enchanting some young man whose name Philippe had already forgotten.

Odd, but he didn't feel a twinge of jealousy.

"Will you do the assignment now? Search out a substitute for my role in it? As if any could be found." Flint tried for a jest.

"I don't know," Philippe said absently. He truly didn't.

"You should marry, Philippe," the earl said, following the direction of his gaze. "You're lonely."

As a matter of formality, Philippe snorted at such an unmanly assertion. They both knew the earl was right, however.

They said nothing for a moment.

"Do you think," Philippe said slowly, "that marrying the wrong person can make you feel lonelier?"

This made the earl turn his head slowly to study Philippe.

Philippe carefully did not meet his eyes.

"All I can tell you is this. I was an orphan. And remember, I married the only person who would have me. But I can tell you that it's infinitely better to feel as though you belong to something. Or someone. And I think you know that all too well, too."

Philippe said nothing. His eyes flicked toward the withdrawing room, and just the thought of Elise was like a taste of something sweet and narcotic. It made him feel better, freer, more peaceful, for just that moment.

"You're smiling now at something. What is it? Who is she?" the earl demanded.

Philippe turned to him, resignation and surrender on his face. Confirmation.

But he wasn't about to give up her name.

The earl gave a soft snort.

"This is another thing I know, Lavay. There was a time when I thought I would need to live without Violet, and you know this, too. She was worth the sacrifice."

"Every man has a different definition of sacrifice, I believe."

"Agreed," Ardmay said easily enough.

"Do you think Lyon Redmond still loves Olivia Eversea, Flint?"

"Did we always have these kinds of talks before we became old men?"

"We're not old. Just a bit worn."

Flint laughed. "I think loving Olivia Eversea has been a part of who Lyon Redmond is for so long that even he likely doesn't know. Why?"

Lavay gave a short nod. "Since we're talking of love and sacrifice, I simply wondered."

They fell silent again.

"Limbo is a horrible place to be," Flint said. It sounded like commiseration.

Lavay wondered if Olivia Eversea was in limbo.

"Agreed," Lavay said. "Go dance with your wife, Ardmay. I'm going to dance with Olivia Eversea."

Chapter 18

H<small>E FOUND HER BY</small> a process of deduction: she was surrounded by Everseas he recognized—Colin, Marcus, Chase, and their wives.

From a distance, the storied Olivia was petite and porcelain-skinned, fragile yet somehow regal, like a fairy queen, in deep blue. Closer he could see that she was a bit too thin, which made her eyes large and bright in her face. She was like a jewel, faceted, sparkling, hard, remote.

"Lavay!" Lord Landsdowne, her fiancé, greeted him. "Thank you. Such a pleasure to see you looking well."

Philippe exchanged bows with all of them.

"Thank you, Landsdowne. And thank you, Miss Eversea, for coming this evening. I wondered if you would be so kind as to give me this dance?"

"To reward you for interrupting the winter doldrums with an assembly, there's little I wouldn't do. I would be delighted. You won't mind?" she said to Landsdowne.

"Of course not."

He probably did, but the woman was going to be his for the rest of his life, and Philippe wanted to know why Olivia had said yes to that proposition.

Because this was the woman for whom Lyon Redmond was engaged in staggeringly dangerous heroics. The woman who had allegedly broken his heart and caused him to disappear, stirring the centuries-old enmity between the Redmonds and Everseas, and making her the subject of the alleged curse: that an Eversea and a Redmond were destined to fall in love once per generation, with disastrous results. Lyon Redmond had abandoned his family and birthright to prove himself worthy of this woman.

And Lyon Redmond, as of two months ago, had been in London.

"May I congratulate you again on your engagement, Miss Eversea?"

"Thank you, Lord Lavay. And are congratulations for your own in order?"

He'd heard that she was disconcertingly direct, Miss Eversea, which, combined with her alarming good looks and her penchant for passionately taking up causes, particularly antislavery causes, frightened off all but the most stalwart of men. A tactic she'd employed in part as a defense, Lavay suspected, as Lyon Redmond had taken her heart when he'd left and she wished to be left alone so that no one would notice her heart was gone.

The little orchestra was surprisingly competent,

and a man with dramatic dark curls was teasing pathos from the "Sussex Waltz" with a violin. Philippe and Olivia had circled the ballroom twice now. In his peripheral vision, other couples spiraled around them. Like clockwork gears.

She hadn't once looked at Landsdowne.

Not a single glance toward him.

Landsdowne had never truly taken his eyes off her, even as he exchanged pleasantries with other guests. As if she was true north.

"Have you chosen a date for the wedding yet, Miss Eversea?"

"Spring, which will allow for all of our guests to travel comfortably. The second Saturday in May."

"Will you be married here in Pennyroyal Green?"

"So many questions about my nuptials for a man who claims his aren't imminent. Yes."

"One must prepare for the inevitable by doing the proper research."

She laughed.

It was easy to see how Olivia captivated. A sort of effortless intelligence, and charm, a hint of impatience that suggested she would never gladly suffer fools, that suggested she knew so few men who were anything other than that.

He wondered what Olivia Eversea would do if he told her that no less than two months ago, by the dark of the moon, Lavay had looked up into the blue eyes of Lyon Redmond from the ground where he lay bleeding. "You won't die." Redmond had issued the words with steely calm. He was a man accustomed to commanding all manner of things, even death. A man much like Philippe. A man to whom Lavay owed his life.

And he would never truly know peace until he'd discharged that debt.

He wondered if Olivia Eversea, who had remained in Sussex while Redmond had taken to the seas, would recognize the man Lyon had become.

Was love something you helplessly fell into, like quicksand? Was love for another person something you could learn, like Latin? Or was love for one particular person something you were born with, or, like a fever, lay dormant, until that one person for you happened along and released it?

He didn't know, and he suspected Olivia didn't, either. Not knowing absolved neither of them of making the choices life forced them into making, so that life could move, as was its nature, ever forward.

"IF YOU WOULD hold this please while I see to my hair." Lady Prideux thrust a shawl at Elise without looking at her or waiting for a response. It was not a question.

This made it easier to study Lady Prideux up close. Her nose was a perfect incline ending in an insouciant tilt above a pale blossom of a mouth. She had a slight and quite fetching overbite. Her skin was Sevres fine.

She was absolutely stunning.

For an evil person.

And then Alexandra looked up sharply, as if she'd felt the heat of Elise's gaze.

She froze.

Ah, so she recognizes me, after all.

To the credit of her conscience at least, Lady Prideux went a little pink.

"Oh, it's you, Mrs. . . . . Fountain."

"Yes. We meet again, Lady Prideux." Elise curtsied.

"My apologies. I didn't recognize you out of context. This is quite a different position for you, isn't it?"

There was a hint of cold glee in her tone.

"I suppose it is."

"I didn't know you were working for Phil—that is, Lord Lavay. I call him Philippe, of course."

"Of course," Elise said smoothly. Her back teeth clamped down. The word felt wrong, wrong, wrong when Lady Prideux said it. The word belonged to *Elise.*

"I'm so glad to see you landed on your feet," Alexandra enthused insincerely. Confident, apparently, that Elise was now invisible because she was a servant.

Lady Prideux settled in at the vanity and turned her head this way and that, either admiring herself for the five hundred thousandth time, or seeking any imperfections that might have sprung up between her trip from her home to Alder House.

Elise studied her, too, imagining with relish where she would first jab Lady Prideux with a pin, if she was so inclined.

Lady Prideux whirled, and Elise schooled her face to stillness.

"I trust there are no hard feelings over what transpired about my sister," Lady Prideux said with a gushing and wholly manufactured warmth. "It is just that our family is so very particular about the moral education of our girls, and Colette is so very, very sensitive. I'm sure you understand why I did what I did. Given that you're a . . . mother." She purred all of this.

Colette was in fact a beautiful, stupid, and mean little girl, and Elise normally gave the benefit of the doubt to her students at least a dozen times before drawing any such conclusion about any of them. There *might* be hope for her. She refused to believe there wasn't, but with a sister like this one, Elise despaired of this.

But this wasn't why Lady Prideux had gone to such cold and calculated lengths to ensure that Elise was removed from her position. As she had told Lavay when he'd probed, Elise had indeed spoken out of turn, in the heat of caring about a student, and had apparently gravely insulted Lady Prideux. Who, not content with being merely beautiful, wanted also to be thought intelligent.

"Let us put it all behind us, shall we?" Lady Prideux didn't wait for Elise to agree to that. "I expect to become engaged very soon," she confided on a girlish whisper. "Perhaps even tonight. I should like to look my best." She gave a self-conscious little laugh. "What do you think?"

"Your coiffure is *beautiful*, Lady Prideux."

"It took four maids and half an evening to achieve it," Alexandra said with some satisfaction. "And still it seems to be coming loose." She fussed with one of the diamond-tipped pins. "If you would assist?"

She said this imperiously. And likely just for the pleasure of giving Elise an order.

With shaking hands, Elise took the proffered pin and slid it back where it belonged, though she sincerely thought it belonged jabbed somewhere into Lady Prideux's soft skin. Her stomach turned, imaging Philippe touching this woman's hair, which presumably he would do if he married her.

"Well, I'm off to dance with Philippe," Alexandra said. She studied Elise, as if to make certain she was still more beautiful. Elise had noticed that women like Lady Prideux often did this, assessing where their beauty fell in comparison to other women's beauty.

Apparently satisfied, Alexandra turned to leave.

Elise stopped her. "Oh, Lady Prideux—I fear your hair is still sliding a bit in the back."

Alexandra halted.

"Oh, dear. Would you please, Mrs. Fountain?" She presented her slender back to Elise.

Elise slid a pin from its place, carefully detached one of the fine braids from its latticed position, pulled it gently, surreptitiously upward, and pinned it very, very carefully so that it thrust vertically up from the center of Alexandra's head.

"There. Now you look *perfect*," Elise said warmly.

Perfectly like a unicorn.

"Thank you, Mrs. Fountain," Lady Prideux said, as if there had never been any doubt. Then she sailed back into the ballroom.

"I FIND I should like a breath of fresh air. I don't suppose you can call your gathering a crush, Philippe, but I find I am breathless anyway. Perhaps you can escort me to an open window, or . . . the garden?"

Philippe gave a start when he saw her.

A narrow braid rose up from the middle of her head, not unlike a cobra preparing to strike. Then again, the caprices of fashion often eluded him, and she was, after all, fresh from Paris.

"*Certainement*," he agreed warmly. His eyes warily on the rearing cobra braid, he extended his arm.

He led her toward the crowd to the French doors that opened out on the garden.

"*Aarrgh!* It's looking at me!" a young man said, pointing at Alexandra's vertical braid. "It has an antenna and it's looking at me!"

"Don't mind him—he's drunk," his friend said. But he eyed Alexandra uneasily.

"Splendid," Philippe said smoothly. "I'm glad you're enjoying the evening."

"What was he talking about, Philippe?"

"Probably an hallucination of some sort."

Heads turned and eyes widened as they proceeded through the room, but Alexandra took all of it as flattery.

AFTER LADY PRIDEUX departed, Elise fled the cloakroom—leaving an excited Mary and Kitty in charge of it—and scrambled up the stairs to peer in at Jack.

She exhaled a breath she hadn't realized she was holding and paused to watch him. Jack's even breathing was the best song in the world. She lingered for a stolen moment, basking in the perfection of him and in a pure cleansing blast of love.

She moved to her own chamber, dragging her hand across the back of her friend and beautiful gift, the brown chair, then paused to look out the window.

A pair of shadows was strolling in the garden below.

Carefully, slowly, she raised her window a few inches.

The voices became audible. Not the actual words; just the low rumble and lilt of conversation.

She heard laughter.

A woman's laughter.

She saw the tip of a lit cheroot move in the dark, like a firefly. A man was gesturing broadly about something.

Being French.

The night was cool and clear and stars hung like tiny icicles, an echo of the chandeliers inside.

She felt as isolated from those aristocrats in the garden as one of those stars, suspended millions of miles away from them, up in the quarters of a housekeeper. Powerless to do anything but watch.

So she watched them, almost as a form of penance.

She had no doubt that was Lady Prideux. Elise wondered if the moonlight made her vertical braid cast a shadow at her feet as they walked.

How many times had Philippe done this throughout his life—how many parties and balls had he attended, how many women had he held in his arms, taken into his bed, walked with in gardens?

He might find happiness with the awful Lady Prideux, who was, after all, a member of his species. But Elise didn't want to witness it. The very thought made it feel like the ground was opening up beneath her feet like a trapdoor into oblivion.

"Fallen woman." The term made a sort of poetic sense. Once the fall started, it seemed it never stopped.

She closed her eyes and remembered the kiss, and how his eyes had been hot and bewitched and uncertain, and how he had tasted, and how he had trembled when he'd touched her, and how hurt and closed his face had gone when she'd pushed him away.

And as the sensations surged through her, hot and bright and as dangerous as the edge of a blade, she brought her fingers to her mouth, pressed her lips against them, and closed her eyes.

As if kissing him good-bye.

PHILIPPE AND ALEXANDRA trod along the moonlit path toward a bench between a pair of tired shrubbery.

A distant giggle told Philippe they weren't the first couple to have this idea.

"Philippe, I haven't yet asked—how are you enjoying Pennyroyal Green?"

"How do I like Pennyroyal Green . . . let us say it's no wonder the Eversea family is known to be so wild. They've gone wild out of necessity, due to boredom."

She laughed softly.

"Surely it's not as awful as all of that. The pretty hills, the view of the sea, the picturesque buildings, the picturesque villagers . . . the picturesque housekeepers."

He shot her a sharp sidelong look.

"*Certainement*, the Redmonds and Everseas are easy to look at," he said evenly.

"And cannot you go out and do manly things? Shoot creatures, and the like?"

"The weather hasn't cooperated with those kinds of activities, unfortunately. Perhaps I am restless, now that I am feeling more myself. It will be a pleasure to be in my own home again, or to be on my own ship. I have never been comfortable in limbo."

"I understand," she soothed. "One does like to have one's own things about, and men do not abide well when trapped in little country houses, like pets. And you've grown so accustomed to having dangerous men leap out at you."

"The squirrels do a fair amount of leaping. Other than that, my reflexes remain unchallenged."

"And the options for servants are so limited here in the country that service is wanting, and how do you say, *avoir le mal du pays*. One feels more at home in the hands of servants who were trained, who come from a lineage of servants, like my dear butler Francois. I do think a talent for serving your betters is inbred, don't you? Instead, you must settle for that common woman running your current household."

He paused then.

"That . . . common woman?" he repeated mildly.

The words echoed with a peculiar dissonance. Never in a million years would he ascribe "common" to Elise.

The back of his neck prickled a warning.

"Yes. Though she seems competent enough in her present role." Alexandra waved a gloved arm about to indicate the general success of the festivities. "You look well fed, and the house hasn't yet burned down. I suppose it is all one can hope for from the staff one can find here in the country."

"Forgive me, but your tone of insinuation puzzles me. Do you have a prior acquaintance with my housekeeper?"

She tilted her head to study him there in the cloud-filtered moonlight, then made a little moue and gave him a sympathetic little tap with her fan.

"Ah, forgive me, Philippe. It hadn't occurred to me that you hadn't heard. I thought perhaps you had simply settled for the lesser of all the evils presented to you when hiring a housekeeper. But then, one wouldn't expect you to indulge in local, provincial gossip. A very few people do know and have been all that is discreet about it, so it should not reflect upon you or *your* character. I assumed when you hired that woman you knew why she was removed from her position at the school and had made your decision accordingly."

"Her name is Mrs. Fountain."

He said it almost silkily.

If Alexandra called her "that woman" again, he was afraid he'd do something rash.

Only the Earl of Ardmay would have been able to tell just how utterly furious Philippe was now.

And Elise, perhaps.

"Of course it is. *Mrs.* . . . Fountain." Alexandra gave an unpleasant little laugh.

Philippe's patience expired. "It is unlike you, Alexa, to be coy. Mrs. Fountain's character was represented to me as unassailable by the Redmond family, which was sufficient for me to hire her, and I have thus far found no fault in her ability to run the house. She has in fact made me quite . . ." There was, in fact, no single word that encompassed just exactly what she'd done to and for him. ". . . comfortable."

What a ridiculously inadequate word. Nearly a lie. He almost laughed. He'd felt a good many things in Elise's presence, but comfortable, lately, wasn't one of them.

"It is clear she cannot be faulted for the way she has managed your establishment," Alexandra al-

lowed magnanimously. "And she's doubtless certainly more than qualified to be a housekeeper, of
all things. She was raised gently enough and was
apparently hired to teach young ladies a number
of subjects at Miss Marietta Endicott's esteemed
academy. It's just that her character doesn't *belong*
in an academy for young ladies. Below stairs is
just the place, among those of like temperaments.
I just don't believe women who possess, shall we
say . . ." She lowered her voice discreetly, though
they were entirely alone. ". . . *low impulses* . . .
ought to be teaching young girls, especially those
troublesome enough to be admitted to the academy. Though I maintain the girls are merely high
spirited, not, as popularly assumed, recalcitrant."

He knew Alexandra's youngest sister had been
admitted to the academy.

"Low impulses?" he repeated, incredulously.

"Yes."

Alexandra was serious.

Suddenly he thought of Elise's laughter, the rise
and fall of it, so like music, so like a reward that
he thought he would do nearly anything to earn
it. The songs that careened off melody but were
impressively well rhymed.

The apple tarts.

The look on her face when she watched her
son—a look that tightened his throat.

The little sound she'd made in her throat when
he'd kissed her.

The soft, God, the soft, generous yield of her lips.

His impulses seemed to originate from a place lower on his body.

Hers seemed to emanate from some inner grace. Some innate warmth.

A variety of emotions, now stretched him on some sort of internal rack, each fighting for supremacy.

The one that prevailed was a very nonspecific, cold fury.

Listening to Alexandra, he suddenly understood the rabble's *low impulse* to divest aristocrats of their heads.

"I'm sure you'll understand when I ask you to expound, given that she is an employee of my home," he said smoothly.

"Oh, I'm certain she's harmless enough, and her ability to perform her current duties seems unquestionable, but her past . . . well, I fear it's rather . . . *unsavory.*"

She whispered that last word.

He was tempted to do something shockingly violent, like reach out with both hands and vigorously muss Alexandra's hair. He could imagine the shrieking.

"Rest assured, my dear Alexandra, that I am impossible to shock. Providing your delicate sensibilities can withstand revisiting the occasion upon which you learned about Mrs. Fountain's . . . low impulses . . . would you be so kind as to elaborate?"

She blinked at his tone, which, granted, was

rather more militant than usual. Then she drew in a long breath, clearly enjoying the notion that her sensibilities were delicate, and lowered her voice and spoke in a rapid hush.

"His name was Mr. Edward Blaylock. He was the son of a solicitor, training to be a solicitor in London, and he came to see his young sister settled in the school. I'm told he was quite handsome—he was the talk of the teachers. But his attention settled upon Mrs. Fountain. They walked out together, he came to call evenings . . . well, let us just say that apparently the courtship wasn't a secret. And then one day he was gone. And nine months later her son was born, though it was somehow kept very sub-rosa, you see, and very few people knew, and she continued on in her position there. And . . . well, as you know, her name isn't Mrs. *Blaylock*. For a reason."

The sensation seemed to leave his limbs. He recognized it as quite similar to that infinitesimal moment between the time the sword goes in and the time the pain starts.

Suddenly the beautiful starry sky seemed terrifyingly infinite and impersonal.

What must it have looked like to Elise when she'd learned she was pregnant?

Jack's father is gone, she'd said.

Jack's "quite handsome" father was gone.

"Philippe?"

Apparently he hadn't said anything for quite some time.

"From whom did you learn this, Alexandra?"

His voice was even and steady, but he heard it as if from a distance. He still felt peculiarly empty, waiting for the right emotion to pour in. He wasn't certain how he felt.

There was an interesting pause.

"One of the servants at the school shared the information."

He remained silent.

Which seemed to puzzle Alexandra, and she expounded in a rush.

"The academy apparently conspired to allow her to keep her job for some time despite her moral transgression, which seems very risky, don't you think, since they depend upon the contributions and tuition fees of wealthy benefactors?"

"I imagine they had an excellent reason to keep her on."

"And an excellent reason to finally remove her," Alexandra said tartly.

It was the strangest sensation, these words strung together to tell a story about a woman who had become more real to him than any other. He wanted to claw at them as if they'd been a net that had dropped down over both him and Elise.

Where had she made love to Edward Blaylock?

His hand slowly curled into a fist.

Where the hell was Edward Blaylock?

"Imagine a woman and a man making love. How very shocking," he said.

Alexandra completely missed the bite in his words.

"I suppose it's what men and women *do*," she said lightly. She laid her fan gently on his arm, as if claiming future rights to doing just that with him. "But it certainly speaks poorly of her judgment. Or at the very least her control. *Poor* thing," she added, with a great and unconvincing show of compassion. "How could a woman be so careless, when in truth it is really all someone like her has to offer a man?"

He turned slowly and stared at Alexandra.

"Someone like her?" he repeated, as if she'd just said something in a confounding language, like Turkish. "I confess I have never known anyone like her."

Tension was coiling ever more tightly in him.

"Good heavens! Nor have I," Alexandra said emphatically, as if reassuring him, with a little shudder. Alexandra, who not only presumably had her beautiful self and her virginity to offer a man but also a vast, life-saving, dynasty-saving fortune. "But at least she has found a place here, for now. I suppose we all find our place, eventually."

" 'We all find our place eventually,' " he quoted on a drawl, with great irony. "What a surprise to discover that you're profound as well as beautiful, Alexandra."

As his tone didn't quite match his compliment, she turned to him, her head tilted quizzically.

She parted her mouth. Then closed it.

"You're too kind," she said, her breeding providing him with the benefit of the doubt. The sort of thing she'd never allow Mrs. Fountain.

He had the grace to feel abashed.

He looked at Alexandra then, her exquisite little face so familiar, her responses and opinions predictable, and all of it was *almost* comforting. There was beauty in tradition and duty, in rhythm and expectation. When one's life had been comprised of cutthroats lurking around corners and pirates creeping onto the decks of ships under cover of morning mist, when relatives lost their heads, when his fortunes these days often depended on the turn of the dice or whether a ship sank before its cargo could be sold . . . he couldn't deny that predictability could be soothing.

Perhaps his emotions weren't meant to be contorted or stretched like the muscles in his injured hand. Perhaps it was better this way. Perhaps it was unnatural for a woman's laugh or kiss to flay him open, revealing raw, new layers to his being he never dreamed existed, each of them exquisitely, painfully sensitive.

As if such feeling could be legislated.

"The night sky is beautiful everywhere, even in dull places like Pennyroyal Green," Alexandra said softly.

He gave a start. He'd been looking up at the stars again. He usually glibly steered a given conversation. He'd been utterly silent.

He did need to leave Pennyroyal Green. This was not his habitat. No wonder he had lost his way. He had no rudder here; it was like a foundering ship.

"And what fitter setting for the Lady Prideux,

jewel of Paris, than a sky full of diamonds," he said reflexively.

This was the Philippe she'd always known. She smiled whimsically, her teeth bright in the dark, and he lifted her white-gloved hand to kiss the air above her knuckles.

It was all a bit like reciting lines from a play.

But if she'd hoped he'd surrender to his low impulses and try to kiss her on those blossomlike lips, she was destined for disappointment this evening.

"I'll return to Paris inside a month, Philippe," she said softly. "And I'm returning with Lord and Lady Archembault to London in a fortnight. I do hope you'll return with—that is, return, too."

It was as much a warning as a hint. It wasn't as though Alexandra would go wanting for suitors if Philippe didn't make a formal offer.

"I shouldn't like you to catch a chill, Alexandra. Shall I escort you to the house again? I haven't had nearly enough to drink yet, and I believe I've more dancing to do."

Chapter 19

THE EVENING HAD SEEMED interminable, but as Elise leaned again out her window, listening to the last of the carriages rolling away amid shouted farewells, she knew a surge of pride—for herself and for Philippe—that it had been a success. She thought she'd heard someone retching somewhere outside in the shrubbery. She saw a cluster of men farther up the road staggering along, singing "The Ballad of Colin Eversea."

Two men behind them were having a fervent exchange.

"Have I told you I love you, Jones? I do, ol' man. You're the *besht* friend. The very besht."

"No, *you're* the besht."

"I swear to God man she was a unicorn. A unicorn! A very pretty unicorn!"

"I saw it, too, old man, don't let anyone tell you otherwise."

Elise laughed softly, then lowered the window all the way, like closing a curtain on a play. And on, perhaps, a chapter of her life.

And then she scrambled downstairs to give final instructions to the staff, who were likely exhausted.

She found them all in the kitchen.

"It can wait for tomorrow. Please do go on up to bed, and thank you for your help. You all did a wonderful job this evening, and I know Lord Lavay appreciated it."

They all beamed at her, weary and pleased, and she beamed back at them, suddenly unutterably touched by their hard work and support and their kindness, all in all, that she'd helped uncover.

"Mrs. Fountain, Lady Merriweather was so pleased with my help with her coiffure she inquired as to whether I'd had training as a lady's maid," Kitty confided on a hush.

"Cor!" Mary exclaimed. "Lady Lumly said the same thing to me!"

They squealed, and Elise gave a delighted clap for them.

Just then Elise's bell jangled, and they all gave a start.

They all eyed it wonderingly. Nobody moved.

"You'd think his lordship would be drunk by now and want to sleep," James yawned.

"He just wants a nice cup of tea, I suspect," Elise said smoothly. Her heart was ahead of her, already flying up the steps to the room. "Off to bed with all of you! Our day starts in but a few hours."

And just in case he did want a cup of tea, she put the water on to boil.

Let him ring twice, if he wanted her that much.

SHE FOUND HIM in his study, lounging on the settee, arms flung over the back of it.

"Good evening, Lord Lavay." She settled the tray down on the little table next to him. "I anticipated you might enjoy a cup of tea."

He didn't even look at it.

"Thank you, my dear Mrs. Fountain. You kept me waiting. That isn't like you."

His voice was odd. A bit ironic. A bit abstracted.

He'd flung off his coat and left it draped across a chair, and his cravat was nowhere to be seen. He was in shirtsleeves, and he'd rolled them up and unbuttoned two buttons.

All of which was quite uncivilized for Lord Lavay.

He'd never looked more thoroughly enticing.

She turned to leave so abruptly that she was nearly fleeing.

"Will you come and sit beside me for a moment, Mrs. Fountain?" He all but drawled it.

She turned back again.

He gave the settee a pat.

He said it so companionably, so softly, and made it sound like such a reasonable request, that saying no seemed churlish.

She settled in and pressed herself against the corner of the settee, as far opposite him as possible, curling her feet up beneath her.

He was silent. Studying her. There was a different quality to his silence, however.

She was concerned it was the silence of a cat about to toy with its prey.

"How did you enjoy the assembly?" she ventured.

"It was a triumph."

His tone was so grim that she laughed softly in surprise. "I thought you enjoyed balls and soirees."

"Oh, I excel at them, this is for certain. I spread my charm about, like so." He made a strewing motion, as if he were feeding chickens in a barnyard. "I am considered delightful, I am told. I danced with countless women. All beautiful. All as delightful as me."

He'd gotten awfully voluble and French, and she was both amused and dangerously enchanted.

And more than a little wary. Because there was an edge to his tone.

His face was flushed. His hair had fallen rakishly over one eye, while the other was peering at her speculatively.

"Are you bragging or complaining, Lord Lavay?"

"Merely reporting," he said. "I did not shame myself with clumsy waltzing, thank you."

Perhaps the memory of one little kiss had dissolved amidst the sea of beautiful women with whom he could make new memories.

She doubted it.

Head thrown back against the chair, he stared across at her and studied her through slitted eyes. She wondered if he was about to doze off.

"I've always wondered what it would be like to attend a grand ball," she said, when it seemed he would never speak.

"I've always wondered what your hair looks like unpinned and spread out all over a pillow," he replied.

Her jaw dropped as if the hinges had snapped.

She managed to clap her mouth shut before he could look closely at her tonsils.

"It does not *want* to stay pinned, you know." He said this crossly, as if she'd been inflicting tyranny upon it against his objections, and he was arguing the case before a magistrate. "Look, even now!" He leaned slowly forward, and she was as mesmerized as if she were a snake and he a charmer. He reached up and drew a curl out between his fingers, straightening it then letting it go. "It bounces! Like a spring! Do you see? Why do you even try?"

She was too astounded to do anything but laugh. But it emerged breathlessly. He was so close she could feel the heat of his body, but she'd gone breathless.

There was no mistaking the fact that her heart was beating a rapid, futile warning.

Leave. Leave. Leave. Leave.

"You're a little drunk, aren't you, Lord Lavay?"

"You are as astute as always, Mrs. Fountain. I am, indeed, *un peu* foxed. Your hair is very soft."

There ensued a silence, a soft one, perhaps as soft as her hair.

"Thank you," she said cautiously.

He gave a short, ironic laugh.

"So many thoughts in your head now, I would

wager, my dear Mrs. Fountain, but the words you say are 'thank you.' We are so careful with each other. Or rather, you are so careful, always."

Now she was irritated. "What else would you have me be? I am your housekeeper. A servant."

"I would have you be Yourself," he said instantly.

"Which is?" she demanded, forgetting to be careful.

"Tart, like a persimmon, yet sweet, like a lovely, warm . . . *pêche*. A peach." He hefted his hand and cupped it to illustrate. "So very, very kind. Clever and witty. Annoying. Delightful. Beautiful." He again said all of these astounding things irritably, as if she'd asked him something she ought to have known. Something he'd said to her over and over.

She gaped at him and resisted the temptation to bring her hand up to touch her face.

The man knew how to conjure a blush.

He watched the blush intently, with a good deal of pleasure, as if it were a sunset. He smiled crookedly. "Ah, you see, I know you, and I know how to make you turn red. You would look magnificent dressed in red. The things I know, Mrs. Fountain. The things I know."

"You certainly *have* had a good deal to drink" was all she said.

He shrugged with one shoulder. "Some women might say thank you, others might comment on my state of inebriation. Such is the world."

She laughed, astonished. Utterly at a loss.

He didn't laugh. He didn't smile. He merely studied her through hooded eyes. "And honest," he purred. "I should like you to be honest."

Ah. And here it was.

She suspected he'd been disarming her for a reason.

She pressed herself more deeply into the corner, and they perused each other from opposite ends. It might as well have been a metaphor for their social spectrum.

"I have never lied to you. And . . . I haven't the luxury of being anything other than careful, as you say, Lord Lavay."

His brow furrowed faintly, then cleared.

"You have not— Ah. I see. You were once carefree, and someone has been careless with you, Mrs. Fountain. And now you no longer trust. This person was Jack's father, perhaps. And now you think I will do the same to you."

He suggested this almost lightly.

As usual, he'd leaped right to the crux of the issue with startling swiftness.

Her head rang as if he'd dropped her suddenly, hard, from a great height.

She said absolutely nothing.

"Jack's father . . . this man . . . did he take advantage of you?"

"No."

Alas, that answer, she realized, was only going to result in myriad questions.

"Did he seduce you, then?" asked the man who

likely knew precisely how to seduce anyone, and could, in fact, do it with one hand tied behind his back. Might be, in fact, doing it now.

She drew in a long fortifying breath, then let it go.

"In the spirit of honesty, Lord Lavay, and in the hope that you'll forget by morning what I'm about to say: No. If seduction implied strategy was needed to overcome my maidenly protestations, then no. I fear it was quite mutual. I wanted him. Only him. It was unexpected and of course inadvisable, but I was caught up in the moment, I did not say no, and I enjoyed it. And lest you think I distribute my favors about, like so"—she mimicked his strewing motion—"it wasn't as though I had a slew of suitors. It was the very first time I lost my heart, and I daresay could be the last. And I would dare you to say 'slew of suitors,' Lord Lavay, but I think you're too foxed to do it."

She watched the play of emotion over his face—shock and admiration and something like anger, swift and subtle, none of them settling in long enough for her to read them.

"My parents disowned me when I told them the news, and I haven't seen them in six years, either. And in case you wondered, divulging the foregoing was an example of me being something other than careful."

She'd just deliberately indicted herself. She was tired of being sorry, and she wasn't certain she was anymore, because in the end there was Jack. And she supposed this honesty was her way of seeking protection. Because if Lavay was so repulsed by the thought of her cavorting with a man outside of matrimony, perhaps he'd remove the threat to her heart and peace of mind that was his beautiful self.

He was quite still.

When the questions came, they were quick and abrupt. As though he were pulling shrapnel from his skin as quickly as possible.

"Where is he now?"

"God only knows."

"Did you care for him?"

"Yes. Very much."

And as she spoke, she watched Lavay's face go harder and harder, colder, more remote.

"Did he care for you?"

It was getting more difficult to answer his questions.

"I thought he did."

A hesitation at last.

"Do you still care for him?"

She heard the studied nonchalance in this question.

"I fear there is no simple answer."

He mulled this. The silence stretched.

"I have never been in love." He said this almost defiantly.

"I don't recommend it," she said.

He gave a crooked half smile, very ironic, very bittersweet.

Silence.

"Do you think he's still alive?"

This he drawled, sounding thoughtful and cheerfully, faintly sinister. As if he'd be only too happy to run him through, and it would be an easy enough thing to do.

"He's certainly resourceful enough. If I were required to wager on it, I would wager yes."

And on the last word her voice finally broke.

She'd managed to give all of her answers a glib lilt, but it was like taking one too many steps on a wound that hadn't quite healed and might never completely. A man she cared about and trusted had made love to her and then abandoned her whilst pregnant. She, who was so, so clever, and so, so proud, hadn't been able to discern a good man from a feckless, faithless one.

And now she was presented with a *truly* good man she could never have.

The pain caught up to her, and suddenly she couldn't breathe.

She held very still, as if everything inside her was broken and should not be jostled.

Lavay's eyes were glittery and remote, and his regard was merciless. She feared reading his verdict about her character or lack thereof on his face. And yet perhaps it would be a relief.

At last, he leaned back hard against the settee.

He sighed a breath he'd seemed to be holding.

He lifted his hand and held it briefly over his eyes. As if to shield himself from the glare of all that appalling truth. And then dropped it again, and gave his head a slow shake.

"I don't know how . . ." he began. "It's just . . ." His voice was low and scraped raw.

He seemed unable to meet her eyes.

They were aimed at his untouched tea.

And then he turned his head very deliberately to look at her, and the very act of seeing her seemed to pain him.

Her heart did a slow plummet, and she seemed to feel its jagged edges all the way down.

He leaned toward her, hands on his knees. "I just don't know how *anyone* could ever leave you, Elise."

He said it slowly, deliberately, wonderingly, as if handing down a verdict.

And then he gave a short rueful laugh.

As if it was both a realization and a confession and he wasn't quite certain how he felt about it.

Their gazes collided, and a rush of joy roared through her bleakness. He began to smile.

She shook her head, as if she could settle all the old fear and shame that had been stirred into its undisturbed place again, but it was no use. She dashed her hand roughly at her eyes, but a few tears escaped and clung to her eyelashes anyway. She could feel the consequences of everything that came before pulling at her.

He reached out instantly and took her hand firmly, as if to pull her back from the brink of that.

The gesture was all grace and instinct and tenderness.

So very him.

His instinct was always to protect, at any cost to himself.

She gripped his hand like a lifeline, but it was hardly safety, and she knew it.

Desire and joy were twined all through with fear of what she wanted. And as he laced his fingers through hers, she remembered the whisper-soft slide of them over the hairs on the back of her neck, and the fit of his hand at the small of her back, and desire spiked through her so violently that she nearly swayed.

All those hairs stood erect now, very hopeful of being stroked again, apparently.

"There was no shame in passion, Elise. The shame is in abandoning you with the consequences." His voice still had that husky edge. "The shame is all his."

"That," she sniffled, "is not a popular opinion. But if I were trying to seduce me, it is precisely what I would say."

He laughed softly.

But denied nothing.

"Nevertheless, you gave yourself honestly. We reason with ourselves in such moments, do we not? Fortunes are made and lost every moment on such wagers. Lives are changed for the better or worse in moments." He snapped his fingers. "You wagered you could indulge passion and receive trust and honor in return, and lost. Every choice, no matter how small, is a gamble. I wagered the Earl of Ardmay would make me a rich man, and he almost did. I imagine there's still time. I wagered on you restoring order to my household, and here you have upended me completely."

She laughed at that, then gave a rather graceless sniffle.

"You wagered a man you cared for would deal honorably with you. And you lost. We all lose from time to time. It is what makes winning sweeter. The day needs the night in order to enjoy any significance at all, *n'est-ce pas*?"

He gave a shrug.

She stared at him wonderingly.

She did rather prefer his vision of life as one enormous gaming table.

"I'm not a harlot but a gambler?" She managed to say this lightly. "And here I told the staff that life is best played as a long game."

She saw his other hand curl into a fist, almost languidly, at the sound of that word.

"If anyone refers to you as a harlot, would you be so kind as to tell me, so that I may shoot them?" he said almost lightly.

"As you wish, my lord."

He smiled a small, taut smile.

"There is something between us, *n'est-ce pas*, Elise?"

It was more a statement than a question. An understatement, in fact.

"*Oui*," she whispered.

A fraught silence ensued.

"And so, Mrs. Fountain, we have arrived at another such moment of wager, have we not?"

She was still holding his hand. That hard, elegant, scarred hand, that could wield a sword, a pistol, reins, rigging. And had likely touched more women than . . .

Now was not the time to think about that.

In many ways, he was no less frightening now than the day she'd met him.

And yet she could feel his pulse beating at least as swiftly as her own.

Because of her.

Because he wanted her.

She knew he was waiting for a word or a sign. How she wanted to drag her thumb over that hammering pulse, to commit to memory how he felt about her in this moment, to savor the life in him that had almost been extinguished by six men. How she wanted to raise his hand to her mouth and place a kiss there.

She released it instead.

Sliding her fingers from between his, savoring the touch of them as if for the last time.

And when he took it back from her, resignedly, as if he were scabbarding a sword, she saw the light leave his face.

It was closed and hard and still.

The silence that followed was like the sound of the end of the world.

Or before there *was* a world.

And a moment later, with fingers gone suddenly a little clumsy, she reached up and slid a hairpin from her hair.

And she laid it down between them as if it was the card that would decide the game.

Chapter 20

HE STARED AT THE hairpin.

Then raised his gaze cautiously to hers.

His breath seemed held.

She reached up and slid out another hairpin.

And laid it down next to the first.

A spirally lock of hair tumbled down and bobbed over her eyes.

"Well played, Madam." His voice was amused and admiring, but taut with anticipation.

And as slowly, torturously slowly, as slowly as she'd dreamed of sliding her hand up over his hard thighs . . . she slid out another pin.

He followed her hand with his eyes as she placed the pin down next to the first, as if he'd heard her thoughts. And followed her hand all the way back up to her hair.

She withdrew another pin.

He watched, statue-still, a smile beginning to grow.

Several little spirals of hair were freed this way, and she began to worry that what had begun as sensual was now comically Medusa-like. Still, in for a penny, in for a pound.

She reached up for the last pin.

"No," he said abruptly. "Allow me."

He leaned toward her, so close she could see the burnished tips of his dark lashes, and the gold splashes in his eye, so like autumn leaves spiraling in a wind, and she could smell starch and tobacco and warm man and she thought, *This must be how he does it*. One whiff of him was as intoxicating as a snifter of brandy. One sniff and women would fall at his feet. Or on their backs, rather.

His breath came swiftly against her cheek, against her ear, mingling with her own swift breath, and her nipples rose to attention.

And he drew, at last, that last hairpin from her hair, with the same gravity and triumph as Arthur had pulled the sword from the stone. He held it up to her, then tossed it into the pile with the others.

She gave her head a little shake.

He leaned back just a little to review the result.

"Dear God, it's *chaos*," he murmured. "We best put them back immediately!"

She would have laughed, but as he spoke his fingers were already lacing through it, and his voice had gone lazier and softer and more lulling with each word until "immediately" was a confiding whisper, and she was perhaps the happiest creature ever to be caught in a web of her own making.

He let his fingers dangle across the nape of her neck, and just like that little bonfires of pleasure were lit all across her nerve endings. It was a veritable Beltane of bliss.

When his hands were thoroughly wound in skeins of her hair, he tugged back her head.

"I am so glad," he murmured, "that you are a gambler, *chérie.*"

His lips brushed hers.

She moaned softly. It was scarcely even a kiss, but its subtlety held the promise of untold pleasure. It suggested he was a man who knew more about her desires than she did, and could fulfill them. He was a magician.

"I know, *ma chérie.* In good time. In . . ." He brushed her lips with his. " . . . good . . ." He coaxed her lips open and gently pulled a kiss from them. " . . . time."

His lips crushed hers.

With the dive and twine of his tongue, the brush and slide of his lips, layer upon layer of pleasure was revealed to her, heat and satin, cognac and smoke, dizzying musky sweetness, and she tumbled deeper, deeper, deeper into a sweet oblivion. His fingers loosed themselves from her hair and skated down, down, so lightly over her breasts, over those erect nipples, and she arced and gasped as bliss snaked through her veins.

"Elise." His voice was in her ear, a hoarse whisper, and he touched his tongue there. She shivered, and arched her neck, abetting him.

His mouth traveled to that secret, satin hollow beneath her ear where the tempo of her pulse betrayed her desire. He left a slow, hot kiss there, too. She considered herself branded. She was his.

His fingers were at the laces of her dress, fumbling at first, his fingers awkward. He spread them loose, and her dress sagged down the front of her like shameless, drunken doxie, to just above her breasts.

"You are beautiful."

"You are foxed."

"On you," he clarified.

"Very well. I am beautiful."

He laughed softly and dragged his fingertips, a touch soft as a whisper, across her collarbone, across the soft swell of her breasts, and her breath came jaggedly. Teasing.

He took another kiss, a soft one, as his finger skated over the smooth mounds of the tops of her breasts, and she did what she'd long imagined doing—she slid her hands up over his hard thighs and skimmed the tight, burgeoning swell of his cock with her nails.

He hissed in a breath and his thighs parted to allow her access.

Two could tease.

She did it again.

"*Elise*," he groaned against her mouth.

She felt lustful and savage.

He hooked his fingertips into the top of her gown and drew it down hard, and suddenly she was nude to the waist.

"Mother of *God*," he said with great, cheerful reverence, and filled his hands with her breasts.

His thumbs drew hard filigree figures over her ruched nipples, and the pleasure was shocking. She gasped, and her head went back, which gave him an opportunity to drag his lips down her throat. He ducked his head and closed his mouth around one nipple, then sucked gently and traced it with a sinewy, knowing tongue. The shocks of pleasure fanned through the far reaches of her body.

"Philippe . . . God . . ."

He pulled her toward him then, and in a motion as graceful and deliberate as a waltz, he closed his arms around her and rolled the two of them to lay side by side, face-to-face, on the settee, and he hooked his arm beneath her thigh so that it lay across his and they were fused, groin to groin.

And the heavenly shock, the relief, of the press of her body against the hot, hard length of his. She melted into him and pushed her body against the hard cock fighting the confines of his trousers. She could taste the lust, hot and electric, in the back of her throat, feel it coursing through her.

The rush of his breath, the hoarse words, a rush of French and English, very appreciative, coarse and profane. Knowing she had this power over him was excruciatingly erotic, and suddenly she was afraid of how much she wanted him, and what that might mean. His hands slid down to her buttocks and he pushed her against him again. She was likely seconds from her release and yet . . .

She went still.

Still quaking.

Her heart beating so hard that the blood whooshed in her ears. She rested her head against his heaving chest, feeling the thump of his heart against her cheek. She didn't want to meet his eyes.

He didn't question it. She could feel his confusion.

And then his hands slowed and gentled on her back, over her derriere, but never stopped moving.

And then she lifted her head. She could count his eyelashes if she wanted to, or look up his nose, and she could see a tiny scar next to his fine mouth, and a dusting of golden stubble on his chin, because it was already near morning.

"Philippe . . ." She began an apology.

He smiled softly at her. He traced her lips with his finger, a way of hushing her.

"I know so many secret places to kiss you, and so many ways to touch you, Elise. I know how to make you mad, mad with want for me."

The fingertips of his other hand were doing a whisper-soft slide against the vulnerable satiny skin inside her thigh, just above her garter, skin no man had ever touched so sweetly, so skillfully. She quivered with exquisite tension as each stroke sent quicksilver ribbons of pleasure through her.

And then he paused.

"Philippe . . ." And now it was almost a plea.

"I think that when we make love, Elise, the world will burst into flames. But it will not be tonight."

Her vocabulary was lost to her. The only thing

that seemed to have a voice was the slick, pulsing center of her.

His fingers were still skating back and forth, back and forth. So coy. So skilled. So just out of reach.

"You are not certain. Of this. Of us."

It was a moment before she could speak.

"I'm sorry," she whispered.

It was true.

"What are you afraid of?"

"It used to be you. And now I think it's me."

He paused, thoughtfully. His fingers never stopped moving.

"When you are certain, you will come to me. You will ask for it. And I will make you scream with pleasure, and you will do the same for me."

"I won't, Philippe. I can't . . ." The fingers were making her mad, mad, mad with desire now.

"I did not say I wouldn't use persuasion in the interim."

"Philippe . . ."

"And I will not leave you to beg tonight, *chérie*."

He slid his fingers up over her where she was wet and aching, and like a wanton she arched into the hard, skillful stroke.

"Now . . . there . . . *Philippe* . . ."

He didn't need instructions. He knew.

And an instant later she shattered, like a thrown vase, into a thousand sparkling, blissful shards, her body arcing violently with the force of her release. He pressed her face gently against his chest to muffle her hoarse scream.

And for a time they lay together, her cheek against his chest rising up and down, up and down, a little more slowly minute by minute as their breathing evened.

She hadn't screamed like that with Edward, *that* was for certain.

The clock whirred and bonged 3:00 a.m., and it wouldn't be long before the maids would be up to light the fires. She stirred.

"My leg is asleep," he said.

"Sorry," she murmured. She shifted.

"I must ask something of you," he said suddenly.

She turned to him, her hair falling down over his face, and he parted it like curtains, looking earnest.

"Do not worry so about all of the pins in your hair. If you need a ribbon, I will buy a ribbon for you. Postlethwaite's Emporium has dozens."

She laughed. "First a chair, then a ribbon . . . you will lure me into disreputability with a trail of gifts."

A flicker of something that looked like pain crossed his face.

And it was a piercing reminder that nothing at all was on offer apart from this, whatever this was.

She loved him.

She knew, just then, with a startling clarity and thoroughness that was both peace and torment.

She could never make love to him. She couldn't. Not for her sake, and not for Jack's. There would be no return if she did.

"You will come to me," he said softly.

"I won't," she said just as insistently. "I can't, Philippe."

He simply smiled faintly, enigmatically.

"But I'll wear a ribbon, and fewer pins," she promised him gently, as if she'd just told him good-bye.

"*How* you indulge me," he murmured, dryly, after a moment.

"WILL YOU GIVE me a push, Giant Lord Lavay?"

"It is a hammock, not a swing, Small Master Jack. If I push, you will fly out as if fired from a catapult and hit the church bell—*ding!*"

This made Jack laugh so loudly that he nearly fell out of the hammock anyway.

Philippe leaned over to stabilize it.

He'd found a cluster of alders perfect for slinging two hammocks, and though it was still cold, and with Jack's mother's blessing, the two of them had trudged out to sling them up so Jack could see what it was like to be a sailor.

They lay side by side, bundled up, arms crossed for warmth.

"It's grand," Jack pronounced. "Sailors sleep like this? On a ship?"

"*Oui*, the hammock was our bed on the ship. The ship sways on the sea, the hammock sways along with it."

They could see their breath as they spoke, but it was rather peaceful to stare up through the trees at the clear, cold sky. Lavay could remember no other period like this in his life. A calm before everything changed forever. There was the London assignment. There was Alexandra.

And there was Elise.

He didn't search for excuses to ring for Elise. Her assistance was no longer necessary with correspondence, she managed the household skillfully, no more innuendo-laced conversations were necessary.

She knew what he wanted.

Nor had their paths crossed more than once or twice since the night of the ball. But she allowed Jack to spend time with him in the evenings and on days when the weather was too soggy to trudge even across to the vicarage, and there was newness and peace and lightness in this. He had a very good deal of knowledge to impart, Philippe realized, with some surprise. Imagine, he'd gotten wise without realizing it.

What a pity it would be to be killed in London on assignment before he had sons.

And to never know what kind of man Jack would become.

What a pleasure it would be to raise his sons in Les Pierres d'Argent.

If he married Alexandra, the heirs could be imminent.

He pushed all of these thoughts away.

He had another two weeks or so of this strange, peaceful limbo before he needed to be decisive.

He was certain of only one thing at the moment: he wanted Elise in his bed.

"Have you gone to many places, Giant?"

"Oh, I've been all over the world. There are many beautiful lands to see, and not very far away if you sail in a ship. I was born in France, you see. That makes me French. Spain is beautiful and warm, and when the ladies dance, they click castanets." He snapped his fingers.

Jack laughed and imitated him. "Like this?"

"*Oui.*"

"I've only been to Pennyroyal Green," Jack confided.

"Ah. Pennyroyal Green is a fascinating place, too. So many lovely people."

"I think I want to be a sailor. After I can ring the bell."

"I approve of that sequence of events."

"And ride a horse."

"Every man should learn how to ride a horse."

"Or a zebra."

"Zebras will not permit riding, I'm afraid. If you like, I will show you how to use a sextant, which will help you guide a ship all over the ocean, which is how we find our way to new lands."

With a sudden pang, he wished he'd be able to teach Jack how to ride a horse. To watch his face light up with joy and pride and excitement.

Regardless, one way or another, within a fortnight, he would likely be on his way out of his and Elise's life, more or less for good.

"Will you come to the Christmas pantomime, Giant, at the church? I'm going be a sheep. There are angels, too. There's one angel called Colette. From Miss Endicott's."

"Ah, an angel called Colette. Is she pretty?"

"She's *so* pretty," Jack said with unfettered honesty and innocence. It made Lavay's heart squeeze. Oh, to be so guileless.

Suddenly he remembered this was the name of Alexandra's younger sister, the one who had been installed at Miss Marietta Endicott's Academy.

This must be the very same Colette.

"I will come to the pantomime, Jack."

"Hurrah!" Jack said, and thumped his heels lightly in the hammock, making it sway again. "Have you been to Ireland, too?"

"*Ireland?*" Philippe was amused.

"That's where Seamus is from."

"Who is Seamus?"

"Mr. Duggan. I like the way he talks. He knows a lot of songs. And he plays the fiddle and brings flowers to Mama. He'll play the fiddle at the pantomime."

Philippe stiffened. Suddenly the day had gotten significantly less idyllic.

"He does what?" He was aware his voice had gone rather steely.

Jack was blissfully oblivious.

"Plays fiddle. It's like a violin. Mama likes flowers. And Mr. Duggan can rhyme, but not as good as Mama. He sings good."

"He sings *well*," Philippe corrected.

"Have you heard him, too?" Jack was delighted.

"Oh, I intend to."

Chapter 21

Elise took refuge from the tumult of her feelings at the Pig & Thistle during the nights of singing, which magically coincided with her evenings off. She sat at the table with the vicar and his wife, a pint of the dark in front of her, enveloped in the cheery heat from the huge fire and all the bodies crammed into the pub, lulled by the cheerful, inebriated voices of the crowd and Seamus's relentlessly merry band of musicians.

The evening's music was already well underway when a gust of cold air briefly swept through the room, which is what happened every time someone new entered the pub.

She turned idly.

And froze.

Philippe was standing in the back of the room, a greatcoat covering his shoulders, hat in hand. Looking somehow infinitely more right than anyone in the room and more out of place. She'd somehow grown accustomed to his impact. In the context of this humble, centuries-old pub, he looked like the aristocrat he was.

He saluted her with a slow nod, but not a smile.

What the devil was he *doing* here?

"That's Lord Lavay. Get him a table," Ned Hawthorne hissed to his daughter, who had been gawking. Polly Hawthorne scrambled to shoo away a few disgruntled if awestruck young bloods from their spot and bid them stand in the back.

Lavay shook his head, smiled faintly, and waved away the attention. He took up a spot against a wall in the back of the pub.

Everyone reversed their motions and sat again.

Seamus drew his crowd-pleasing jig to a finish with a head toss and a flourish, and the crowd cheered their raucous approval. He bowed theatrically, accepting all of it as his due.

And then he stood on a chair and announced, "I should like to dedicate this song to a particular woman, because I know it makes her weep, and only the tenderest, kindest hearts weep."

He winked at Elise, but the pub was so crowded that a dozen women imagined it was for them, and Seamus's winks were in large part why the musical evenings were so successful.

But when he began, he sang it directly, unwaveringly, to Elise, in a pure, aching tenor:

What made th' assembly shine?
Robin Adair.
What made the ball so fine?
Robin was there.
And when the play was o'er,

What made my heart so sore?
Oh! it was parting with,
Robin Adair.

Damn him. It was a song about how loving someone made everything better, and how the world was so much dimmer when he wasn't there.

As if she didn't already know.

Fortunately, she wasn't the only one sniffling.

A gust of cold air signaled the door had swung open again.

Instinct told her to turn, and her suspicions were confirmed. Lavay had gone.

WHEN SEAMUS EMERGED from the pub a moment later to smoke and recover from the emotion he poured into the song of Robin Adair, he discovered Lavay leaning against the wall, staring up at the stars. Perhaps contemplating whether to go back inside.

Perhaps hoping Seamus would emerge so he could kill him.

"Lord Lavay is it," Seamus said, tucking a cheroot into his mouth.

Lavay said nothing.

Seamus extended a cheroot.

Lavay took it.

Seamus lit it for him.

In total silence, two men united only by their devastating appeal to women and delightful accents sucked on their cheroots.

"I actually enjoy fighting, Lord Lavay," Seamus confided finally into the long, tense, lethal-feeling silence. "I really do. I suspect you do, too. But I suspect you like to win better than I like to fight."

"There will be no fighting," Lavay said, almost lazily. "Because there would be no sport in such an easy kill."

Seamus simply nodded.

The silence and smoking resumed.

"There is no harm in wanting what you want. But wouldn't it be a pity to hurt a woman like that? One who has already been hurt?"

Seamus said it in his lilting Irish accent, which gave everything a bit of an ironic, lighthearted twist.

Lavay turned to stare at him. He would have preferred to be able to dismiss Seamus Duggan as lightweight and frivolous.

The door swung open. "Duggan! Get your arse in!"

Seamus wordlessly did just that.

Lavay took his arse home, walking the entire way.

A SLEEPY HUSH lay over the house when the reverend and Mrs. Sylvaine saw Elise home, before midnight. The rest of the servants had gone up to bed, and after she'd looked in on a blissfully sleeping Jack, she brought herself downstairs to test again the locks on the cabinets, to review the state of the kitchen. It was spotless, everything in its place, all the foodstuffs stored properly.

Not so long ago she'd never dreamed she'd feel so much pride in these kinds of things, but she surrendered to the impulse to bask in the triumph. It had been no small feat.

She had begun to feel as though she could accomplish anything.

She was returning to the kitchen through the passage between it and the storeroom when a shadow appeared at the end of it, blocking the light.

She gave a start.

"Philippe," she breathed. There really was no mistaking him.

For a moment they were merely shadows to each other in the passageway.

With slow measured footsteps, he closed the distance between the two of them.

"Are you . . . are you looking for a tart?" she said softly.

And then she blushed when she realized how that sounded.

He smiled faintly, but he was clearly distracted. "May I ask you a question, Elise?"

His tone was peculiar. A little diffident. Very tense.

"Of course."

"How do you feel about . . . that man?"

"Which man?"

"The man with the fiddle." He raised a mocking invisible fiddle to his shoulder and played, tossing his head.

The funny thing was that it did look quite a bit like Seamus when he tossed his head about.

"About Seamus Duggan?"

"Yes. Are you in love with him?"

"Am I . . . *what*? Why on earth . . . what on earth . . . *what*?"

"He is in love with you."

"He most certainly is not. Or, more accurately speaking, Seamus is in love with everybody. Perhaps most particularly himself."

"I saw the way he looked at you. And sang to you. That is a man in love."

"Perhaps you have confused him with the man you see in the mirror."

That stopped him as abruptly as if he'd run hard into a brick wall.

The truth could sometimes feel like a brick wall.

They studied each other.

And then he moved forward, startling her, backing her against the wall. His hands landed one by one on either side of her, fencing her in.

"How do you feel about Seamus Duggan, Elise?"

"I suppose I feel about Seamus Duggan the way you feel about Lady Prideux."

This won her a smile that bore no relationship to humor.

"How do you feel about Seamus Duggan, Elise?" he repeated softly.

"Seamus is enchanting," she murmured about an inch from his chin.

"Oh?"

"Have you seen how his green eyes sparkle?"

"I have seen," he said grimly.

"And he has a lovely singing voice," she went on.

"If one likes the singing of frogs, I can see how one might enjoy it," he all but breathed directly into her ear, which caused everything on her body to stir in anticipation of bliss.

His hands glided up over her breasts without preamble and with shocking confidence, as if he owned her. Which wasn't far wrong.

"I think that we shall make each other come now, with our clothes on."

It was so matter-of-fact and so coarse and so thoroughly erotic that the blood stampeded into her head and she thought she might faint.

"Who are you thinking about *now*, Elise?" he murmured.

She stared at him, her mind erased, her body already enslaved.

"Who do you think about at night, alone in your room, Elise? I will tell you who I think about. I lie awake and I think about how I would like to do this . . ." His fingers delicately traced the contours of them through her muslin bodice. ". . . for your breasts have a graceful, saucy curve, like so." He savored them with an illustrating caress, then paused to cup them. "And then I think how your nipples are like little raspberries, and I would like to suck them, and flick them with my tongue."

"That is"—she swallowed—"quite a bedtime story. Not at all like Aesop."

"But then I know I can also do this," he murmured into her ear, and then his tongue was there, delving just a little into it, then tracing the contours of it, slowly, dexterously, so sinfully knowingly, which made her moan softly. And he lightly pinched her nipples, then skated hard over them with his thumbs. "And they will go hard as little stones, you see, and you will be wet. So wet for me. Are you wet now, Elise?" he whispered.

"Guh," she gasped eloquently.

Which was really all the answer he needed.

She was either a wanton or he was an arch seducer, infinitely more formidable than she could have anticipated. Probably a bit of both. He was a man who knew what he wanted and knew how to get it, and she was in all likelihood not the most difficult thing he would ever have to get.

And now it was too late to stop, and every ounce of blood in her body seemed to have pooled between her legs and she was aching, burning for him.

He unfastened his trousers with shocking alacrity and hooked an arm beneath her thigh, fitting himself against her. She gasped in shock. The heat and hard length of his swollen cock pressed against her, so excruciatingly tempting.

"And I think," he went on, his narrative made ragged now by his breathing, "how it would feel to be inside you." He moved his hips to slide his cock oh so delicately against her wetness, lightly, teasing, torturing her, torturing himself. She groaned a low, animal sound of pleasure, a plea. "And how sweet that will feel. But for now we will only torment each other, *oui*, because when you want me, *you* will come to me."

"I won't," she whispered.

He slid against her slick heat again. And she ground against him, her limbs shaking and tense with reigned-in lust.

"You will," he whispered.

He slid against her soaking curls again.

He muttered hoarse oaths against her mouth, strings of oaths, all unrelated, all filthy and appreciative and French. "You feel so good, *chérie*." It was a dry rasp.

"Philippe . . . I . . . *please* now . . ." She teetered just on the edge of release. She clung hard to his shoulders and moved herself against him, begging, and he hissed in a breath. But he held her fast, so that she couldn't move. He was in control of this. She whimpered. Their gusting, ragged breath mingled hotly. Her head tipped back hard, and he burned a kiss into her throat. His face was sheened with sweat. The effort not to take her now and take her hard might simply be the death of him.

"Please," she whispered.

He moved again, swiftly, once, twice, lightly, and just like that she shattered with a raw scrape of a scream, and quaked in the throes of it.

Just as he swiftly shifted his hips and she heard his guttural moan of pleasure as he spilled against her thigh. His release wracked him hard.

He allowed himself a minute to breathe, his

head ducked against her throat. He was breathing like a bellows beneath her hands.

She kissed his temple.

But neither of them felt particularly tender or charitable.

It had been a ferocious interlude. All frustrated desire quickly, gracelessly satisfied.

". . . and I think to myself," he said, through gusting breaths, ". . . when she comes to me I will show her the true meaning of pleasure. And she will forget how to even pronounce Seamus Duggan."

Seamus who?

He was gently cleaning her thigh with his handkerchief as he spoke. And then he dropped her thigh again and smoothed down her dress. He buttoned his trousers so matter-of-factly that she wondered how many times he'd done just that, because it was so smoothly executed.

Except she knew she was different from any of the women who had come before.

"It isn't fair." Even as she said them she knew they were petulant, tense, quite obvious and not particularly helpful words.

He gently took her chin in his hand.

"I suppose you are right," he said softly. "But then, *tout est juste dans l'amour et la guerre, chérie.* We have not chosen to want it. But we do. You need only find a way to justify wanting it."

She didn't know how she could love and hate a man all at once.

He kissed her, sweetly, lightly, on the mouth,

and then he turned and left her. She watched him move down the hall toward his study.

FIFTEEN MINUTES LATER, the house echoed with the sound of a vase shattering into a thousand pieces.

He stood in shame amidst the shrapnel of another vase and breathed, wondering at the fact that his life seemed to be closing in on all sides once again, when for a brief shining moment it was as though the sun had burst through.

She was right. As usual.

And it wasn't as though he didn't know it.

Whether or not it was fair was of no consequence.

He had no right to do this to her. To use her passion and sensuality and love for him as weapons to get what he wanted. The desire was like claws in him, and when he inwardly writhed at the injustice of it, the claws sank deeper still.

And he wouldn't ask her again to trade passion for yet more shame. He wouldn't be one more man who partook of her and left, nor would he ask her to live on the fringe of his life, in the shadows, to be enjoyed whenever he could spare a moment. She was a woman who belonged in the light. She was a woman who deserved to be loved and honored for the rest of her life.

So very, very ironic that a shiftless Irish fiddler should in fact have more right to her than he did.

He gave a short, bitter laugh at the burden of being honorable and the caprices of fate.

And yet he could offer her nothing more than pleasure and the fringes of his life, and she knew it.

But if he could, he would give her safety and certainty forever. He would take away limbo so that she never needed to worry again.

And so he set about doing that.

He smoothed out a sheet of foolscap and dipped the quill in. His hand was just now barely fit to perform the fine movements writing required.

And he paused as another truth settled over him, weighted and final: he could not imagine yet gripping the hilt of a sword or curling his hands into fists to throw at men if necessary. It would be weeks before he was fully himself again, and it would require yet more patience of him.

He sat motionless with the realization, final as a death.

He sighed, and began.

Dear Mr. and Mrs. Fountain,

An injury to my hand necessitates brevity, so please forgive the lack of formality. Your daughter Elise is employed as my housekeeper in Pennyroyal Green, Sussex. She has not requested that I write, and I must humbly beg that you never tell her of this letter. She is one of the finest people I have ever met. Her son, Jack, is a handsome, clever, and delightful child, and anyone would be proud and honored to know either of them.

She misses you and her home terribly, though she will not say it aloud. Since you likely know your

*daughter, you know she is proud, and that feeling as
though she has brought shame upon you haunts her.*

*I lost half of my family and most of my
properties in the revolution, so I can assure you
that I know the cost of losing someone you love,
and would not wish it upon anyone.*

*I felt compelled to write to you because you
still have a choice. You don't have to lose her
forever. If it is pride keeping you apart, I assure
you that she would love to see you again. All
you must do is write to her care of this address.*

*I have sailed the oceans and fought wars and
won and lost fortunes. I still know only two things
for certain: Life is short. Love matters most.*

> *Sincerely,
> Philippe, Lord Lavay*

He would send a messenger with it. The footmen could flip a coin for the honor.

He sat back and held very still, the quill motionless in his hand. Never had so few words
seemed so weighted.

And then he dipped the pen in the ink and
wrote one more message to be taken to London:

*It is with deep regret I must decline the offer of
an assignment. I am not yet fully recovered from
the previous assignment.*

He wouldn't sign it. It would have felt a bit like
signing his own warrant, anyway.

Chapter 22

THE DAYS BEFORE BOXING Day and the Christmas pantomime passed in a flurry of costume sewing, as Elise had essentially indentured her spare time to Mrs. Sneath for quite the rest of the season in exchange for being allowed to keep the completed footman uniforms. The Christmas puddings had been prepared well ahead of time, and she planned a feast of roast goose for the servants.

Lord Lavay would be spending Christmas Day with the Countess and Earl of Ardmay.

He'd been scarce, lately. Her bell had been quiet.

The staff spent a merry day bedecking the house with boughs of greenery, and come evening they sat down to a leisurely, delicious, cheerful meal in the kitchen. Everyone drank at least one glass of mulled wine. Elise gave the staff leave to go to bed early, since Lord Lavay wouldn't be home to-night, and she looked forward to an evening of reading to Jack, then perhaps even reading something delightful for herself. A horrid novel would be *perfect*.

She arrived in her room, pleasantly full and flushed from the wine, sleepy enough to drop into slumber without counting Lavays, to brush her hair and tuck Jack in and sing him to sleep.

She moved slowly toward the desk.

And as if she'd been watching it from somewhere above her own body, she saw her hand reach out and touch her hairbrush.

It didn't disappear. It wasn't an apparition, nor was it a dream.

Furthermore, it was tied with a beautiful red satin ribbon.

She sank down in her chair, her heart glowing like a sun in her chest.

"How did he *know*?" she whispered.

She gave a soft, amazed laugh. She gently lifted the familiar, much-loved brush, and held it in her hand as if it were his hand. The initials were soon blurred with tears.

She swiped a hand across her eyes

That was when she saw a small box labeled, "For Jack."

She sniffed. "Jack, my love, this is a gift for you from Lord Lavay."

"For me? Hurrah!" He took it with him to the bed and plopped down to open it. She turned to smile at him, but something caught the corner of her eye.

She'd almost missed the letter beneath it addressed to her.

She recognized the handwriting, and her heart stopped.

Her hand went to her mouth in shock, and all
sensation fled her limbs.

For a moment she was absolutely certain she
couldn't open it. She was afraid of what she might
find inside. Whether it was ghastly news, or more
censure.

Courage, Elise.

She took a deep breath.

The foolscap rattled as she slid a finger beneath
the seal.

Dear Elise,

*We love you and have missed you every minute
of every day since you've been gone. We have
long since forgiven you for your startling news,
but we are a prideful and stubborn family as
you know, and we can be impulsive and quick-
tempered, too. These qualities are the best and
the worst of us. I hope you can find it in your
heart to forgive us. Please come home and bring
Jack. We will love him, too.*

> *Love,*
> *Mama and Papa*
> *Fountain*

"A *lion*! The Giant gave me a lion! I have a lion!
Raaaawwr!" Jack had managed to get his box open.
"Can we act out Androcles tonight with the lion?
Mama? Mama?"

She couldn't speak.

She turned around and tried to smile for him, at the cunning wooden lion with the dyed woolen mane.

She was quite simply too full to speak.

"Yes. Of course, Jack."

He bounded over to her and draped his arm around her shoulder to lean into her. "Why are you crying, Mama?"

She pulled him into a long, squeezing hug.

"I'm just very, very happy about our Boxing Day gifts, Jack, that's all. I will tell you why a little later. Perhaps after your pantomime."

ON BOXING DAY, Philippe slipped into the church just in time to witness the startling Christmas miracle of his own footmen somberly escorting three very short wise men up to where the baby Jesus lay in a manger, surrounded by kindly animals, one of whom was a frisky sheep named Jack. He wore floppy ears and had been bedecked in a great nimbus of fluffy wool.

A host of miniature fidgeting angels, all sporting halos suspended upon stalks, most of whom were missing any number of teeth, one of whom scratched her bum as they sang, hovered around them, and they all collided like billiard balls when they were supposed to queue neatly to sing.

Seamus Duggan played "While Shepherds Watched Their Flocks at Night," and the children sang in their high, sweet voices. And though he'd been instructed not to wave at all, Jack waved to him.

All in all, it was one of the best times Philippe had ever had at the theater.

And damn Seamus Duggan, anyway. But Philippe closed his eyes and let the voices and the fiddle wash over him. It crept into the raw, jagged places in his soul, and for that moment, anyway, he felt a sort of surcease. Seamus Duggan was a ne'er-do-well, but ironically, he was a freer man than Lord Lavay.

When Philippe opened his eyes, he spotted the back of Elise's head immediately. She was wearing a red wool dress, and her dark hair twisted and loosely pinned, the red ribbon he'd given her threaded through it, gleaming like its own halo. He could even now imagine the silk of it against his hands. She was leaning forward, as if she could get closer to Jack if she could. Lending him every part of her support.

He smiled.

Curious heads turned toward him. He saw a contingent of Everseas in the audience, presumably there to lend support to their cousin the vicar. Olivia Eversea was among them, Landesdowne by her side.

Philippe didn't particularly belong here, but he wasn't unwelcome. He was a curiosity, a thing of awe, someone to admire and remark upon and gossip about, a visitor in their midst.

Pennyroyal Green would always have visitors in its midst.

It was better to belong to someone or something, as he and the Earl of Ardmay had agreed.

HE SLIPPED OUT as the evening concluded and hovered outside the door as a flood of little angels and sheep poured out of the church, mingling with villagers. As he waited for them, he felt precisely as conspicuous as he must have looked, ignoring all the curious eyes and goggling stares of various females.

"Giant! You came!"

Usually Jack *bounded* everywhere. Particularly since he'd been recruited to be a sheep. But this time he shuffled over, and it wasn't entirely due to the bulk of the costume. Something seemed amiss.

"You were a brilliant sheep, Jack."

"Thank you, Giant. Thank you for the lion! I love it very much. It made my mama cry."

Philippe looked at Elise in alarm.

"Jack," Elise said in warning. "It was just that the gifts were . . . the gifts were wonderful. Thank you, Lord Lavay."

He merely nodded, too moved by what he saw in her eyes to speak.

Jack really seemed peculiarly subdued, despite the triumph of the pantomime. His eyes were downcast, when usually they darted everywhere, hungry to see everything. His face was clouded and sullen. Philippe had never seen Jack anything but purely delighted to be alive, his face always aglow, like a miniature sun, spreading light.

"Are you not happy about your performance, Master Jack?" he ventured.

"It was fine," he said. It was almost clipped.

"Thank you for coming, Lord Lavay. It was kind of you," Elise said.

"I was unaware that footmen were present at Jesus's birth. I suppose one's education never ends."

"I imagine much of history is still an enigma to us."

He smiled, then turned away, his smile fading into something somber and resigned.

One simply did not engage in lengthy social conversations with one's housekeeper outside of the house, after all. Not without exciting the sort of comment neither he nor Elise could weather. And taking refuge in manners was really all that was left to them.

Meeting. Parting. Meeting.

Parting.

For tonight would likely be the moment everything was decided.

"I have a social engagement this evening, Mrs. Fountain. I will be dining with Lady Prideux and Lord and Lady Archembault at the home of Lord Harry, so it will not be necessary to prepare a meal for me."

He watched her take in the words as if she'd been withstanding jabs with pins. Her spine went straighter, her face went taut and pale.

But he didn't want to lie to her.

"Thank you for the notice, sir."

She meant it in more ways than one.

"And . . . and I have written to the king to decline his offer." He turned away from her when he said it. As if he couldn't bear to see her absorb the news.

Elise stood motionless, suddenly deaf and blind to the milling crowd.

It meant he'd made his choice, and Lady Prideux was it.

She didn't know how long she was silent. The sun might have risen and set a dozen times over, for all she knew.

"It's for the best," she said at last. Her voice was frayed and small. It had needed to pass through what felt like the gauntlet of knives in her gut before it emerged, after all.

And it was such a lie. How could anything that kept them apart be for the best?

She supposed a circumstance in which he wasn't being shot at or dodging sword thrusts was marginally better. Both were horrible.

She stood, strapped to a Catherine wheel of emotion, as Jack shuffled his feet near her. She would never be allowed to show it. She could not afford to sob into a pillow or throw a vase.

She would simply need to find a way to transmute all of that into love. And love him without having him.

"A good day to both of you, Mrs. Fountain." His own voice was a thread, too, faint and hoarse. He somberly touched his hat and turned to leave, like a man heading to a funeral, rather than a festive dinner.

ELISE WATCHED LAVAY go and looped her hand around Jack's shoulder, as if to keep her knees from giving way. She could feel an invisible pull, as if Lavay had her very heart on a red ribbon and was towing it away.

Jack's costume was beginning to list and shed. She had promised Mrs. Sneath to help with the cleaning of the church after, as part of the many things she had promised in exchange for keeping the footman uniforms.

"Are you feeling well, Jack, my love?" Elise lay a hand across his forehead. "It's exhausting to be a sheep, I know, when you've been a boy your whole life."

"I'm fine, Mama." He scowled and slid from beneath her hand as if she'd laid a toad on his head instead.

"Are you constipated? Too many tarts?"

"No, Mama! Cor! Can we just go home?"

"Cor"? Another word she would have to expunge from his vocabulary.

She stared at him, a worried frown between her eyes.

His eyes were on his shoes. Which were still decorated as little hooves.

"Of course, my love," she said after a moment. "But in an hour or so, so we can help Mrs. Sneath clean up after the festivities. We'll have tarts to celebrate."

"I'm not hungry, anyway."

These words more than anything were a stab to the heart, and now she was truly concerned.

"I'll go find Liam," he said, and went jogging off, without waiting to hear what she thought of that.

"I SAW MARIE-HELENE two months ago," Lord Archembault said. "She is a beautiful young lady, Lavay. A credit to your family."

Yes, but how were her gowns? he was tempted to ask. Weren't her gowns tired?

The dinner was a delectably done hare in sauce, and the home was gracious, situated on a rise from which you could look down and see both Alder House and the vicarage, as well as the Pig & Thistle, in the distance.

The company, Philippe thought uncharitably, was stultifying.

"I'm proud to hear that you think so. I hope to see her very soon, when I return to France."

He met Alexandra's eyes across a silver candelabra, the sort of thing refugees from the revolution often seized as they fled.

She gave him an intimate little smile. She knew an understanding was nigh; the air all but buzzed with it. All he needed to do was incant the right words to make it official, and she'd likely heard "when I return to France" as *"when we return to France, and take over the place."*

She would be returning to London tomorrow, and would get passage to France there.

He tried to imagine dinner after dinner after dinner sitting across from her, for the rest of his life. What would they talk about? Their children, presumably. Perhaps all the things they would do with their money.

What would it be like to make love to her?

Everything in him shied away from the notion, and surely that was wrong. Surely making love to a woman like her should not be a chore.

These people bored him, he realized. It felt nearly traitorous, and yet. They spoke to him as though the revolution had never occurred, and for some of them, it had merely struck them a glancing blow. The irony was that his attempts at preserving a way of life they all assumed was superior and to which they were all entitled—his privateering with the Earl of Ardmay, sharing a ship and bloody battles with men like his bald, foul-tempered Greek cook, Hercules, being attacked on the Horsleydown Stairs—had made him nearly unfit for it. They had reshaped him in such a way that he could never be inserted neatly into the slot he'd left behind. It was a rarified, beautiful, comfortable way of life. It was a fine, fine way of life. It was the way of life his sister had come to expect, and the life he wished for her.

But now these people had naught to do with who he'd become.

But perhaps he merely felt this way because

he'd been unmoored for so long. There was no place he considered home.

If he could return to Les Pierres d'Argent, it might restore him to equilibrium. Remind him of all he had fought for.

All evening, he felt as though he was reciting the lines to a play he'd performed a dozen times before.

"Your grandfather brags about you, too, Philippe."

Philippe smiled. "I'm fortunate to still have a *grand-père* who is proud of—"

"Lord Lavay."

They all swiveled in astonishment. One of the footmen who had crept in and out, as silent as cats, all evening, had spoken. It was as if the candelabra had spoken.

"I'm terribly sorry to interrupt, but I'm told it is an emergency. Someone is waiting for you in the foyer."

Philippe looked into the footman's face. Something he saw in it made him slowly rise, folding his napkin very deliberately.

Portent stood his hair up on the back of his neck.

"This way, sir," the footman said quietly.

Philippe followed him and came to a halt on the chessboard-patterned foyer.

His footman-valet Ramsey stood just inside, illuminated by a pair of mounted lanterns, which had bleached his face of color. Rain was pooling on the floor around him.

A buzzing started up in Philippe's ears.

"Is it Elise?" Philippe said abruptly.

The footman looked astonished. "Eli— No, sir. No, sir. Well, sir. I'm so sorry to trouble you, sir. I wouldn't if—"

"Out with it, Ramsey."

"Young Master Fountain is missing."

Philippe's heart froze. "Jack?" The word was hoarse.

"Mrs. Fountain went to look in on him after dinner, and he wasn't in his bed. We've searched the house over, every closet and cupboard, and called and called for him. We even . . ." He gulped. ". . . well, the foot of the stairs. In case he—"

Philippe gave his head a rough warning shake. He didn't want to hear the end of that sentence any more than the footman wanted to utter it.

The buzzing in his ears was louder now, and his heart was slamming as hard as boots coming down in a military parade. All at once he could feel Elise's terror as tangibly as if it were a coming storm, and it wound around his heart like a snake. He knew a peculiar cold fury that anything or anyone, the universe or fate, would dare to harm her. Or Jack.

He would make it right.

"Does Mrs. Fountain know you're here?" he said sharply.

"No, sir. She wouldn't have liked me to trouble you. So I left without her knowing . . . she's still searching through the house, sir, and calling his name . . ." Ramsey swallowed.

Philippe reached out and briefly gripped the man's shoulder. "You did the right thing," he said distantly.

Which is nothing a Lavay would have said or done to a footman prior to the revolution.

Prior to Elise Fountain.

Some notion was moving in the shadows of Philippe's mind, and he fixed on it, desperately willing it into focus, as if it were prey.

"It's very unlike Master Jack. It's been nearly two hours, sir. Maybe longer. We don't know for certain. She's distraught, Lord Lavay." His voice nearly broke. "It's hard to bear. I like her, you see. She's been grand to all of us."

"Philippe?" came an irritated, brittle voice. Alexandra's. Accompanied by the clicking of slippers in the foyer behind him.

"Be quiet," he said abruptly. Shrugging it off as if it were a mosquito. Hardly registering that it belonged to anyone he knew. He was thinking.

Her shocked gasp hardly registered, either.

"I'm not a subaltern or one of those scruffy heathens on your ship, Philippe. You cannot speak to me that way."

"Silence," he said anyway. He couldn't help it. She could have been anyone talking; he would have said it to the king.

Because Philippe had at last drawn a bead on the idea.

And then he had it.

His issued orders came swift, hard, furious, and incontrovertible.

"I know where he is. Go get Mrs. Fountain and bring her to the church, Ramsey. Now. *Now*, man."

The footman turned and bolted as if shot from a cannon. Behind him, the footman who had brought Philippe the message at dinner was already holding his overcoat, and Philippe shrugged into it.

Philippe seized one of the mounted wall lanterns and bolted out the door.

"Phili—"

Alexandra's voice might as well have been the wind.

Chapter 23

HE RAN IN LONG, ground-devouring, lunging strides, across the downs in the dark, the lantern in his fist quickly snuffed by the rain slashing down at him, his boots sinking into the mud. He felt none of it. He felt no pain. His breath roared in his ears. The vicarage seemed so close and yet so terrifyingly far away, and there was no light at all, stars and moon all blanketed by a fat, surly rain cloud.

He never stopped until he reached the door to the bell tower, which was, as he suspected, open just a crack.

And then he scaled in huge bounds the winding steps all the way up to the bell, two at a time, guided more by instinct than anything else. When he arrived he paused, heaving for breath.

He paused and listened. He saw the great, calm, still mass of the bell. He heard the rain striking the wall and the wind rushing through the crevices.

And then at last he heard a soft rustling sound. Accompanied by sniffing and soft sobbing.

And there against the wall Jack was slumped.

The blood nearly left Philippe's head in relief. He dropped to his knees.

"Master Jack. Are you hurt?"

"Good evening, Giant," the boy sniffed. "No. And I'm not crying."

Lavay turned and sank down next to him and pressed his back against the wall, gulping huge breaths.

"Of course not," he wheezed out.

"I can't get the bell to ring," Jack explained. He sniffed. "I tried. It just won't go. I can't do anything. I won't amount to anything."

"Aw, Master Jack. It's frustrating, I know. So many things we have to wait for in life, and it's one of the hardest things in life to learn. Even now, I'm still waiting to be able to do things, and I am a grown man. Here, why don't you warm my coat up for me?"

He peeled off his wet oilskin overcoat and laid it on the ground, then shook himself out of his dry coat and wrapped it around Jack, engulfing him. Jack's head poked out from the dark wool and shining buttons.

They sat together in silence for some time. Philippe's ragged breaths seemed to echo in the bell tower.

"Giant?"

"Yes, Master Jack?"

"What is a bastard?"

Philippe closed his eyes.

Oh, God.

He felt as though he'd just been stabbed clean through again.

"A bastard," he said slowly, "is a person who wishes to make someone else unhappy by saying unkind things. *That* is what a bastard is," he said with feeling. "Where did you learn the word?"

"From Colette, from Miss Endicott's. She's so pretty, Giant. But she says a bastard is someone who doesn't have a father and will never amount to anything. And she says I'm a bastard."

Colette.

Alexandra's sister.

And how would Colette know anything at all about Jack's parentage?

A sizzling, nasty suspicion started somewhere in the recesses of his mind.

And that is the reason Colette is at Miss Endicott's Academy, he thought grimly. The place specialized in difficult girls.

The person to whom Elise must have spoken out of turn was Alexandra.

He shoved this realization aside to revisit later.

"Ah. Well, Jack, that is another meaning for the word, but it isn't a kind one. You know how words can sometimes have two meanings, and other words we ought not say in polite company? It's like that."

"Like 'duck.' It means a bird, and it means to do this." Jack ducked into Philippe's coat and vanished. "And like the bark on a dog and the bark on a tree."

"Precisely. And you are a kind boy, so you won't use that word to describe anyone."

Jack's head popped out of the coat again. "The one that starts with a *B*?"

"Yes."

They sat together for a time.

"I don't have a father," Jack said miserably, his voice a hush, as if he were confessing a shameful secret. "Almost everyone else does. I think I'm supposed to."

And then Philippe could almost literally feel his heart breaking. Cracking like the surface of an ice pond.

He fiercely gathered Jack into his lap, wrapped his arms around him, and rested his chin on top of Jack's head. And this was how one put hearts back together again, he thought. By simply loving.

They were quiet together for a time. Jack's sobs were tapering off into ragged hiccuping.

"I don't have a father either, Jack."

"Did your father go away, too?" Jack sounded sympathetic.

"In a manner of speaking."

"Are you a bastard, too?"

"Some might say, Jack. Some might say. But here is the important part about not having a father. And I want you to listen closely, because I'm a clever man and I speak only truth. Do you believe me?"

Jack nodded.

"When you don't have a father . . . you must

learn to be stronger and braver and more resourceful, which is a word that means you will always
know best how to take care of yourself and the
people you love. And sometimes it's a bit lonely to
not have a father, but when you have a big heart,
and you do, you will never be lonely for long."

He could tell Jack was listening intently. He'd
gone mostly still, though he'd begun to pluck at
one of the buttons on Philippe's coat.

"The thing is, Jack, your *maman* loves you
enough for two people and . . . I've never met
anyone who loves as well as your mother does.
Her heart is enormous, and she is as good as a
mother and father all put together. You are so fortunate, Jack, and so special, and that is why the
two of you were given to each other to love. And
you will amount to anything you want to be. I
know you will be a fine man indeed, because you
are already strong and brave and resourceful, as
well as bold and kind and clever. And we shall
pity and be kind to Colette, because only unhappy
people say such unkind things, *oui*? All right?"

"*Oui.*" Jack sounded considerably cheered.
He heaved a great sigh and leaned back against
Philippe's chest.

"Sometimes we feel things very strongly, *non*?
So strongly that we want to run away from them,
or throw things. But you must stop and think
before you do to decide whether someone who
loves you might be scared or miss you. You can
always tell your *maman* what it is that is troubling

you. Your mama is very worried, Jack. And . . ."
He hesitated. ". . . and so was I."

"I'm sorry, Giant."

"I will take you home now, all right?"

"All right, Giant."

Neither Jack nor Philippe hadn't even noticed
the sounds of the footman and Elise climbing the
stairs, following the flickering light of the lantern
in the window.

THE RAIN EASED a bit after the initial vomiting
downpour, and despite the vicar's pleas for them
to wait by the fire in the vicarage with him and his
wife until morning, they all just wanted to be home.

Lavay carried a sleeping Jack all the way across
the green, and Elise carried the lamp, which managed to stay lit.

They were silent the entire way. It was a subdued, humbled, awed, soft, very resigned silence.

Neither of them felt the cold.

Philippe hadn't thought. He simply hadn't
thought.

He'd simply bolted through the dark, like an
animal sprung from a trap, because he would do
anything for her. He simply could not differenti-
ate what was best for her or for himself, because
they seemed one and the same.

And he supposed that was what happened
when someone else was your heart. You couldn't
help what you did.

And he suspected Elise had heard everything
he'd said to Jack.

A cloud whipped past a half moon, exposing its face long enough to give them light for the walk home.

"I'm sorry, Mama. I love you, Mama."

"I know, sweetheart. I love you, too. You won't do it again?"

"No, Mama," Jack slurred sleepily.

Elise had peeled Jack's wet clothes from him and scrubbed him down with a dry warm cloth, then installed him in a warm sleeping gown. She put him to bed with hot bricks and a cup of sipping chocolate and his lion.

And she held him in her arms until he fell asleep again, which was nearly instantly.

She listened to his even breathing. She counted his breaths, as if she could make up for the ones she'd missed while he'd been in the church tower, futilely trying to ring the bell.

Trying to amount to something.

And that's when she started to tremble.

She slipped out of bed, undressed, and unbound her hair. She shook it out until it poured down her back.

She wrapped herself in her night robe and lit a candle, then made her way down the stairs, almost like a sleepwalker, toward the one person in her world who felt like safety.

She tapped on his door three times. Softly.

There was no reply.

So she tried the handle.

It gave.

She pushed it open a few inches, and it went without squeaking.

Philippe was sitting by the fire in his great wing chair, a snifter of brandy cupped loosely in his palm.

Looking into the fire the way she'd once seen him look out the window. Perhaps he hadn't heard the soft knocks over the rain, which had started up again with a biblical vengeance. He'd changed his clothes, and he sat now in a shirt and trousers, bootless, his hair still a little damp and curling almost whimsically at the temples.

He looked up.

And then went still.

He lowered the brandy snifter carefully to the table next to him.

His eyes tracked her slow progress to him as if she'd been a holy visitation.

She stood before him long enough to allow him to see the shadowed outline of her body through her night rail.

She looked down into his beloved eyes, which were heated like the brandy and reflected the dancing flames.

If nothing else, her tenure here had resulted in reliable fires in all the rooms.

Both of the literal and figurative varieties.

She dropped to her knees before him and lay her head on his lap. He stroked her hair, gently, softly, in silence, for some time.

She didn't know when she began weeping, only that she was, and she couldn't stop. All the terror and not knowing, the shame of the word "bastard." She couldn't bear it if she was the reason he lost everything he wanted. Everything poured out at once.

He stroked her hair softly, murmuring endearments. "*Chérie*, do not cry. *Ma coeur*, it is safe now. He is safe. Shhh . . ."

"I was so afraid." She was shivering and shivering, a delayed response to terror.

"I know. I know. I am sorry. Come here. Come here."

He raised her up and pulled her across his lap, wrapping her tightly in his arms, willing the warmth of his body into hers until the shaking subsided and the sobs at last had their way with her.

And in silence, for some time, she leaned her head back against his shoulder and was held. She remembered wondering if any woman had ever taken refuge there.

It seemed like the whole world took refuge there.

"I tried for so long to protect him from that word, Philippe. He was hardly likely to be judged at the vicarage. It is my fault. I have done this to him."

"You have done nothing but love him. His father did this to him. You cannot protect him from the world. But you can teach him how to move in it. You can teach him that he can still be kind when other people are not. And who knows that better than you?"

She turned her head to look into his eyes. With a single finger she traced the line of his jaw, and then the lyrical shape of his mouth, and he let her. He simply watched, his eyes hot, the reflection of the fire dancing in his pupils. For a while they simply gazed at each other. Who ever would have dreamed that a man this hard would have a heart so vast and beautiful?

She kissed him softly on the mouth.

And then she reached for the button on his shirt.

Time seemed to have slowed to a velvety crawl, and she thought she might remain in the Purgatory of the Undone Button forever.

And the button at last gave way.

She spread his shirt open with a sigh of relief and slid her hands down the satiny, hard chest and sighed. She kissed him.

"How I want you," she murmured.

He threaded his fingers through her hair as she placed a single kiss at the base of his throat, where his heart was drumming hard, fast and fiercely, appropriate to the warrior he was.

And as their lips met and blended, as the kiss became hungry and fierce and tender, her fingers softly followed the seam dividing the smooth muscles bisected by a scar. The wound could have killed him, but it was the road that had brought him to her, so she skated her finger over it softly. It was a bit like following the path that had led her to this moment.

He shifted as his cock swelled and stirred.

She slipped from his lap, kneeling between his thighs so she could trail her tongue along that fine seam of hair that disappeared into his trousers.

And then reached for his trouser buttons.

Which fortunately surrendered quickly to her awkward fingers.

His cock sprang free into her hand, and she closed her mouth over it.

His breath sawed in sharply, then.

She dragged her mouth down over the length of it, following it with her fist. And did it again.

And again.

He arched upward with a soft moan, his hands twisting in her hair. His head went back hard, the cords of his neck taut. His words came in short harsh bursts.

"Mother of God . . . so good Elise . . ."

And his excitement banked her own, until she could feel her body taut and shivering now, not with fear but with power and savage want.

She did it again, with her mouth, her hands, her tongue, dragging her tongue along the swollen shaft, tracing the contours of the silken dome.

His hands reached out and seized the arms of her night rail.

"Take it off," he ordered hoarsely. "Or I will rip it from you."

She staggered to her feet and pulled it off. It

dropped into his hands as if it stood in the way of everything he'd ever wanted, which in some ways it had, but being a night rail, it didn't go far. It fluttered like a shot pigeon to the ground, and he gave a short laugh.

"Oh, my love, dear God."

It sounded like a hosannah. She liked it, so she stood before him a little longer, nude, utterly vulnerable, as his hot eyes feasted.

He looped his arms around her thighs and pulled her roughly into him, closer, placed his lips on her belly, then, without preamble, dragged them down lower, and gently but insistently parted her thighs and slid his tongue hard between her cleft.

She was unprepared for the raw shock of pleasure, which nearly buckled her knees.

"*Philippe . . .*"

He did it again, as his fingers skated lightly over the tender skin of her thighs. She gripped his hard, hot shoulders. Surge after surge of scorching pleasure fanned through her veins, pleasure building upon pleasure, as his tongue darted, glided, and stroked with relentless skill and knowledge.

She was whimpering now, a craven creature comprised only of need.

"Please . . ."

He sucked. "Is that what you want, my love?" he murmured. "Is that why you beg me?"

"Yes . . . oh God . . . *please* . . ." Every word a tattered rasp.

"You will scream," he vowed.

His voice a dark, commanding rasp.

I will do anything you want, she thought.

He pulled her forward until she was straddling his lap. And as he gripped his cock and guided it into her with one hard thrust, he seized her hips and moved her over him. Her head whipped back hard at the extraordinary feel of him filling her, and she moaned softly. He held fast to her as his hips bucked upward again and again and again and again, and then her fists were thumping his shoulders as her release made glorious wreckage of her senses, bowing her backward, tearing from her a hoarse scream of triumph. She nearly collapsed over him.

"Oh, God . . . Elise . . . I am . . ."

And while he broke apart in the throes of his release, she was the one who held him.

Chapter 24

She was more of a rag than a woman, astonished, sated, a bit sore.

She savored the feel of their rib cages rising and falling in rhythm with each other.

"Am I hurting you?" she asked.

"Only a little. Don't move yet. I love the feel of you."

He was still inside her.

She rested her head on his shoulder, and his hands roamed her back. The two of them were sheened in sweat.

"I meant it to be more artful," he said through her hair, which had fallen all over his face. "And it will be. Perhaps the third or fourth time."

His dream was coming true. And now that he had her, he sensed he would never, never quite get enough.

He could feel her smile against his shoulder.

His fingers lightly trailed the blades of them, skimmed the elegant taper of her waist to her hips, then paused to circle, slowly, deliberately, that oh-so-exquisitely alive spot at the very base of the spine, until she shifted and began to moan softly again. "Philippe . . ."

He arched her gently backward in the cradle of his arms and touched his tongue to her nipple. She gasped. How he loved that sound.

He nipped. "I want to taste every inch of you," he murmured. "There is pleasure to be had from every curve, every hollow, every secret place."

"Show me."

"Come with me," he said abruptly.

He gave her a little push.

She slid from his lap. She took him by his hand, pulled him up out of the chair, and led him to the bed. He followed behind so he could watch the silken sway of her unfettered hair tapering to a stop just above her delectable, round white arse, and he knew how he would next take her.

He sank down on the bed with a sigh and pulled her over him.

"We must get rid of these first," she insisted.

She pushed his shirt away from his shoulders and flung it away much the way he'd flung her night rail. He made short work of his trousers, and they became a wad on the floor.

"Cover me," she whispered.

And then he captured her, engulfed her completely in his arms, and rolled her over to face him.

"I've always wanted to lay down beside you for a night," he murmured. His finger traced her jaw, the line of her nose, the little nautilus of her ears.

"Always?"

"After I'd ravished you a dozen different ways."

"Are there a dozen different ways?"

"Oh, *ma chérie*," he said in mock pity. "If only you knew."

"Ravish me," she decreed on a whisper.

His mouth took hers hard, and he pushed her hair back from her face.

Her hands were gliding tantalizingly over his thighs, exploring, relishing in the feel of him, and his lungs drew in swift, ragged breaths as desire ramped.

The glorious friction of her sweat-slick bare skin, the chafe of her nipples against his own made him moan softly. She was a heaven of softness and lithe curves. And his cock was hard again, curving up toward his belly against hers, and it made him wild.

He moved suddenly and rolled her over on her belly and straddled her thighs, trapping her hands, leaning over her to trail kisses along the pearls of her spine, followed by the glide of his fingertips. Her breathing heaved, too.

"Philippe . . ."

He raised her hips off the bed and trailed a finger between the divide in her arse, nipped first one cheek, then the other. *"Comme une pêche,"* he said.

She groaned. "Please, Philippe, I want . . ."

And then he slipped a finger between her legs to find she was hot and wet. It made him savage.

She groaned gutturally, a low animal sound,

feral and so erotic it was like a long, hard stroke down his shaft.

"Do you want me, Elise?"

"Yes."

"How do you want me?"

"*Now. Now.*"

"Like this?"

He tormented her and himself by sliding his cock lightly, lightly along her cleft.

Her hands curled into the counterpane. Her back swayed with the hard gusts of her breath. She slapped the counterpane, half groan, half laugh. "Damn you . . ."

And then he thrust hard, sheathing himself in her, and she groaned softly.

He considered tormenting the two of them with finesse; he knew how to amplify pleasure with anticipation . . . and he tried. He withdrew slowly, allowing her to feel every inch of him, savoring every inch of the cling of her flesh.

But need had its claws in him.

He sank into her again, pulling her hips hard up against his, reveling in her gasp.

"Shall I stop now, Elise?" His voice was a raw rasp.

"Oh, God, no. *Please*. Faster . . ."

He drew back, and sank into her again, slowly, slowly, slowly. Sweat beaded his body. The cords of his neck were drum tight.

She shifted her hips to take him deeper and moaned in sensual torment.

He unleashed himself. His hips drummed into her, and the world was the raw, primal sound of the slap of their skin together, the ragged saw of their breathing, the moans of pleasure and pleas for more more more.

His release nearly yanked him from her body, and as hers tore through her, she screamed, her body arcing toward his, fingers curling into the counterpane. He felt ripped from his body. He heard his own harsh cries as if he were on the moon.

HE AWOKE WITH her hair across his lips; they must have slept for a time. Her head was on his chest, and her arm was flung over his shoulder. Her thigh was draped over his. She was breathing softly, her breath was warm against his chest, and desire kindled like a match to a rushlight. He shifted as his cock began to stir. He trailed his fingers over her spine, over the curve of her hip, savoring, arousing, waking. Wanting. Wanting. Dear God, wanting.

And she woke with a sigh and lifted her head with a murmur. "Philippe."

She lifted her head and softly, teasingly, kissed his mouth. He smiled against her lips, then pulled her bottom lip gently between his and splayed his hands across her buttocks, pressing ever so slightly so she could feel how aroused he already was. She smiled, too. She rippled with him as he stroked her back, her thighs, knowing how to move to make him wild, to make herself wild.

He rolled her over on her back and hovered over her.

"Slowly," he said.

"We'll make time stop," she agreed on a whisper.

He was inside her in a leisurely thrust, and she locked her legs and arms around his back, pulling him close, pulling him ever deeper in.

They moved together almost languidly; he drew his hips back, she arched to meet him. Prolonging, as best they could, that inevitable, savage, ramping of pleasure, the greedy run toward ultimate bliss. Savoring the feel of each other, drunk on deep, hungry kisses. Prolonging the time when they would part again.

For as long as he could. And then it was upon him, pressing at the very seams of his being.

"My sweet, I cannot wait . . ."

By way of answer, she arched against him. "Faster, Philippe."

As the tempo escalated, their bodies collided, and she took him as deeply as she could, her head thrashing back, her fingers digging into his arms, her legs locked around him as he drove the two of them to release.

THEY HAD STOLEN time.

They had not stopped it.

"Stolen" did indeed seem to be the word for it. Because neither of them had the right to each other, given their stations and . . . oh, yes, that word: "circumstances."

"What of Alexandra, Philippe?"

She couldn't believe she'd been able to utter the name, but as the fire burned low and the perspiration cooled on their bodies, and as sleep fought for the right to them, a certain ruthless clarity had taken over Elise's consciousness.

For a moment the word rang there in the dark, a sudden shock, like the sound of a distant gunshot.

It seemed to have nothing to do with the two of them. It was an intrusion of reality into the stolen fantasy of the night.

It was a long time before Philippe spoke. His voice was thick. As if he'd needed to unwillingly drag the words to the surface.

"She has gone to London. I will make it right with her in London."

Elise said nothing more.

And at last she took in a long breath, as if drawing in his very essence, and sighed.

His hand absently swept her back. Sleep was claiming him.

A certain merciful numbness, a finality, a resolution, set in for her.

This had been an elegy, of sorts, this night with him.

No one knew better than she the consequences of diverging from duty, responsibility, and station. She would never fault him for it. She would not ask it of him, ever.

But she now knew what to do. And she supposed there was peace in that.

THIS TIME HE must have slept like the dead. For when he awoke, he was alone, and a gray light was beginning to slip through the curtains.

He slid his hand over to the side of the bed. It was still warm. And he left his hand there, as if she were lying there still. And he remembered. Why did he feel so very weighted, when he'd just had Elise in his bed?

He woke again when there was a tap on the door.

He sighed at the intrusion of the real world. "Enter, please."

In sprang a dapper and alarmingly alert footman with coffee and an apple tart on a tray, which he deposited on a little table.

"You're off to London today, sir?"

Ah, of course. That was why.

"Yes, James, it's London." He'd told both James and Ramsey of his plans last night as Elise had taken Jack up to bed.

"Horrible day for it, sir," he said cheerily. He whipped back the curtains to reveal yet another curtain of rain.

"I've seen worse," Philippe yawned.

Today he was inured to it. He wouldn't feel the rain or the cold. He would go through the motions of duty, and as he rode in the Earl of Ardmay's loaned carriage—a slow journey to be sure in this weather—the memory of last night would sustain him. With luck, he would be in London before Alexandra.

And that was where he would do right by everyone.

ONCE IN LONDON again, after a truly unpleasant trip, much of which he'd slept through, and after he'd made himself presentable at the Redmond Townhouse, where he was admitted by Jonathan, the only Redmond currently in residence, Philippe called upon Alexandra.

He found her in the sitting room of her family's town house, arranged picturesquely on a blue settee that made her eyes look extraordinarily bright. The house was so thoroughly heated he was surprised steam didn't rise from his coat.

She rose and allowed him to bow over her proffered hand.

"I wasn't certain whether to expect you, Philippe."

"Please forgive my unorthodox departure the other night. I know it was uncharacteristic."

"I should hope so! How tremendously odd and, I daresay, rude of you to dash off so, Philippe. And yes, so very unlike you. You were hardly off to deliver a baby." She gestured to a Chippendale chair and rang the bell.

It was odd, but his heart gave a reflexive little anticipatory leap at the sound of a ringing bell.

He sat in the fragile, elegant chair.

"It was indeed rude, and for that I apologize sincerely. A friend of mine was in distress and I could ease it, Alexandra. Surely you've come to the aid of a friend in distress before?"

Even as he said it, he had difficulty imagining her doing that, or what precisely the occasion might be in which she would leap to help a friend.

She was silent, studying him coolly.

"I heard you use the word 'Elise.' Isn't that the given name of your housekeeper?"

"Yes."

There was a peculiar, brittle, little silence, into which a woman, presumably a housekeeper, crept bearing tea and a plate of scones.

Alexandra settled a scone onto a plate and handed it to him, then she poured two cups of tea. Neither of them spoke.

"Alexandra," he said idly, after a sip of tea, "where do you suppose your sister learned the word 'bastard'?"

She froze.

But only momentarily. She lifted the tea the rest of the way to her lips, sipped, then settled it leisurely upon the table.

"Whatever do you mean?"

"I mean that she called my housekeeper's son a bastard."

"Well . . . isn't he?" She was genuinely confused. She pointed to the teapot. "Teapot." She pointed at the settee. "'Settee.' 'Bastard.' Like that. Perhaps we should be grateful my sister is demonstrating a command of the language, since she has struggled with her lessons."

He wondered if she meant to be witty.

He explained slowly, as if she were a witless child, "It was meant to be hurtful."

She straightened. "Please do not feel free to use that tone with me," she said icily. "He's just a—"

Philippe settled the china cup down so abruptly that the clink echoed in the room.

She blinked.

They regarded each other in silence.

"Why don't you tell me how you got my housekeeper removed from her position at the academy, Alexandra?" he said softly.

She froze again. She regarded him unblinkingly.

"'Elise'?" she quoted, on a scoff. With a nervous little laugh.

"Elise."

"Well . . ." She seemed confused again. "It was a simple thing to accomplish, Philippe, for people such as us. I suggested that my sister was merely an unusually gifted child of delicate sensibility, and should be allowed to proceed with her lessons how and when she saw fit. And your 'housekeeper'—you will love this, Philippe—said it would be stupid to remove her from a circumstance of order and discipline, as it was exactly what she needed. Stupid! I ask you. Imagine her calling *me* stupid. And so when I learned of her circumstances through a servant, I threatened to expose Elise and her son to all of the parents of children attending Miss Marietta Endicott's Academy. Which would have spelled financial ruin for the school, as no decent parent would want their children taught by such a woman. That woman needed a lesson in learning how to address her betters."

Philippe was silent. He couldn't speak. He needed to breathe through the anger, as if it was new pain visited upon him.

"Betters" had never sounded so ironic.

He could so easily imagine Elise in a moment of passionate caring suddenly saying the wrong thing to the wrong person.

How he wished he'd been there.

"How *did* you learn of her 'circumstances,' as you call them?"

"Servants are eminently bribable, Philippe. They have such amorphous morals."

"Ah, yes. Unlike the aristocracy."

Alexandra flushed. "She implied that I was *stupid*." Even now the memory clearly raised her hackles.

He remained coldly silent.

She gave a little laugh. "Is that how you would like me to be treated? You would have a common schoolteacher, a common housekeeper, *insult* me?"

"She has a *son*." He said this almost hoarsely.

"Yes, I know," she said patiently. "The bastard."

He closed his eyes and counted to five to steady his temper.

"Do let's not argue, Philippe," she soothed. "We have been friends for so long and I know we would rub along well together. I think you know it, too. I believe you came here for a purpose. Do let's move on to it."

Her eyes were soft and placating, and she made to lay an entreating hand on his arm.

He stared a threat at it, so she retracted it, astonished.

"I came here to thank you, Alexandra," he said shortly.

"To thank me?" Her face began to light, anticipating some recitation of her virtues.

"Yes. Because if you hadn't gone about removing Elise from her position, I never would have met her."

She stared at him. And then as realization set in, her face slowly flooded with scarlet, and her eyes narrowed to slits.

"You have been sleeping with that whore," she all but hissed.

"Have a care," he warned silkily. "Have a care."

She was gasping for breath through her own shock and anger. "Surely you don't intend to marry . . . you will be the laughingstock of everyone you know, you will bring shame upon your great family with that common little—"

"*This* . . ." She jumped when he took his fist and lightly thumped his scone, shattering it into a million little crumbs. ". . . is all that is left of my life and my great family. And that is how much I now care what you or anyone else thinks of what I do now."

She was breathing hoarsely. "You will leave now."

He nodded and stood looking down at Alexandra, for it was likely the last time he would see her.

"If you are disappointed or hurt, Alexandra, I do regret causing you discomfort. I have cherished the friendship between our families."

"Get out," she hissed.

"And there is nothing common about love, Alexandra," he said gently. "I do sincerely hope one day you learn it for yourself."

He bowed shortly and showed himself out.

Chapter 25

THEY HAD SO FEW things between them. Their clothes. Her hairbrush.

A toy lion.

A brown velvet chair.

Packing would proceed swiftly.

She'd read her parents' letter again, and she didn't know how she'd missed it the first time.

Please come home and bring Jack. We will love him, too.

How had her parents known the name of her son?

Philippe must have written to them.

The *devil*.

She laughed softly, and it filled her again, that glorious light that came with being loved. Because she knew he loved her. And no matter what, no matter where they were, whatever became of either of them, she knew she could call upon that feeling whenever she wanted to remember how loved she'd been.

The day after Philippe departed for London, she decided to tell Jack.

"Jack, sit beside me and let's have a talk."

"Am I in trouble, Mama?"

"Not at all. Now, I know you are concerned about your father, Jack, and how he doesn't live with us."

"That's all right, Mama. I love you and you love me and that's just fine."

She gave a soft laugh and squeezed her son. God bless Philippe and his wisdom.

"That's true, and it is quite fine. And I have some truly splendid news. Other people love us, too. You've never met them, but we are going to live with your grandmother and grandfather, and be a family. They are wonderful, wonderful people, and you will love them, too."

Jack took this in, his eyes round, studying her face. She didn't know it, but the searching gaze was disconcertingly like her own.

"But I like it here, Mama. The Giant!"

"Remember when we left Miss Endicott's, and I told you you would love it here? Was I right?"

He thought about this. "Yes, Mama."

"I promise you will *love* your grandmother and grandfather, Jack. They are so funny and wise, and the house is just a little bit smaller, but you will have a bigger room of your very own, and I can show you the banister I slid down when I was a little girl, and the river where I caught fish. There are so many wonderful places to play, and they even keep a horse you can learn how to ride."

"Cor—I mean, hurrah! Will the Giant come to see us?"

Elise hesitated.

Philippe had been so certain she would come to him.

He'd been so right.

And now she was very nearly certain that what she was about to tell Jack was true.

She crossed her fingers for luck. "If the giant can find his way down the beanstalk, I'm sure we'll see him again."

IT WAS A long, slow trip back to Sussex from London—almost two days of travel. Though the weather was clearing, the roads had yet to recover from the last of the storms and were still soupy ruts in parts.

He'd spent nearly a fortnight in the city, looking in on *The Fortuna*, dining in establishments with people who would have horrified Alexandra but who had crewed their ship. Men he would trust, and had trusted, with his life. He'd stood on the dock beneath glowering skies alongside Jonathan Redmond and the Earl of Ardmay, and they had shaken hands on an agreement to use their ship to transport silks and spices rather than chasing down pirates, an endeavor that would prove profitable in a few months' time. They would hire a captain for her, or anoint a member of their crew, while Philippe and the Earl of Ardmay would remain on land.

Besides looking in on his ship, Philippe had also written to Monsieur LeGrande.

Dear Monsieur LeGrande,

I thank you kindly for your patience and consideration, but I now give you leave to sell Les Pierres d'Argent. I wish the new occupant many years of happiness and health. It is a beautiful home.

He'd posted it before he could change his mind.

And because he now knew a bit about love and sacrifice, he knew now how he intended to repay Lyon Redmond for saving his life.

Alder House was a dark hush at one in the morning, which was when Philippe finally arrived home in Pennyroyal Green. And it did feel like home, oddly: he drew in a long breath and took in linseed and lemon, the faint scent of snuffed candles, some lingering aroma of what he could swear were apple tarts, but that could simply be wishful thinking. It all settled over him like the softest, sweetest of blankets, soothing and loving. He crept up to his rooms and flung off his clothes and crawled beneath the blankets, immediately sinking into a dreamless sleep for what felt like five minutes before there was a tap on his door.

He jerked his head up, blinking.

"Enter," he croaked in an exhausted morning voice.

And in bustled . . .

"What the devil . . . who the devil . . . what are *you* doing here?"

"Good morning, sir. I understand you like an apple tart and coffee in the morning. I'm Mrs. Winthrop, if you'll recall sir—we've met—and I'm on loan from the Earl and Countess of Ardmay until we find a new housekeeper for you."

"Loan? A new . . . I *have* a housekeeper."

He shot bolt upright. Surely this was a dream. Or perhaps he'd dreamed everything between Mrs. Winthrop and Elise. Did Elise even exist? Was Mrs. Winthrop a dream?

If so, this was definitely not his favorite dream so far.

Poor Mrs. Winthrop was wholly unprepared for the glory of his torso at this time of the morning. She dropped the tray.

He winced at the clatter and thunk.

They both watched the coffee land and spread inexorably on the carpet, eyeing it as if a murder had taken place there.

He stared at her. "Never mind that, Mrs. Winthrop. Where the devil is Elise?"

The Christian name made her widen her eyes in alarm.

"*Mrs. Fountain* has returned to her people in Northumberland. Didn't she leave you a letter, sir?" Her voice quaked.

"I've been in London. I returned only last night. Letter? What letter?"

Surely this was still a dream.

"Well, Mrs. Fountain wouldn't dream of leaving without telling you, she's right responsible, she is. She said you would have anticipated it. Oh, and you ought to know a young lady arrived yesterday evening."

"A young *lady*? Ramsey! James!" he bellowed, as if he was trapped in a nightmare. It was too much information to take in five minutes after he'd opened his eyes.

Poor Mrs. Winthrop had been informed that Lord Lavay had become charming and had stopped shouting and throwing things. She felt betrayed by how untrue this was.

His footmen scrambled into the room.

At least they were there and appeared to be real. Dressed in midnight blue livery.

And if it wasn't a dream, then it must be true: Elise was gone.

"The young lady says she's your sister," Mrs. Winthrop said, her voice quavering.

"My sis—Ramsey! James! Get me dressed and shaved."

Mrs. Winthrop, who couldn't bear all the shouting, slipped out. Things really were in a fix if the former Violet Redmond seemed like a mild-mannered employer.

HE'D JUST ARRIVED in his study when a tornado in muslin rushed through the door at him.

He grunted as she caught him midtorso in an embrace. His arms were trapped. She was muttering a tangled torrent of incensed and worried French and English.

"Marie-Helene," he ground out through his teeth from the confines of her embrace, "what in God's name are you doing here? *How* did you get here?"

She released him and stood back.

"Where does it hurt, brother, and I will not punch you there!"

"Why must you punch me at *all*?"

"Why didn't you tell me you were hurt, at death's door, Philippe? I am not a child. Do you think I'm so callous and shallow that I see you as only a tree that shakes out money? I used the money you sent to buy passage, not gowns. I arranged it all on my own. You see, a child wouldn't have been able to do that. It was easy. I just order people about like so." She waved her hand airily. "I don't know why, but they want to do what I ask."

He knew why. She was beautiful and imperious and charming and willful. And yes, he had underestimated Marie-Helene. Looking at her now, it seemed to him almost incomprehensible that he had underestimated her. As Elise had pointed out, she *was* his sister.

"How on earth did you find out about the cutthroats in *London*?"

He knew his *grand-père* would never tell her.

"It was in your letter. Have you forgotten? Were you injured in the head?" She produced it and shook it at him as if it were a royal decree.

Only his sister could get away with saying

"were you injured in the head?" to him in that tone of voice. It was in fact lovely to hear it.

"It was in my *let . . .* give that to me now, please."

He snatched it out of her grip and scanned to the final paragraph.

I am recovering well enough from my attack by cutthroats in London. Many parts of me are still sore and may never be quite the same, but I bless all the pain, as I could have easily died. I thought of you as I lay near death's door and miss you, Marie-Helene, as you have been a good sister.

Good God. That was a bit much. He could picture Elise laughing even as she wrote it. That *minx.*

And he *never* would have been so sentimental. No wonder it had panicked his sister into boarding a ship and coming to Sussex straightaway.

And now that she was here, he didn't want her to ever leave.

"I will stay here," Marie-Helene said breezily, looking around the house as if she already owned it. "It is not the same in Provence or Paris without you. *None* of it is the same, Philippe," she added softly. "And it never will be again. Surely you know that."

He did. Oh, he did.

He blinked warily. "You will stay here? In Pennyroyal Green?"

"And why not? London is not so terribly far, and London is not Paris, but it is not provincial.

The house is remarkably clean and comfortable, your footmen are handsome, and the townspeople seem very friendly. A delectable-looking man by the name of Mr. Duggan, I believe? Outside the vicarage? Assisted me when one of our trunks came loose and fell from the carriage. How very fortunate he managed to be nearby when we rolled into town."

Oh, God.

Philippe gave a short laugh. "And grand-père . . ."

"Oh, he will never leave Paris, but we can go to him and see if we can persuade him, Philippe."

And then he stared at his sister, in whom he could see his mother, his father, himself.

"Why are you staring so?" she asked uneasily.

"I am just . . . unutterably glad to see you, Marie-Helene." He seized her by the shoulders and kissed her on both cheeks. "Even if your gowns are last season's gowns."

She swatted at him. "You *were* injured in the head."

"In the heart," he corrected. "But I'm about to see about mending it."

Chapter 26

WINTER WAS SHOWING A little willingness to give way to spring, and as evidence, the sun poured into the cozy kitchen of the Fountain house. Toasted bread and kippers and eggs and sausages were heaped on platters, and the pot of coffee placed in the center of the table by the maid was enthusiastically greeted.

Jack had already found a few new friends in Northumberland, but he yearned after a church with a proper bell.

He was lunging across the table for the marmalade when he looked out the window and—

"It's the Giant!" he bellowed, and Elise's father's scrambled eggs shot into the air on the way to his mouth, much like that fateful morning when Elise had told them she was pregnant.

Jack dashed out the door, leaving it wide open, and ran like a shot up the path, hurtling himself into Lavay's thighs.

Lavay hoisted him easily and strode up the path with Jack, big as he was now, tucked in the crook of his arm, almost as if he were in fact real, not a hallucination or a dream, which would really be the only reason he was striding up the path to this little house in Northumberland nearly a month after she'd left him, she thought, for good.

She froze and waited for him to disappear. Surely he must be a dream.

Her parents stared at Lord Lavay as if he were indeed a giant.

Then rotated in unison to stare at Elise.

"Don't worry, it's nothing like the last time," she said distantly.

Which really didn't do much to reassure them.

Lavay stood in the open doorway, Jack in his arms.

Elise couldn't speak. Her heart had leaped up and flown away like a dove released from a cage, and clearly it had taken her voice with it.

Centuries of breeding all but rolled off him in waves. He was still the vast, hard, arrogant, beautiful man, and he somehow both dwarfed and elevated everything in the house.

"The Giant is here, Mama," Jack said quite redundantly.

"So I see," she said softly.

He was wildly out of context in this quiet Northumberland doctor's home.

"Mother, Father, this is . . . this is . . . my former employer. Lord Lavay."

"What a pleasure it is to meet you," he said to them.

His voice echoed for a time all by itself in the kitchen, that familiar, much-beloved baritone, the soft *s*'s, the exquisitely constructed consonants, like diamonds.

Finally her parents bowed and curtsied like toys wound and set loose.

"If I may have a private word with your daughter," Philippe said in that pleasant way of his that made people reflexively leap to do his bidding. Her parents collided with each other in an effort to leave the room. "Jack, will you go with your *grand-mère* and *grand-père*?"

He lowered Jack to the ground with a little grunt, and Jack dashed after them up the stairs.

They heard his voice following his grandparents up the stairs. "He gave me a *lion*!"

"Come outside with me, if you will, Elise."

She would have gone straight to Hades with him if he'd asked, but she couldn't quite find her voice. She followed him.

They stood outside, blinking in the clean sunlight, surrounded by the land of her birth, by everything she'd known and loved.

They simply stared at each other for a time.

"I like your ribbon," he said. "Is it new?"

She smiled faintly. "This is your conversation?"

He didn't laugh. He was looking at her as if he'd located the grail.

"I think your laugh is my favorite sound in the world."

Oh. Well, that went straight into her heart.

He looked so deadly serious when he said it.

"That, and that little gasp you made when I first kissed you. And the sound you make when you—"

"Philippe, you must tell me why you're here." Her entire body was covered in a sort of soft, feverish heat that he could inspire so quickly. Her heart was slamming against her breastbone.

"My sister has arrived in Pennryoyal Green."

"Oh, she *came*?" Elise was delighted.

"That was quite a risk you took with that letter, Mrs. Fountain. But then you have always known me better than I know myself."

She was silent.

So was he.

"Did you come here to tell me that, Philippe?"

"No."

"To complain about your sister?"

"No."

She still seemed unable to make him smile. She realized he was tense as a drum skin.

If he were any more still, he'd grow roots like a tree, and the birds would come to sit on his shoulders.

"It's just . . ." He took a deep breath and thrust his hands into his pockets. "I am here because there is life, and there is death, but they are one and the same without you, Elise."

Oh.

She gave her head a little shake, because the tears had begun.

"I thought I needed everything I once had . . . I thought I owed it to my family to preserve it as it was. But the only thing that gave those places meaning was love. My family has scattered or died, gone on to make new lives elsewhere. All the memories I wish to keep were comprised of love. And home, Elise, is anywhere love is." He stepped toward her urgently and looked down. "And you are my love."

He was blurry now. She dashed tears away from her eyelashes. The breeze lashed at her hair and whipped it about gaily, and she almost missed her hairpins, because she didn't want to miss a second of his face during this moment.

"I love you, Elise. You knew even *that* before I did."

He still didn't smile.

The short remaining distance between them had begun to seem unbearable.

But there was more to know before he crossed it.

"What of Alexandra?"

"She will prosper wherever and with whomever she pleases." He airily waved away Alexandra as if she hadn't been the cloud over Elise's world. "It will not be me. I have told her how I feel about you. I even thanked her for bringing you into my life, for now I know what happened."

Elise said nothing. Happiness had rendered her mute. For the moment, she wanted only to feel this way forever, as if she was made of light and peace.

"We can make our *own* history. Our own house,

our own dynasty, if we choose. If . . ." His voice was a husk, and nearly broke. "If you love me."

She didn't want to torture him, but her voice couldn't yet find its way to the surface, so stupefied with happiness was she.

"I love you." She choked the words, and they sounded so small, when they ought to have been delivered accompanied by celestial trumpets.

He drew in a long breath, like a man who'd just been released from a locked box. He released it, and closed his eyes.

In seconds, he had closed the distance between them, and suddenly she was in his arms as if she'd never left them.

He murmured things to her in French, non-sense words, endearments, as he brushed away her tears so she could see his beautiful face, and remember forever how he looked the moment she'd told him she loved him.

He looked into her eyes. "And will you be my wife?"

"And I will be your wife."

"Are you certain of that, *chérie*?"

"Oh, yes. As you pointed out, I'm a gambler."

"Ah, very good. And I have learned how to play the long game."

"Perfect. Between us, we are certain to always win."

It was then he kissed her, tentatively at first, as if it had been the very first time he'd kissed her.

And then he claimed her with a kiss so thorough and passionate that birds were flushed from nearby trees, as if a fire had begun below.

Her parents and Jack had, in fact, watched and heard the entire thing from the upper-story windows.

"She takes after you," her father said to her mother, who was dabbing at her eyes with a handkerchief, and her mother elbowed him in the ribs.

THEY WERE MARRIED in the church in Pennyroyal Green by the Reverend Sylvaine. The wedding was attended by a very surprised but surprisingly sentimental Earl and Countess of Ardmay, and witnessed by happily weeping family members and servants.

And when they burst triumphantly from the church to the cheers of gathered onlookers, Philippe and Jack promptly climbed the bell tower together.

And then Philippe hoisted Jack up, and together they made that bell peal so joyfully it was heard in nearly every corner of Sussex.

And at the great celebration in the hall after the wedding, some noted that Seamus Duggan was a trifle more subdued than usual, and that his fiddle sounded a little more plaintive whilst playing the "Sussex Waltz."

IN LONDON, LYON Redmond, also known as Mr. Hardesty, a successful trader, was preparing to board his ship when a man in midnight blue, silver-trimmed livery strode up the gangplank.

All around their captain, hands went to swords and pistols, and the footman, to his astonishment, met a bristling phalanx of hard-faced men.

The footman bowed. "I seek Mr. Hardesty."

"I am he."

He bowed.

"For you, sir." The footman extended the message.

"Hold," Lyon said to the footman, who had, with great but unfounded optimism, turned to leave.

Poor Ramsey, who had won the coin toss, remained obediently motionless, face admirably impassive, while the tips of a half dozen swords glinted in the sun at him.

Lyon broke the seal.

He went still.

"Pay the man," he said absently.

Someone flicked a guinea at Ramsey. He caught it neatly.

Nine words.

She's getting married on the second Saturday in May.

And thusly, Lavay discharged his debt to Lyon Redmond.